"That blanket of yours doesn't look very warm.

"It'll be tight, but there's room for two in my sleeping bag. Want to join me?"

"No!" Tara almost shouted out her quick refusal. She hadn't forgotten the comments he'd made while trying to convince her not to accompany him. "Thank you. I'll be fine. It's warm enough," she lied through her already chattering teeth. The cold she could manage well enough. She wasn't at all sure of her ability to continue to refuse him.

"Suit yourself."

The eerie cry of a wolf pierced the silence. Tara sat bolt upright.

"Don't worry," came Kent's reassuring voice. "Sounds travel in the mountains. I'm sure the wolves are farther away than you'd think. They won't bother us."

Tara hoped he was right.

"Unless they're really hungry."

She chose to believe that the chuckle following his alarming comment meant he was only teasing her.

"My offer about the sleeping bag still stands."

Dear Reader,

When two people fall in love, the world is suddenly new and exciting, and it's that same excitement we bring to you in Silhouette Intimate Moments. These are stories with scope and grandeur. The characters lead lives we all dream of, and everything they do reflects the wonder of being in love.

Longer and more sensuous than most romances, Silhouette Intimate Moments novels take you away from everyday life and let you share the magic of love. Adventure, glamour, drama, even suspense— these are the passwords that let you into a world where love has a power beyond the ordinary, where the best authors in the field today create stories of love and commitment that will stay with you always.

In coming months, look for novels by your favorite authors: Linda Howard, Heather Graham Pozzessere, Emilie Richards and Kathleen Korbel, to name just a few. And whenever you buy books, look for all the Silhouette Intimate Moments, love stories for today's woman by today's woman.

Leslie J. Wainger
Senior Editor and Editorial Coordinator

FRANCES WILLIAMS

The Road to Forever

SILHOUETTE·INTIMATE·MOMENTS®

Published by Silhouette Books New York

America's Publisher of Contemporary Romance

SILHOUETTE BOOKS
300 East 42nd St., New York, N.Y. 10017

THE ROAD TO FOREVER

ISBN: 0-373-07378-X

First Silhouette Books printing April 1991

Printed in the U.S.A.

FRANCES WILLIAMS

was born in Montreal, Canada, and now lives in the Washington, D.C., area. An addict of suspense and adventure stories, Frances has won the Georgia Romance Writers' Maggie Award, the Delaware Romance Writers' Diamond Award and the *Romantic Times* Award for New Romantic Suspense Author. Her last book was nominated by *Romantic Times* for the Reviewer's Choice awards.

For Camilla, Cara,
Carole and Patricia

Chapter 1

Through the disorienting haze of a thousand flickering butter lamps, Tara caught a glimpse of the man she'd been sent to Tibet to find. She hadn't yet been able to see his face, but the tall, dark Westerner strung with cameras had to be Kent Masterson. Aside from a few Europeans in the tour group ahead, most of the pilgrims winding their way through the former palace of their god-king were Tibetans. She started to pick her way in the prescribed clockwise fashion around the group of bronze statues of Buddha, but lost sight of the photographer in the smoky interior of the chapel.

Tara came out, blinking, into the brightness of a small courtyard. Above her the morning sun blazed off the Potala's golden roofs and intricately carved finials pointing like fingers to the clear blue sky. From somewhere inside came the low, droning chant of pilgrims, and she caught a whiff of smoky incense mingling with the rank odor of the butter lamps.

Tara Morgan delighted in discovering the strange and wonderful. In arranging adventure tours for her specialized travel agency, she'd traveled with the Masai and watched a Papuan shaman drive out a devil. But seldom had an experience affected her as deeply as wandering through what was still one of the most inaccessible structures in the world. The remarkable, centuries-old building, which looked at once wildly exotic and strangely contemporary, soared from its rocky outcrop as if its builders had piled up its mud bricks in an attempt to reach the sky gods of their ancient, mysterious kingdom.

But she was supposed to be attending to Roger Elliott's business, Tara reminded herself.

The hotel clerk had told her Kent Masterson had left for the Potala only a half hour before, and she'd come after him. To follow the man she assumed must be her quarry, she forced her tired legs to carry her up yet another flight of stone steps.

She'd considered herself in excellent shape until she began the long climb up the steep zigzag staircases of the palace. But it was beginning to dawn on her that she might have made a mistake by hurrying to connect with Masterson. The once-forbidden city of Lhasa was over two miles above sea level and the altitude was making her head ache. Even with frequent rest stops, her lungs couldn't seem to drag in enough oxygen from the thin air. Moreover, the sweet-sour odor of burning yak butter was making her stomach queasy. Still, she refused to allow the symptoms of altitude sickness to dull her exhilaration at being in a country that was one of the world's most fascinating and remote.

A movement on the parapet above her caught her eye. The man she was searching for was leaning against the low wall as he snapped a photograph. Anxious to reach him before he disappeared again and forced her into yet another climb, Tara took two or three quick steps upward. She stopped, alarmed, as her heart jogged into a sudden wild thumping, and put her hand to her head to steady it against the dizziness threatening to take over.

If a strong arm hadn't appeared from nowhere to circle her waist and hold her steady, she'd have fallen. As it was she had to brace herself against the man's lean, hard body for support.

"Easy, girl. I've got hold of you," a smooth baritone voice assured her. "You won't fall." Tara looked up into the face of the man she'd been following. "It looks to me like you're suffering from the effects of high mountain sickness." When she wobbled on her feet, his grip on her tightened.

"I'm all right," she protested, not at all sure she should be allowing him to hold her so intimately, although she was glad for the solidity that held her upright.

"You don't look all right. You look as if you're ready to toss your breakfast."

Since the man's assessment of her condition was all too distressingly accurate, Tara thought it brave of him not to quickstep away from her. Instead, with a single competent movement, he swept her up in his arms and carried her back down the steps. Tara didn't have the strength to lift her head from his shoulder. Nor did she want to. His clean, woodsy scent was helping to counteract the sickly odor of the burning yak butter. Just inside a white-awninged entrance he deposited her gently on a long, cushioned couch covered in faded red silk. A resting place not nearly as comfortable as the stranger's arms.

"Close your eyes and rest a moment," he ordered as he slid the strap of a large camera case from his shoulder to the floor and unlooped another camera from around his neck.

Tara was only too glad to comply.

"Now take several very deep breaths."

She did.

In a few minutes, whether as a result of the way the man was briskly rubbing each of her hands in turn or simply from lying down, she began to feel better. Since her stomach had stopped churning, she decided it was safe to open her eyes. When she did she found herself gazing into a pair of intriguing brown eyes. Her Good Samaritan had gone down on one knee beside the couch and was bending over her, his eyes full of concern. She'd always thought brown eyes fairly commonplace. Not these. These were deep and dark and flecked with gold. And looking into them stirred a fluttery little circle of warmth into existence just below her rib cage.

Evidently satisfied with his inspection of her face, the man nodded approvingly. "You're getting a little color back." Inexplicably, Tara felt just the slightest tinge of regret when he moved back from her to rummage through a leather bag jammed with photographic equipment. He brought out an orange, peeled it, pulled off a segment and handed it to her.

Tara bit into the fruit cautiously. Its sweet juice freshened her mouth and settled her stomach. After a moment, she started to sit up and he slipped a hand behind her back to support her. Slowly she lowered her legs to the floor.

"Thank you. I really needed your help." On tour with clients, she was usually the one to take care of people with problems. She could have done without learning what it was like to be on the receiving end.

"I take it you've just arrived in Lhasa," he said.

Tara nodded carefully so as not to instigate a recurrence of the dizziness that had plagued her earlier.

"You should have given yourself a couple of days to acclimatize before tackling the Potala."

"I know that." The romantic whitewashed terraces of the imposing structure had drawn her to it with an enchantment she hadn't been able to resist. She hadn't expected the altitude to pose any great problem, since she was accustomed to highland treks and usually experienced no more than mild mountain sickness.

This wasn't the first time her enthusiasm for delving into a new environment had led her into trouble. Once her friendliness toward the old headman of an African village had darn near made her his fifth wife. Although Tara knew her rescuer was right, the dry note of reproof she'd heard in his voice put her on the defensive.

"I shouldn't have done it, but when I woke this morning and saw this amazing building framed in my hotel window, I couldn't wait to get to the place."

The man glanced over his shoulder at the magnificent chamber painted in lush colors of cinnabar red and bright blue. "Yes," he admitted, "the Potala will do that to you. To tell the truth, it did much the same thing to me this morning. But I acclimatize quickly."

"I've just finished an exhausting tour of China," she explained. Her rescuer did look somewhat like the photographs she'd seen of Kent Masterson, and she didn't want a man with whom she'd have to work to think her a complete idiot without the sense to pace herself. "I guess I'm a little more worn out from three weeks on the road than I thought."

"You'll be okay. Just take it easy for the rest of the day."

The lopsided smile flashed wider, baring a row of perfect white teeth. Earlier she'd felt too sick to inspect the owner of the strong arms that still sustained her. The man's face, tanned and rugged, was strikingly handsome, its squared-off, jutting chin suggesting a competent self-reliance.

A jacket of buttery soft black leather draped beautifully over shoulders whose breadth, she'd discovered when her arms were around him, were shaped more by solid flesh than by padding. The expensive jacket was paired with gray cotton twill slacks that molded lean hips and muscled thighs. Apparently, though, looking stylish wasn't high on the man's agenda. The shaggy strands of dark brown hair that curled well below collar length hadn't seen a pair of scissors in months.

A distant, measuring look came over the brown eyes studying her face. They flicked to the vividly colored patterns on the wall behind the couch on which she sat, then back to her.

"Mind if I take a few shots?" he asked, reaching for a camera. "This will make a great picture."

She could hardly refuse to pose for a man who'd kept her from hitting the pavement. Besides, he was already circling her, clicking off shots from several angles with quick dexterity. She only hoped a picture of her, captioned American Tourist Collapsed on the Roof of the World, wouldn't show up in some national magazine.

"Maybe I should point out," she offered, "that according to my travel guide taking photographs in here is not permitted."

"A sizable stack of yuan plus a letter from the head man at the Ministry of Culture bought my permission to take all the photographs I want." Though he lowered the camera, he continued to peruse her face. "You know, with that great bone structure you could be a model."

"I'm too short." The man's earlier inspection was discomfiting enough, but the way his gaze was now traveling over her body with undisguised male interest brought a flush to her face.

"I don't think so. You've a beautifully proportioned figure." He thrust out his hand. "Forgive me, I haven't introduced myself yet, have I? The name's Kent Masterson."

Tara wasn't surprised. But she heartily wished she'd been able to track Masterson down before he'd found her instead under such embarrassing circumstances. Only a slight dizziness afflicted her when she stood up and grasped his hand. "How do you do, Mr. Masterson. Tara Morgan."

The firm hand enveloping hers was lingering much longer than necessary, but strangely enough she was rather enjoying the continuing tactile connection between them.

"A pleasure, Miss Morgan. It *is* miss, I hope?"

"Actually, it's Mrs. But I'm divorced."

"You're an American."

She nodded.

"So am I."

"I know who you are, Mr. Masterson." On the verge of identifying herself, she remembered Elliott's warning that the photographer wasn't expecting her and might be a little prickly about her presence. Maybe this wasn't the right time to divulge her true purpose for being here. Better to establish more of a rapport with the man before tackling the job of explaining her mission. "I'm sure just about everyone has seen a photograph by Kent Masterson. Your pictures capture the spirit of the world's wild places like no one else's. And I have a couple of your books."

From the look on his face, her comment both surprised and pleased him. "You do? Which ones?"

"The book on the Masai and the one on Egypt." She owned all the Kent Masterson books of pictorial essays, but there was no point in making herself sound like a gushing fan. "In fact, I use them in my work."

"Really. What kind of work is that?"

"I'm a travel agent."

"Ah. So that's why you're here in Tibet. You're not just the usual tourist."

Tara lowered her eyes. She wasn't really engaging in deception, she told herself—only postponing the disclosure of her purpose for a little while. Still, deliberately misleading the man even for the moment made her feel uncomfortable.

"Yes," she said quickly, turning away in her discomfort to pick up her tote bag. "I've been working out a travel itinerary in southern China. I thought we might add a loop into Tibet for our more adventurous clients."

The sound of low conversation just beyond the entrance awnings warned them that others were approaching the chamber. The Chinese had turned the Potala into a museum, but to the Tibetan natives making their way through the halls that had once been home to the Dalai Lama, it remained a holy place.

A young Tibetan family hesitantly entered the gallery. The adults carried small prayer wheels whose every turn lofted a thousand prayers to Buddha. The soft *kerching* of the small stones whirling inside the copper cylinders added to the timeless atmosphere of the exotic building.

Tara knew they were nomads—people who lived a life so removed from hers that they could be from another

planet. The little boy with almond-shaped eyes peeked at
Tara from around the safety of his mother's long black
skirt. She guessed the child had seen no one with pale skin
and round eyes until his family's visit to Lhasa. Apparently her long mass of red hair and definitely non-Tibetan
green eyes were provoking his curious stare. She smiled at
the boy, who rewarded her with a giggle and a gap-toothed
grin.

Kent turned to investigate. *"Tashi deleg!"* he said.
When the little boy grinned his hello in return, Kent tossed
the remaining half of the orange to the child, who might
never have tasted the expensive fruit. The boy held the
orange up to his father, who nodded his permission and
gave Kent a quick bow.

"Too-jay-chay."

Kent returned the man's nod. "You're welcome."

Tara was impressed. "You can speak Tibetan?"

"Only a little," he said shortly, picking up his camera
bag to hook it over his shoulder. "Maybe we should let
these folks worship in private."

"Yes. I think I'd better skip the rest of the tour for today and start back down. Could I prevail on you to come
along, Mr. Masterson? Just for insurance, in case I start
feeling woozy again."

He slipped his arm around her waist with an unwarranted, yet unobjectionable, familiarity. "Believe me, lady,
I've no intention of letting you run off without me." The
suggestive rasp in his voice shivered a curious ripple of
pleasure down her spine. "We won't have to walk back to
the hotel. My motorcycle is parked down below. I've paid
a kid to keep an eye on it."

"You've rented a motorcycle?"

"Not rented. It's mine. I take the BMW with me on my
travels. A motorcycle gives me the freedom to tool around
in places where paved roads are nonexistent. I imagine
you're staying at the Lhasa hotel."

Tara bridled. "Why did you say it that way?"

"What way?"

"As if you were intimating that I must be the kind of person who'd only travel insulated within a comfortable Western-style cocoon." Ordinarily she'd have preferred to live among Tibetans at the guest houses to get a better feel for the country. But on this trip her mission for Elliott dictated that she blend in with other Western tourists at the Lhasa. Besides, she hadn't wanted to cause a stir with the China International Travel Service, which had booked her into the place.

"I'm sorry if I sounded condescending. Maybe I've just run into too many tourists who never bother to interact with a country's natives. Actually, I'm staying at the Lhasa myself."

"I know."

He gave her a sharp glance. "How do you know that?"

Elliott had told her, but she shouldn't have let it slip out so readily. "I imagine members of the illustrious Philadelphia Masterson family travel first class all the way, don't they?"

"Not always." Amusement sparked into the dark eyes. "I'm the black sheep of the family. I've even been known to mingle with the common folks from time to time. Right now the idea of...mingling...with an attractive travel agent is extremely inviting."

Rather than slide her hands around his waist as Kent guided his motorcycle through the crowded, narrow streets of crumbling old buildings at the foot of the Potala, Tara held lightly to his sides.

"Will you meet me for dinner after your rest?" he asked as she was leaving him in the hotel lobby to go to her room.

"I'd like to." She had to. They had an important matter to discuss.

As Kent had prescribed, a couple of hours in bed and the use of her room's oxygen tank banished most of the symptoms of high-altitude sickness. Her stomach had been too upset for lunch, but she was ravenous when Kent held out a chair for her at dinner in the hotel restaurant.

Her companion turned out to be charming and easy to talk to. They discovered that they'd traveled to many of the same places and he recounted amusing stories about them with a captivating boyish enthusiasm. She admired a man who'd been to offbeat locations that even an experienced traveler like herself would hesitate to enter.

He had a habit, she'd noticed, of squinting slightly in concentration as he spoke, as if he were constantly framing the scene in front of him for a photograph. More often than not that narrow-eyed scrutiny fell disconcertingly on her, producing within her a curious combination of discomfort and satisfaction.

"I'm here to take photos for a new coffee-table book on Tibet," Kent told her. She knew darn well he was here to do more than that. "The Chinese hope it will promote tourism. You probably know that they've lost billions of tourist dollars since the Tiananmen massacre."

Tinny Chinese pop music whined in the background. Tara was sure the same song had assaulted her ears everywhere she went in China. Tonight, though, its torturous repetition didn't bother her as much as it usually did. Kent's voice, a deep, pleasant rasp, resonated against the base of her skull in a most interesting way.

"Yes," she answered absently, her mind busy pondering not the subject of travel in China, but Kent's attractiveness. She'd assumed the black-and-white photos of him on the dust jackets of his books were the usual glamor job. They weren't. But the posed, airbrushed studio portraits hadn't captured an interesting gritty dynamic edge about the man. She knew him to be only a couple of years beyond her own age of twenty-nine, but he looked older. Evidently Masterson wasn't a man who worried much about the effects of constant exposure to wind and sun on his face. But he was waiting for her to finish her response to his comment about Chinese tourism.

"Their tourist service has been going all out to woo us back," she went on. "Which is why they invited a group of travel agents over here, hoping we'd push China as a destination to our customers."

Did that chiseled face always carry a look that seemed to dare the world to throw him a challenge? And had that strength wavered at all during his well-publicized ordeal with kidnappers a few years ago when his family had been forced to pay a million dollars for his safe return? The thought made her shudder.

"Chinese officialdom is of two minds about the whole tourism thing, though," Kent observed, bringing Tara back to the here and now. "They particularly don't like having outsiders wandering through Tibet alone, as I'm doing. They desperately need hard currency, but the presence of foreigners makes it difficult to control the population. Tourists don't take kindly to seeing innocent people gunned down in the streets."

Kent sat back and perused the lovely flame-haired woman sitting opposite him. He liked the femininity of the swingy black skirt that showed off a pair of shapely legs, instead of the jeans or pants of most of the other tourists. And he'd certainly noticed how well the kelly-green sweater hugged her tantalizing curves. In another context, he'd like to spend more time with her. On this trip, unfortunately, he had business to attend to. Business that precluded any further involvement with her.

However, the night promised an unexpected pleasure. He didn't usually come on to women he'd just met, but he had an astonishingly strong urge to hold her supple body in his arms again, as he'd done this morning. And what man wouldn't be overcome by the soft power of those startling jeweled eyes fringed with incredibly long, dark lashes? Maybe the lady was unaware of the numerous times she'd touched him, but the way she was looking at him right now indicated her mind might be running along the same lines as his.

If only he could erase the smile that had crept over his face since meeting her. By now, he suspected, it was starting to look a little silly. And he wished his seduction skills weren't so rusty. The embarrassing truth was that Tara Morgan very likely enjoyed a love life much more interesting than his. Since his divorce he'd spent most of his time photographing in remote areas with, at most, a native guide for a companion.

"What permits do you have?" he asked idly as he slid his hand smoothly over the top of hers. She trembled slightly at his touch. And when she spoke, he was pleased to hear the hint of breathlessness in her voice.

"The usual spots. Shigatse. Lhatse. I didn't need the Alien's Travel Permit to Lhasa since I was already in China on a three-month visa. If there's time, I might try to hit Everest Base Camp. Some of my mountain-climbing clients would be interested in that."

Exceedingly conscious of Kent's fingers circling over the pulse point on the inside of her wrist, she hoped they wouldn't pick up the quick jog her heartbeat had just taken. Or at least that he wouldn't think its irregular rhythm had to do with anything other than her excitement at being in a strange land.

She had to admit, though, that the ridiculously pleasant tingle weaving its way up her arm was due entirely to the gentle motion of his slightly roughened fingers. She'd never realized the tender skin between a person's fingers could be an erogenous zone. Kent's pleasurable stroking, however, was demonstrating that it was. The alert tautness growing in her thighs made her sit up straighter to counter it. The man's quirky smile played lazily around his wide, sensual mouth, hinting that he was well aware of his effect on her. When he slid his finger between two of hers to trail slowly down their length and back upward to her palm, she understood perfectly the meaning of his unspoken query.

The fact that she didn't immediately reject the subtle invitation to visit his bed, but found herself giving it much more thought than it deserved, was surprising enough. That she actually felt a twinge of regret at having to refuse it was unprecedented. Engaging in a brief affair with Kent Masterson might be interesting, Tara allowed. But even before the perils of casual sex became well-known, she'd been careful to keep her relationships with men under strict control. That hadn't proved to be any great problem—until now.

Kent definitely wasn't the kind of man who could give a woman the time needed to develop a relationship beyond the purely sexual level. He was into serious wandering. Oh, she went off to remote places for a week or two with a group of clients. But this fascinating man had macheted his way through the Amazon jungle and crunched across the frozen Arctic tundra for weeks, even months on end, all by himself. And he came out with breathtaking photos of headhunting Indians or vanishing traditional Inuit life that showed less venturesome souls scenery and ways of life they'd otherwise never see.

No. The internationally renowned photographer was admirable, but he wasn't a man she'd want to get involved with. She slowly began to slide her hand out from under his. He moved quickly to recapture it. Leaning forward on his elbows, he clasped her hand between both of his and lifted her fingers in front of his mouth. Alarm spread through her, followed by something she absolutely refused to acknowledge as a tiny thrill of delight. Wasn't he gentleman enough to accept a lady's refusal?

Surprise lifted one of his dark eyebrows. She worried that his speculative gaze might uncover her ambivalent feelings about her refusal. Innate honesty forced her to admit that she wasn't entirely sure she could continue to resist those feelings if he pressed his suit. Holding her eyes captive, he brushed his lips across her knuckles. An arousing tide of heat washed over her as strongly as if he'd actually pressed his mouth to hers.

Then to her great relief he released her. But not until a small heft of his shoulders spoke of his disappointment. A disappointment Tara wished she didn't share quite so strongly.

It was long past time, she decided, to disclose to him who she was and why she was here. She'd been quick to accept Elliott's offer to pick up the hefty tab for her trip to Tibet in return for her performing another service for him. She could never have afforded the side trip from Beijing on her own. Besides the money, she didn't mind taking on these courier assignments. In her line of work it didn't hurt to have someone like the deputy chief of American intelligence owe her a favor. If a Third World country suddenly became dangerous while she had a group on tour there, Elliott could do a lot to guarantee their safety.

"Our meeting wasn't exactly accidental, Kent," she said, curling her fingers safely around her tiny bowl of Chinese tea. "We have a mutual friend in Washington."

"Oh?" Masterson responded indifferently, as if he were still entertaining thoughts of their previous subject, excitingly real though never actually stated. "Who?"

She lowered her voice. "Roger Elliott."

The immediate stiffening of Kent's body told her this was not news he was pleased to hear. His dark eyes narrowed warily.

"What do you have to do with Elliott? What's going on here?"

"He sent me to contact you. His orders were to obtain the film from you and carry it back to our embassy in Beijing."

Their earlier rapport melted away beneath Kent's scowl. "Damn it. You're one of Elliott's spies, aren't you?"

It might not do, Tara thought, to let him know that she was not much more than a fill-in agent like him. She'd acted as courier for Elliott a few times. The assignments were simple enough: pick up a letter or a package from a certain person at a certain place and deliver it to another person in another place. But that's as far as her agent expertise went. Anyway, Kent didn't wait for either her confirmation or denial.

He leaned toward her, his low, angry voice carrying no farther than her ears. "I thought I'd made it clear to Elliott that I wanted to work alone on this project."

"There's no point in arguing with *me* about it, Kent. I'm simply here to carry out his instructions."

"Dammit, I—hell, we can't talk here." Kent's eyes lasered into the inattentive waiter, and the man jumped to it as if he feared some physical retribution from the tall, suddenly mean-looking foreigner. Kent scribbled his name on the check and scraped back his chair.

Tara followed him through the hotel lobby out into the street.

"Look," he said after waiting for a strolling Japanese couple to pass them. "I don't want your help. I don't need your help. I told the man I'd get the photographs to him and I will."

"There's no need to get huffy about this. I don't intend to get in your way. My only job is to carry the film to Beijing."

"Your job is not my problem. When Elliott asked me to tackle his mission, I laid out to him exactly how I intended to proceed. And that doesn't include becoming involved with any of his regular agents."

Tara pressed her lips tightly shut for a moment to avoid making an angry rejoinder. "Look, Kent. Be reasonable. Elliott just wants to be sure the film makes it out of China, and he probably assumes I can do that faster than you might. It's not too hard to figure out why. Let's face it. Kent Masterson has been known to become embroiled in headline-making situations. Look at the time you were kidnapped by bandits in Africa."

In the light of the street lamp, she could see a tiny nerve working in his jaw. "Before going there I checked with the State Department, who assured me the region was perfectly safe."

"I didn't say you were responsible for your own kidnapping. I said it made news. And just last year you popped up in the middle of a Central American revolution."

"I was only there to photograph the erupting volcano. And even your friends the intelligence experts hadn't foreseen that the local guerrillas would pick that time to stage a new offensive."

"Nevertheless the State Department apparently had to do some pretty fast talking to save your hide."

"Okay, so getting the perfect picture is more important to me than to most other photographers and sometimes I take personal risks to do that. That's a weakness of mine. Just one of many, some would say. But because of my family name incidents involving me tend to provoke press coverage where another man can make his mistakes in private.''

Masterson was quick to accept full responsibility for the incidents, Tara noted, but that responsibility didn't lie entirely with him. It sounded as if he'd taken the sensible precautions any traveler in dangerous places could be expected to take.

He shoved his hands in his pockets and shook his head in annoyance. ''I should have known Elliott would pull something like sending in a pro to keep tabs on me. He obviously wasn't happy about being forced to use a civilian, even though I already had the perfect credentials plus all the necessary travel clearances from the Chinese.''

''Can't you see that cooperating with me will only make your job easier?'' Tara argued. ''After you've taken your photographs, you give me the film. I go on my way, leaving you free to wander at will taking your pictures all over the country—and with a greater degree of safety to yourself, I might add.''

''I can handle my own safety,'' Kent shot back. ''I was quite willing to help our government score one against the invaders of a country that has special meaning for my family, but I intend to do it *my* way.'' He pulled a hand from his pocket and made a sharp dismissing motion.

''The discussion's over, lady. Enjoy your stay in Tibet. From here on it has nothing to do with me. I'm leaving for Shigatse early tomorrow morning and I won't be seeing you again.''

Tara understood from the hard set of his face there'd be no moving him. ''All right. I can't force you to cooperate. If you change your mind about accepting my help, I'll be here for the next couple of weeks.''

Without so much as a courteous good-night, Kent stalked away.

Tara stood gazing after him. Why was the irritating man so dead set against accepting her help? she wondered. His quick anger at learning who she was seemed a curious overreaction after the very pleasant evening they'd shared up to that point. Did he think that she was intruding on his personal turf? Although Elliott hadn't clued her in to the details of Kent's mission, she obviously knew he had one. So why was the photographer acting for all the world like a man with something to hide?

So much for her job as courier, Tara thought glumly. A milk run, Elliott had called it. He'd assured her she should encounter no problem getting the film back to American officials in Beijing for inclusion in diplomatic pouches to Washington. All her previous missions for the intelligence officer had gone off without a hitch, but this time she'd hit a snag in the person of the infuriating Kent Masterson.

And there didn't seem to be very much she could do about it.

Chapter 2

Kent tossed his few belongings into the small, detachable plastic suitcases that fitted onto his motorcycle. He'd long ago learned to travel light. The greater part of his pack was always his photographic equipment. Evidently carrying out Randall's request wasn't going to be as easy as he'd first thought. By agreeing to take on Elliott's mission he'd already added a serious complication to his real agenda. Now Tara Morgan had arrived to add another.

He could see now that he never should have acted on his immediate attraction to the woman. His annoyance at himself grew. Why the hell wasn't he able to avoid thinking of her? Fortunately, she was a complication he could do something about. Leaving the hotel they shared and not seeing her again would get that problem, at least, off his back.

The last thing in the world he needed right now was to have Elliott's lovely agent hounding him. He hadn't hesitated to accept the mission to photograph the secret Chinese installation in Qinghai. His grandfather, with even less love for the Communist Chinese government than he had, had resoundingly seconded Elliott's intelligence-gathering operation. But what Elliott and his pretty spy didn't know was that their temporary enlistee had reasons of his own for his trip to Tibet. And he didn't intend to let either of them interfere with his plans. Plans that had begun with the terse message from Randall Masterson.

So unusual had been his grandfather's urgent summons that Kent had quit in the middle of a shoot in Borneo to hurry back to the stately Philadelphia mansion that had served as home to Mastersons for two centuries. White-haired Randall, the family patriarch, had scarcely greeted his favorite grandson before herding him into the library, shutting the door behind them and pulling an envelope out of his pocket.

"I've received a letter from the high lama."

Kent couldn't have been more surprised. His grandfather's Tibetan friend had for so long been a part of family folklore that he seemed more like a character of legend than a real man.

"From Songtsen? After all this time?"

"Hand delivered to me personally by a monk from his monastery. You'll see the reason for such secrecy when you read the letter." Randall handed his grandson the folded sheet of paper.

Somehow Kent had expected a communication from the lama who'd saved his grandfather from freezing to death in the Himalayas to consist of something more exotic than a few typewritten lines.

"It says here he wants your help in smuggling some kind of religious treasure out of Tibet." Kent gave his grandfather a wry smile. "In writing only one letter in almost forty years, you'd think he could spare a little more in the way of details."

The old man gave a dry chuckle. "Songtsen never was very talkative. As I recall, when he found me in the snow he just picked me up and carried me to the monastery."

"What kind of treasure is he talking about? Gold? Jewels?"

"I doubt that. Most likely he's referring to a *thangka,* a sacred scroll painting depicting a deity. Perhaps he wants it exhibited in a museum to remind people of Tibet's on-going destruction. Maybe he wants it sold. A fine antique *thangka* painted by a master could fetch a princely sum from a collector. That money would go a long way toward helping out the Tibetan refugee communities in India and elsewhere. You'll find out when you meet him. I only hope it isn't a scroll several yards wide meant to hang on the outside wall of a monastery."

For a moment Randall Masterson's bright blue eyes narrowed in the same kind of thoughtful squint his grandson often fell into when considering a problem. "I owe the man my life, and this is the first time he's ever asked anything of me. I only wish I could undertake this task myself."

"I'll do it, Grandfather."

"I hoped you would, boy. Trekking around the Hima-layas isn't the sort of thing your father or brother could do. I see this as a matter of family honor, Kent. In my opin-ion the Mastersons are forever indebted to Songtsen of Tibet."

"I agree, Ran. I'll be glad to do what I can to repay that debt. Not that smuggling out a painting can equal saving your life." Kent sank to one knee by the old man's chair. "Quite aside from anything we all owe Songtsen, Grand-father, I want to do this for you personally. I owe you a debt of my own."

"How's that, boy?"

"You've always supported me in my desire to go my own way. The rest of the family weren't happy when I refused to enter the foreign service or the law, but you took my side in those arguments. I'll always be grateful to you for that."

"It was the right move. You were never very good at following other people's rules. Not even mine," the old man added ruefully. "Like when you insisted on getting a degree in engineering when no Masterson before you ever had."

"Maybe that was why I did it, Grandfather."

The old man's eyes crinkled in amusement. "I suspect it was. Especially since you apparently have no desire to build a bridge or a dam. No. I could see you were hell-bent on running around the world taking your pictures. No argument would have stopped you.''

His grandfather understood perfectly. Mastersons had played their roles as ambassadors and advisers to presidents since the first American Masterson had served as aide-de-camp to General George Washington. But Kent had never wanted to go into the family business. The rigidity and formality of the diplomatic life embraced by his brother, his father and his grandfather had never appealed to him. And many would agree that diplomacy and tact had never been his strong suit. He preferred to call the shots as he saw them.

''We're more alike than you might think, boy.''

Kent took his grandfather's hand and gave it an affectionate squeeze. ''I kind of like that idea, Randall,'' he said as he stood up. ''I'll leave for Tibet as soon as possible.''

''We'll have to pull a few strings to get you the broadest permits for independent travel, but I think we can manage that. The American ambassador in Beijing is a friend of mine. He owes me one.''

''You'll write the lama to let him know I'm coming?''

''No. It would be too risky. I'm sure the Chinese keep a man like Songtsen under surveillance. They'd intercept any letters coming to him from outside Tibet. Oh! By the way, the messenger told me my old friend had been recognized as the reincarnation of a dead lama and because of his wisdom has been given the honorific *rimpoche*.''

''So I'll address him as Songtsen Rimpoche?''

''Yes.''

''I assume I'd better use the cover of taking photographs as my reason for being in the country.''

''Definitely. Not only do we not want the Chinese to get wind of this, we'd best keep the State Department in the dark about it. I haven't mentioned Songtsen's letter to anyone but you. The thing is, what Songtsen has asked us to do isn't legal, although in my mind it's certainly moral. The Chinese government won't allow Tibetan artifacts to

be taken out of the country—not even by the people who
rightfully own them. They'd like to get their hands on all
of them and put them in a museum or destroy them. You
can bet that if Songtsen is asking for outside help with this
object, it's bound to be important. And if our government finds out about it they'll try to stop you in order to
avoid provoking an international incident. I'm afraid,
Kent, that if you're caught on Chinese soil, the State Department will not be able to intercede on your behalf.''

"I understand, and I'm willing to take the risk. My
publisher has been pushing for a book of photographs of
the Himalayan region. He'll be delighted to hear how soon
I'll be ready to do that.''

Tara had learned her lesson about altitude problems.
She felt fine, but decided against any more high climbs for
a while. Today she'd visit a monastery located at the *bottom* of a mountain, and she'd make her trip by taxi. According to the guidebook, the lesser-known monastery
wasn't as large and impressive as some others, but it was
one of the most ancient. She liked the idea of discovering
a place most other tourists wouldn't bother to see.

The demolishment of Elliott's plan clearly wasn't her
fault, but she didn't like being unable to carry out her end
of their deal. She was even more dejected about how mistaken she'd been in her assessment of Kent Masterson.
She'd always considered herself a good judge of character, but she'd certainly struck out with the photographer.

Even before she'd met him, she'd admired the man. His
concern for her at the Potala had made her like him, and
their interesting dinner conversation had increased that
liking. What a disappointment to discover that he was such
an arrogant, macho loner that he refused to accept even
the simplest kind of help.

There was still a chance that she might be able to obtain
the film from Kent. Elliott had told her the time frame for
receiving the package depended entirely on the photographer. Almost any way out of Tibet involved returning to
Lhasa to catch a plane or a bus. The Chinese seldom al-

lowed people into or out of the country any other way. She'd stay here and wait for a couple of weeks to see if he turned up again. Meantime she'd enjoy the sights and experience of the strange and exotic area associated with the mythical Shangri-La, the hidden paradise of James Hilton's *Lost Horizon*.

Outside the monastery, Tara almost stumbled on a man sprawled in the dirt. She thought he might be injured and was about to bend down to help him when he stood up and chanted a mantra. To her astonishment, he then took a few steps to the point his leather-mittened outspread hands had reached and threw himself down on the ground once again. When she noticed the wooden knob tied onto his forehead she realized he was a worshiper who would encircle the monastery in this painstaking way to atone for past sins or to build up good karma for his next incarnation. Tibet was full of such sights so foreign to Westerners.

Tara paid the toll collector at the entrance to the monastery and entered the main chamber where she joined a long line of Tibetan pilgrims winding its way through the chapels. Following the lead of the Tibetan woman just ahead of her, she spun the squeaking bronze prayer wheel that was as tall as a man.

The rattle of the prayer wheels, the sounds of shuffling feet—more of them encased incongruously in high-top sneakers than in the traditional soft Tibetan boots—and the murmur of prayers underscored the respectful hush the place commanded. Occasionally visitors would stop to pour a little of the melted butter they carried in thermos bottles into a bronze lamp basin to keep the floating wicks burning. Pilgrims believed the smoke carried their prayers to the gods.

Tara's wandering gaze caught on a dark head towering above the others ahead of her in the throng, and her heart gave an odd little double beat of recognition. What was Kent Masterson doing here? He'd told her he was leaving Lhasa to photograph the monastery at Shigatse, almost two hundred miles in the opposite direction. Evidently he'd made that excuse simply to get rid of her. After he'd learned her identity, he'd made it painfully clear he didn't want her around. For some peculiar reason his rejection of her had felt personal. And it still stung.

The monastery's pervasive calm suddenly shattered as a phalanx of armed men marched into the large chamber, their metal-shod boots pounding a harsh rhythm into the stone floor.

If Tara's gaze hadn't immediately darted back to Kent she might never have seen him duck behind a green-painted column, as if to avoid being seen by the uniformed intruders. He was carrying a *kata*, she noticed, a white ceremonial scarf with long fringes that devotees draped over statues and offered to highly respected lamas.

Indifferent to the sacred surroundings, the Chinese marched down the hall. The hard black eyes of the military officer who led them darted back and forth scanning the line of Tibetans who scurried out of his way. The commander's gaze landed sharply on Tara with a coldness that made her shiver. His inspection lasted only a second or two, but Tara knew a complete picture of her was filed away in the officer's mind. The thought did not cheer her. It was only natural that the man should notice a Westerner, she told herself, but she was glad when the military group had stomped off.

Wondering if the Chinese had given Kent the same sense of unease they'd produced in her, she saw him move unobtrusively away from the crowd and slip furtively behind the heavy drapery covering a doorway.

Immediately her curiosity flared. What on earth was the man up to? Was he going to commit the sacrilege of trying to photograph forbidden sections of the monastery? Maybe he didn't know that parts of the buildings were off-limits to visitors, especially to nonbelieving foreigners. Or maybe he was one of those—like some of the Everest climbers—for whom the very fact of being denied easy accessibility acted as a spur to overcome whatever barrier existed.

Kent had reacted strangely last night when he'd learned who she was, and he'd lied to her about where he'd be this morning. Might there be something going on with Elliott's enlistee that the intelligence officer didn't know about?

She decided to follow him and find out. Trying to look nonchalant, she hung back and slowly made her way over to the doorway. She stopped and quickly turned away when a monk approached. But he simply brushed past her on silent feet on his way to continue his endless devotions.

As a woman, she was even more of an intruder into the private sections of the monastery than Kent was, but she slipped behind the awning to find herself at the top of a stone staircase. The photographer was nowhere in sight. But he could only have gone down the steps that led to a long hall, dark and heavy with the smell of incense and lined with many shrines. A young novice chanted at one; the others were empty.

She turned a corner just in time to see Kent, accompanied by a monk, disappear into another corridor, and she hurried after them. But after walking quickly down the hall she'd been sure was the one they'd taken, she halted. This couldn't be right. The hall was even darker than the others and totally silent. She turned to retrace her steps, but soon found herself lost in a labyrinth of deserted corridors.

Tara fought down increasing nervousness. Instead of just wandering down one shadowy hall after another, the best thing to do, she decided, was to wait in one of the chapels. At least they were lighted, if dimly, and sooner or later one of the monks who lived here had to show up and lead her out.

The basins of butter lamps in the next chapel allowed her to get a good look at her eerie surroundings. A swirl of violent colors clashed in front of her and she wished she'd chosen a less horrific room in which to wait. These murals weren't for the fainthearted. In one, a ring of skeletons danced around a fearsome, multi-eyed goddess wearing a cloak of flayed human skin. The guidebook had informed her that these terrifying spirits were nonetheless considered protectors, but it was hard to believe.

A bright light suddenly flared in front of her. Tara jumped. The young monk carrying the flaming torch seemed every bit as startled as she to find someone in his way. She couldn't understand the words he was saying, but his annoyed shooing motion made his meaning clear.

"I'd love to get out of here, sir, but I don't know how." She raised her hands, shook her head and hunched her shoulders in what she hoped was a universal sign for *I'm hopelessly lost*.

The monk brought his torch closer and gazed seemingly awestruck into her face. With a bow that seemed to Tara unusually deep and respectful in view of the irritation he'd demonstrated a minute ago, the man gestured for her to follow him. She was more than ready to get out of here. Kent Masterson could fend for himself.

Kent gathered that his wait to see the high lama was caused by the inopportune visit of the Chinese military contingent. Blast his luck. He'd hoped to meet Songtsen without the knowledge of Chinese officials. Perhaps they hadn't seen him. At last his guide reappeared to lead him into the presence of a shaven-headed monk of great age and dignity seated on the floor with his legs crossed in front of him in the lotus position.

"Welcome to Tibet, my son," Songtsen said in perfect—if strongly accented—English. Though he was the head of this lamasery, the lama was swathed in the same dark red robe as the other monks.

Kent bowed and presented the lama with the customary gift of a *kata*. "It's a great pleasure to meet my grandfather's friend, Songtsen Rimpoche." He'd tried to keep his demeanor serious, as befitting the occasion, but he felt such pleasure at finally setting eyes on the old man that he couldn't keep himself from smiling broadly. He was glad to see his host's answering smile.

"I, too, am most happy to meet the grandson of Randall Masterson. I hope the years have treated my old friend well."

"My grandfather finds it difficult to follow his doctor's orders to take it easy after suffering a heart attack, but otherwise he is well."

Kent could see that time had been kind to the lama. Though his body was slight, and the hand he offered Kent shook a little, the old man's black eyes were every bit as bright and alert as Randall's.

"I saw the Chinese officials, Rimpoche. Are they a problem for you?"

"The invaders are a problem for all Tibetans. Our Chinese masters do not allow us to teach our people even our own language. Wu Chen, the Chinese colonel who was just here, hates us. It is his pleasure to harass us at every opportunity. He seeks the new Gendun Lama." The rimpoche's gaze took on a sharper intensity. "Do you know of the Gendun Lama?"

"Only that your people hold the Gendun Lama third in religious reverence behind the most revered Dalai Lama and the Panchen Lama."

Songtsen nodded approvingly. "Randall has taught you well. However, let us talk no more of the Chinese."

The high lama gestured Kent toward the small rug next to his. "Come, sit with me, Andrew Masterson. Will you take a bowl of *po-chay,* our Tibetan tea?"

Kent folded his long frame onto the proffered space. "Thank you, I will. But I'm not Andrew, Rimpoche. I'm Kent Masterson."

The lama blinked rapidly and there was a moment's uncomfortable silence. "You are not the older of Randall's two grandsons?"

"I'm afraid not."

To Kent the benign expression on the old man's face changed very slightly, but that momentary look of confusion evidently was enough to bring on a quick question in Tibetan from an elderly monk standing nearby. With his small knowledge of Tibetan, Kent couldn't follow the rapid-fire conversation, but it was clear from the way the three monks in the room were regarding him that they were dismayed to learn that their guest was not Andrew Masterson.

Songtsen held up a hand to stem the tide of anxious comments from his companions. "We knew that age would prevent Randall from making the journey," he said. "And that his son, your father, could not come because of the back injury he suffered years ago, but we expected that Randall would send the elder and more important of the two grandsons."

Kent was used to being odd man out in his family, but it was disconcerting to find these Tibetans so clearly chagrined that he wasn't his highly respected brother.

"I'm afraid Andrew couldn't come. He's heavily engaged in arms limitations talks with the Russians just now, so Randall sent me instead." There was no point in adding that Andrew's element was the diplomatic circuit, definitely not poverty-stricken, Third World areas where decent plumbing and comfortable means of transportation were at a premium.

"So you are the younger son, Kent." The lama digested this information for a moment. "But you too have diplomatic immunity, do you not?"

The lama looked so hopeful Kent was sorry he had to give him more bad news.

"Again, I regret that I must disappoint you, Rimpoche. I carry no diplomatic papers, only a plain American passport."

"Are you at least a married man, Kent Masterson?" Kent thought the high lama's voice was taking on just a hint of desperation. "You have children, yes?"

This conversation wasn't doing a whole lot for his ego. Kent shook his head.

Songtsen's gentle sigh told Kent what a disappointment he was turning out to be. "I'm sure I can serve your needs as well as Andrew could have done, Rimpoche," Kent protested. In fact, he thought wryly, though the Tibetans didn't know it, they were getting a much better deal with the younger brother than the elder. This wasn't Andrew's kind of mission at all. "I'm quite willing to smuggle your *thangka* out of the country."

The lama looked blank. "My what?"

"Forgive me. Perhaps I'm not pronouncing the word correctly. Your *thangka,* the sacred symbol you referred to in your letter to my grandfather."

"Ah, yes, of course, the Light of Buddha."

"Right. I'll get your Light of Buddha out and deliver it wherever you say. But first, Rimpoche, I must ask a favor of you in return. Before I leave Tibet with the *thangka,* I must travel to the province of Qinghai to perform a service for my own country."

Evidently years of meditation and religious exercises hadn't yet resulted in the holy man's mastering of all his emotions, because Kent's words produced a crease of what looked suspiciously like anxiety between Songtsen's eyes. And if Kent's announcement of his identity had produced consternation among the rimpoche's companions, Songtsen's relaying to them the statement their visitor had just made resulted in their expressions of downright alarm.

"We prefer that you not go to Qinghai," the high lama said after another quick conference. "We wish you to take the . . . the Light of Buddha and leave Tibet immediately."

This kind of thing was exactly why he'd never entered the diplomatic service, Kent thought. He was getting just a little tired of having the Tibetans insinuate he would be a total washout at accomplishing the task they'd set him. He wanted to tell them that his intelligence mission would strike a much stronger blow against their conquerors than would smuggling out their painting—no matter how sacred to them—and that he was perfectly capable of doing both. Instead he forced himself into the tactful kind of argument his ambassador brother would make.

"I understand your concern for your treasure, and I share it. However, it's necessary that I make the journey I spoke of. I must discover what the Chinese are building in the wilderness north of the town of Amdo." Maybe his intelligence gathering could start right here, Kent thought.

"Have your people mentioned a large construction site in that region?"

Songtsen nodded. "No one is allowed near it. Our nomads are chased away from land which has been theirs for centuries. Tibetans would never desecrate the land by scraping and gouging huge holes in it as the Chinese do. To us the earth must be treated with respect."

"I agree that the earth must be treated with respect," Kent offered, glad to have found an area where he could live up to Tibetan expectations. "One of the reasons that I make my living taking scenic photographs is that I hope my pictures will instill in others more reverence for the beauty of our world."

The rimpoche considered this for a few seconds. "Then yours is a profession worthy in the sight of Buddha, my son."

Some of Songtsen's distress seemed to be leaving, Kent noted, holding his eyes steady under the priest's penetrating gaze. The moment seemed right to press his case.

"I was hoping you could furnish me with some assistance for the long trip, Rimpoche. I'll need information concerning nomad trails leading from the road to Golmud westward to the construction site." He had committed Elliott's map of the site's location to memory, but getting to an area where there were no roads except for the newly built one leading to the installation wouldn't be easy. "Depending on the weather, I may need a place to stay. Even—I must be honest—a place to hide should I be discovered by the Chinese."

His intensive study of Kent over, Songtsen nodded slowly. "Perhaps it can be done, my son."

A young monk hurried into the room. His obvious eagerness to speak to the high lama didn't make him forget to drop to his knees and touch his forehead to the floor in the gesture of respect due his superior. The monk spoke rapidly in Tibetan, and at Songtsen's nod, returned to the door.

Kent had caught enough of the message to cause him to leap to his feet even before the monk led Tara Morgan into the room. So much for his attempts to evade Elliott's agent. "No, Rimpoche," he protested hurriedly. "This woman mustn't—"

"Please introduce our guest to me, my son," Songtsen interjected.

Since the lama was evidently bent on receiving Tara, Kent had no choice but to bow to the inevitable. "Songtsen Rimpoche, may I present a fellow American, Mrs. Tara Morgan."

The glance of amazement the monks darted at each other gave way to their reverent whispers and deep bows in her direction. Only Songtsen appeared unmoved, although even he bowed his head a little deeper than Kent thought was strictly necessary in acknowledging the introduction.

"Your presence does us honor, lady."

A curious greeting, Tara thought, nodding respectfully at the old man whose air of calm, gentle goodness relieved some of her anxiety.

"The rimpoche is the high lama of this monastery," Kent explained.

Tara stepped back in alarm when the young monk who'd led her into the room fell on his knees in front of her. A quickly spoken command from his superior kept the monk from prostrating himself completely at her feet.

Tara regarded Kent nervously. "Have you gotten yourself in trouble with these people?"

"You had no business following me."

The presence of the monks forced her to hold her tongue. This was no place to resume their argument.

"You were sent to assist Kent Masterson on his mission to the Chinese construction site in the north," the high lama said. "Is it not so?"

Tara's eyes widened in surprise. "Uh, well..." She gave Songtsen a dubious smile. "Will you excuse me a moment, uh...Rimpoche? If you don't mind, I'd like a word with Mr. Masterson." She sidled over to Kent and kept a diplomatic smile on her face as she stage-whispered to the photographer. "What's going on, Kent? They know why you're here?"

"I'll need their help on the journey. Don't worry, Elliott's mission is safe with them. These people have no love for the Chinese. They'll do anything they can to thwart their conquerors."

"He is here at our request," Songtsen interjected.

Kent winced. If the old man kept this up he'd unwittingly torpedo their smuggling project.

"What does he mean, you're here at their request?" Tara asked, her suspicions evidently sparked by Songtsen's unfortunate comment. "Does Elliott know about all this?"

There was a whole lot both Elliott and Tara didn't know. Kent wanted to keep it that way, but the situation seemed to be slipping out of his control. He turned to Songtsen.

"Rimpoche, I must speak to you...privately." The frown he aimed at Tara made it clear whose presence wasn't wanted. To Kent's dismay, instead of asking Tara to leave, Songtsen simply crooked his finger, inviting Kent to bend and speak quietly in his ear.

"You don't understand, Songtsen," Kent pleaded. "This woman is an official of our government. If she learns about the *thangka*, she will inform officials who would try to prevent my taking it out of the country."

Oddly enough the old man, who'd been so perturbed about Kent's identity and his trip into China proper, didn't seem too upset about the appearance of Tara Morgan. Knowing what he did about the culture of Tibet, Kent had a good idea why. He only wished Elliott had chosen a courier with a different name.

The high lama was regarding her with deep consideration. "You say the young woman is a representative of your government?" he finally asked.

At last he was getting somewhere, Kent thought, relieved. "Yes. And you can understand that an official must have no involvement in an illegal act. That was another reason why Randall didn't send my brother. I'm sure you know that it is against the law to remove Tibetan objects from Chinese soil.''

"We do not recognize the laws of the invaders," the old man said dismissively. "We have laws and customs of our own. I sense no evil purpose in the young woman, my son." A flick of a wrinkled hand waved aside Kent's objections. "And I believe the lady can be of help in your mission."

Kent looked hopefully at Songtsen's companions but saw that he could expect no support for his position from them. Their previous dismay had evidently left them. Now all the monks were stealing worshipful glances at Tara and softly mouthing their standard mantra, *Om Mani Padme Hum.*

Tara was growing more confused by the minute. Even for an alien country, this whole scene felt weird. Although their faces reflected no threat whatever, the way these monks were staring at her—or rather, trying so hard not to stare at her—was making her nervous. Moreover, she had the distinct impression that Roger Elliott didn't know about whatever was going on between Kent Masterson and the monks, and wouldn't like it if he did.

It was beginning to look as if she'd better keep tabs on Elliott's photographer. The intelligence chief was depending on her to bring out his film. She'd never failed him before, and it now occurred to her that there was one way she could be certain of accomplishing that.

She came to a decision. "You're right, Songtsen Rimpoche," she said as she stepped forward. "I have been sent to assist Mr. Masterson with his mission." She turned to Kent with a determined lift of her chin. "From here on, Kent, wherever you go, I go, until I have the film. Then you can go your way and I'll go mine."

In a couple of quick strides Kent was by her side and glowering down at her. "Good Lord, woman. Don't be ridiculous. This trip north will be no picnic. It will take at least two days each way, probably more. We'll run into freezing weather in the passes and I'll be traveling on my motorcycle."

"I'm going with you."

"There'll be no room for you or your baggage. I'll have to carry my own food, a sleeping bag, an extra can of gasoline."

Tara looked up at the brown eyes that retained no trace of last night's warmth. She was taking this step, she told herself virtuously, only out of a desire to uphold her end of her bargain with Elliott. Any muddled personal feelings for Kent Masterson had absolutely nothing to do with it.

"Then you really need me. I'll provide two extra arms for holding equipment, and carry some of the pack on my back if need be. Plus I'll bring only this." She held out her handbag—a large black nylon tote. "It won't take up much space. Besides, I can drive a motorcycle, so I can spell you when you get tired."

From the grim look on Kent's face she could see that he wasn't about to let her take any space whatever. "I don't think you understand," he said with dangerous control. "This isn't the kind of leisurely trip you arrange for your clients. I'll be pushing to use every available minute of daylight. I'm heading into the wilderness. There'll be no hotels, no restaurants."

Kent frowned down into the jade eyes that had disturbed his equanimity from the first moment he'd glanced into them. Blast the woman. He wasn't used to having people contradict him and didn't like having to contest a case that he thought was self-evident. He shot home the argument he was sure would do the trick. "Even more important as far as you're concerned. There'll be no ladies' rooms along the way. Like other travelers, we'll simply have to squat by the side of the road."

To his satisfaction, his lovely adversary paled. He'd won the debate. But against all reason a part of him regretted that he wouldn't be spending the next few days with the woman who continued to exert such an unexplainable tug on his emotions.

But she was still glaring up at him. "If you can handle it," she announced, a bit weakly, "I can."

Damn! He was having as much trouble dissuading the woman today as he'd had yesterday trying to persuade her to spend the night with him. Remembering her refusal then gave him an idea. He stepped closer to her, deliberately crowding into her personal space. He was so close his chest brushed against her breasts and he could feel the heat of her body. He had to work to keep from betraying the fact that an answering heat was curling through his loins. He smiled down at her and pitched his voice low.

"You can, huh? Well, let's just see if you can handle this. For a long period of time we'll be out there in the wilderness ... alone ... together ... just you and me ... camping out at night ... sleeping side by side ... all alone. Sounds real interesting, doesn't it?"

He delivered his comments in short, hard bursts, hammering home details of a situation that should worry her. He felt like a heel for using her own vulnerability against her. He respected her for refusing the advances of a man she hardly knew. But aside from the need for secrecy, he really did want to spare the woman. He hadn't exaggerated the toughness of his proposed trip.

Tara wanted to back away from Kent's overwhelming nearness. She forced herself to hold her position and look up at him boldly. She liked neither the man's suggestive remarks nor his provocative smile, but she'd be darned if she'd let him scare her off. She was used to taking care of herself. And if she wasn't entirely sure of being able to do that with him, she didn't intend to let him see it.

"Then I'd better get over to the Barkhor and pick up a sleeping bag of my own," she said with equal finality.

The woman was a nuisance all right, Kent allowed. But he couldn't help admiring her grit. All his objections continued to run up against the stone walls of both Tara's insistence on remaining with him and the rimpoche's calm assurance that her presence was all part of the wisdom of Buddha.

Kent put less faith in the wisdom of Buddha than he did the machinations of the American intelligence chief and his beautiful but exasperating agent. However, it was possible that her presence on the difficult journey north might prove useful in some way. And he had to admit that the prospect of spending several days alone with her did have its intriguing aspects.

Chapter 3

The red-and-white BMW motorcycle sped through land that hadn't known wheeled transport until this century. On the Chinese-built road they were able to make sixty miles an hour even with Tara's added weight. The first part of their drive through the lush Lhasa valley proved to be pleasant, and warm enough so that neither Kent nor Tara needed to wear their jackets.

Photographs of the snow-capped Himalayas led people to think of Tibet as a northern country. In fact, Lhasa shared the same latitude as Cairo, Egypt, Houston, Texas and Daytona Beach, Florida. Tara was grateful for the sun visor of the helmet Kent had provided that blocked out the hot, direct rays of the sun beating down on the Tibetan plateau. He'd bought the helmet from a French tourist who was leaving the country.

There were still patches of tilled fields to be seen against the backdrop of the brown and barren mountains ranging away to the horizon. They'd been riding for hours when Kent drove off the road to park the heavily laden motorcycle on the side of a hill. Saving their packets of dried food for farther into their journey when they'd encounter no villages, they'd stopped at a tiny shop a mile down the road to buy containers of refreshing yogurt and fill their thermos with hot water for instant coffee.

Tara doffed the protective helmet and shook out her hair. She was glad for the break. Glad that for a while, at least, she could put a little distance between herself and her driver. Spending the past six hours pressed up against Kent's warm, strong back on the dual seat that left no room whatever between driver and passenger was all too enjoyably bothersome. She'd simply have to work harder at ignoring those feelings.

If only she didn't face several more days of the closeness that made it difficult to remember that she was with him for one purpose only, and that her decision to remain with him had nothing whatever to do with the unwanted attraction he continued to hold for her.

She knew perfectly well that Kent had agreed to take her with him only under duress. And when she'd left the hotel early this morning to meet him in the Tibetan quarter a few blocks away, she'd half expected to find herself waiting for a date who never showed. But he'd been waiting impatiently for her, astride his powerful machine. He hadn't even made her carry anything. He'd just taken her bag and strapped it securely to the small luggage rack in the back of her seat.

Her companion had spoken little on their journey. The roar of the motor and the necessity to focus his concentration on driving on a road that twisted and turned treacherously around and up mountainsides kept conversation to a minimum.

Kent was eating standing up to work out the kinks brought on from spending hours on a motorcycle seat. As he gazed at the tumbled ruins of a monastery on a mountainside on the opposite side of the river, his thoughtful almost-squint deepened and his face grew even more grim.

"Look, Kent," Tara finally said, irritated. "I know you're not happy about having me along, but do you have to keep on looking so darn mad about it? Like it or not, I'm here, so let's make the best of it, okay?"

He glanced down at her. "What? Oh. No. That's not it. Don't think I'm not still highly annoyed that you insisted on coming along, but right now—" he nodded toward the ruins "—that's the sight that's making me both angry and very sad. Only a few years ago that monastery housed hundreds, perhaps thousands of monks. It flourished until the sixties when hordes of young Chinese Red Guards rampaged through the country bent on destroying all vestiges of Tibetan culture."

Disgust tinged his voice. "That monastery, and others that had stood for centuries, were dynamited into rubble. They burned scriptures and stole tons of gold and silver religious objects and melted them down." The wondrous, mysterious Tibet Randall had known was gone forever. Systematically exterminated by the Chinese invaders.

"I'm glad my grandfather will never see the terrible things that have happened to the land he remembers so fondly."

Kent was providing her with one surprise after another, Tara thought. He'd mentioned something about Tibet being meaningful to his family for some reason, but she hadn't known he harbored such deep personal feelings for the country. Nor that any member of his family had been here before him. "Your grandfather has been to Tibet? When?"

"He was sent here by President Roosevelt during the Second World War. The American government was seeking alternative supply routes to our Chinese allies. It was a useless mission, of course. Even then Tibetans weren't eager to do the Chinese any favors. And the Himalayas were still too great a barrier to men and matériel. Randall almost died trying to get through them. If Songtsen hadn't found him in the snow, he would have. He made another trip here in the early fifties, just before the Chinese overran the place."

"So that's what you were doing at the monastery yesterday? Relaying your grandfather's greetings to the high lama?"

Kent averted his eyes and spooned up another mouthful of yogurt. "Now it's the faith of Tibetans that keeps the soul of their country alive. The power of their religion is the only weapon they have to fling against Chinese military might."

Kent's eloquent defense of a conquered people made Tara ashamed she hadn't paid more attention to Tibet's struggles for freedom. She remembered the news reports of the Dalai Lama's winning of the Nobel Peace Prize but, like most Americans, she knew little about his country's history. That reminded her of yesterday's curious meeting with the monks.

"Kent? There was something strange about that whole scene in the monastery. The way those monks looked at me..."

"Most likely it was because of your name. It's perfect for this country."

Tara looked blank.

"Tara is the name of one of the most revered of Tibetan goddesses."

"Is it? I doubt if my parents knew that when they gave me the name. They think it's Irish."

"Come to think of it," Kent said, "from the way the monks were acting yesterday, there may be more to it than just being impressed with your name. You know that Buddhists are strong believers in reincarnation?"

Tara nodded.

"It wouldn't surprise me if they've come to the conclusion you may be a manifestation of the goddess."

Tara was stunned. "You're telling me that they actually think I'm a goddess?"

"Could be. The idea of a living goddess isn't unknown in the East. In neighboring Nepal a little girl is chosen as an incarnate goddess. She's kept pampered in a temple, her feet never touching the ground, until puberty."

"You can't really mean they'd apply something like that to *me*."

"I do mean it. To Tibetans, the supernatural is as real as these rocks are to you and me. And who's to say they're wrong?'' The anger that had hardened Kent's face a moment ago was gone. Now the sexy grin again played around his lips. ''How does it feel to be a goddess?''

''Don't joke about it, Kent. I find the whole idea disturbing.''

Kent shrugged. ''I may be mistaken. Their reaction may simply have been due to the fact that they'd never seen a woman with your coloring.''

''That must be it. Remember the child in the Potala? When the little guy saw me, he looked like he couldn't believe his eyes. In any case, I'd just as soon not have any more people bowing to me.''

Tara wasn't the only one who'd noticed some strange undertones during the meeting with the high lama, Kent conceded. Why Songtsen and his monks should have been so upset that the man they were about to trust with their sacred scroll wasn't a married man with children was beyond him. But even Randall had admitted that Tibetan ways were often mysterious to outsiders. As near as Kent could make out with his small knowledge of the language, the monks were working from the words of Tibet's last State Oracle, who apparently had made some murky prophecies about the religious object they wished smuggled to the West.

''And what did Songtsen mean yesterday when he said you were there at their request?'' Tara asked.

He had to keep her mind off those kinds of questions, Kent decided, until he'd given her the blasted film she seemed so set on retrieving and she disappeared from his life. He sauntered over to sit beside her on the boulder. ''Remember what I said yesterday about us being all alone out here?'' he asked casually as he gently fitted a finger into the interesting little hollow that showed above the opening of her shirt collar. The rapid pulse he could feel fluttering under the soft and silky skin made him wish he weren't only playing a game with her. ''Right now we have enough privacy to engage in any activity that might come to mind.''

He wasn't in the habit of thrusting himself on women who weren't entirely willing, but she didn't have to know that. A pink flush rose quickly to the lightly freckled, creamy white oval of her face.

"Stop that."

The slight tremor he heard in the weakly delivered objection provided him with a victory of sorts. However, he found it took surprising effort to keep himself from carrying his investigations lower to the enticing swell of her breasts. But he managed to draw back his hand.

"Move it, woman," he said gruffly, getting up to stride back to the machine. "We've lots of miles to cover. We can't just sit here and chat for the rest of the afternoon."

Tara's question, which he had no intention of answering, had prodded a question of his own. As they were leaving Songtsen's room yesterday, he'd caught the old man's last muttered words. "So it begins," the rimpoche had said. "May the Lord Buddha grant a happy conclusion to our great and perilous undertaking." It seemed to Kent like a rather heavy-duty prayer to lay on in view of the fact that his carrying a rolled-up painting out of the country couldn't prove all that perilous. But then Tibetans did set great store by the most important of their *thangkas*.

Tara was now convinced she'd done the right thing by coming with the photographer. She hadn't missed the fact that he'd deliberately avoided answering her last question. She was willing to bet that Roger Elliott didn't know everything there was to know about his man in Tibet. Her suspicion was growing that Masterson might have reasons of his own for being here beyond the obvious one of taking photographs of the country and the secret mission for American intelligence. She intended to find out what those reasons were.

The landscape grew more barren and the temperature much colder as their vehicle strained into the passes. Every so often Kent had to stop and adjust the motorcycle's carburetor for altitude.

Tara layered on a sweater. Later she fastened the collar of her down parka tightly around her neck. Kent zipped the fur lining into his leather jacket. Both added gloves. Kent kept going long after nightfall, slipping into the wake of a truck to allow its larger headlights to cut a swath through the darkness. The wet snow that had pelted them for the past hour was beginning to trickle uncomfortably down Tara's neck and into her sleeves.

Angling his face over his shoulder, Kent shouted so his passenger could hear him over the sound of the motor and roar of the wind. "The road is getting too slick for safe driving, and we can't sleep out in this tonight. Let's try for shelter in that village up ahead. I hope my Tibetan will be good enough to let them know what we want."

Calling the few small, crumbling houses clinging to a hillside a village was giving the place an importance it didn't deserve. But a friendly and hospitable resident, delighted to find himself unexpectedly playing host to Western visitors, offered the weary travelers a corner of his tiny house.

Kent's arms and shoulders already ached from the effort of holding the motorbike steady in the face of constant pounding by the wind, and he knew tomorrow's leg of the trip would be even more difficult. He looked at the young woman curled up already asleep next to him and smiled. His enforced traveling companion had been less trouble than he'd expected. No trouble at all, really. She hadn't complained once—not even about these bottom-line accommodations.

There was something about Tara Morgan, he mused, waiting for sleep to claim him—an appealing vibrancy that matched the most colorful sights of this alien land. At the same time he sensed a softness, a vulnerability about her he wouldn't have expected to find in an intelligence agent. He'd been all too electrifyingly conscious of her soft body pressed along his back and her arms clasped in front of him during the long day. He wasn't about to tell her, of course, but he'd enjoyed her company, enjoyed having someone to talk to on their breaks. If only she didn't ask so many questions he didn't want to answer.

* * *

When Kent shook her awake in the morning, Tara was sure she'd been sleeping for no more than ten minutes. She had to admire the seeming relish with which he downed the breakfast of *tsampa* and tea their host provided. Her coddled Western stomach recoiled after one sip of the Tibetan tea boiled from shavings of the iron-hard dark green tea brick and flavored with salt and a dollop of rancid yak butter. She did manage to eat the *tsampa*, which was a kind of gruel made of roasted barley flour moistened with tea.

When they were ready to leave, Kent repaid the old man's kindness by offering him a photograph of the Dalai Lama. The tears of gratitude welling up in their benefactor's black eyes made her glad that her companion had disobeyed guidebook warnings that the Chinese forbade the importation of photos of the god-king. The man's response to Kent's gift belied Chinese hopes that Tibetans would soon forget their former ruler and religious leader.

Riding pillion behind Kent once more, Tara ducked her head against his back to avoid the cold wind that robbed her of breath. She was wearing long underwear under heavy cotton pants but the rushing wind chilled the outsides of her thighs to numbness.

Only the long gray ribbon of tarmac stretching away to the horizon linked them to any level of human contact. Occasionally they'd catch glimpses of small groups of nomads herding their yaks across the grasslands edging the bleak, wind-scoured wastelands of the Chang Tang—a rugged wilderness deadly for the unprepared or the unwary.

"Heads up, Tara!" Kent called, slowing the machine. "There's a Chinese work gang up ahead repairing the road. There'll likely be a càdre with them. Low-level officials like to lord it over foreigners and he'll probably demand to see our papers. My permits were signed at the highest levels, so there shouldn't be any problem. I'd just as soon they didn't get a good look at you, though, so keep your visor down and don't speak unless you're spoken to."

They drove slowly by the group of dour, shovel-wielding Chinese, whose work slowed perceptibly. As Kent had feared, the unkempt cadre in a blue Mao suit strutted into the middle of the road and imperiously waved them down. Kent passed his papers into the man's bony hand. Tara followed Kent's orders to keep quiet. Fortunately the official seemed less interested in examining their papers than in giving the Westerners' luxury motorcycle an envious inspection.

Tara breathed easier when they'd left the road crew far behind. The scenery grew ever more desolate—endless miles of gray-brown hills streaked with coarse grass dotted by grazing sheep. Boredom became her biggest problem. From time to time the drone of the engine would lull her into a doze. Whenever Kent felt her slump against him, he'd shout back at her to stay awake or she could fall off.

Tara had no illusions about what would happen if they had any kind of accident out in this deserted area. No police helicopters would descend to whisk them away for rapid lifesaving procedures at a well-equipped hospital. It could take hours, even days, to obtain even the most primitive kind of medical attention.

That thought always sprang to mind in the moments of stark terror when they'd round a bend to find a truck hurtling down on them. The trucks, many painted a garish blue, all looked as if they dated from the fifties, and they didn't seem to follow any discernible rules of the road.

Kent always managed to veer out of harm's way, but often he shouted curses after the vehicles that threatened to end their journey—not to mention their lives—out in the middle of nowhere. Tara's respect for the photographer grew. The motorcycle's sleek white fairing provided him some protection from the wind, and its heated handgrips kept his fingers from freezing, but only his sheer determination and strength held their vehicle, shuddering in furious gusts, on the road.

She remembered her father warning her that the main hazards of motorcycling lay right between the ears of the biker. Maintaining concentration became a serious prob-

lem on long trips. Kent's concentration never seemed to
falter. The back she rested against from time to time never
lost its posture of alert readiness. The powerful machine,
sometimes called the rich man's dirt bike, suited its owner's rugged masculinity, she thought. The idea of the lone
cowboy reveling in the freedom of the open road and
broad, fenceless vistas defined him better than did the
pampered, privileged life-style to which he was born.

Hour after hour they plowed through countryside that
possessed its own kind of desolate beauty, past distantly
spaced villages that seemed medieval in their squalor.
Often she was ready to plead with Kent to take a break.
Not only for her sake but for his own. The man had to be
exhausted. She certainly was. But remembering his expec-
tation that she couldn't hack the journey, she merely gritted her teeth and held on to him literally for dear life.

When he finally did pull off the road into the dubious
shelter of a small stone structure topping a small hill, daylight was fading and she was ready to drop.

Tara gazed up at the strange little building brightly
painted on all four sides with huge staring eyes. "What is
this place, Kent?"

"It's a *chorten*. A place where a saint is believed to have
stopped, or perhaps it houses some kind of holy relic. The
chorten is to Buddhists what the cross is to Christians. It'll
give us some protection from the wind."

As soon as Kent had cut the motor a deep silence descended on them. Here, at what seemed like the end of the
world, there wasn't even the rustle of trees, and they were
far enough from the road that no sound of the few passing motorized vehicles reached them.

"We don't have enough water left in the canteen for
both soup and coffee," Kent informed her. "Which gets
your vote?"

Their tiny camp stove supplied only enough heat to
warm their soup, which they spooned companionably out
of the cooking pot. Dessert was a handful of trail mix.

"We've made better time than I expected," Kent said. "We'll reach the construction site by tomorrow afternoon."

"What construction site? I don't even know where we're going." At this point she didn't much care what their destination was. She only wanted to have it and the trip back to Lhasa behind her. She did, however, want Kent to keep talking. The pleasant sound of his voice lightened the lonely, deserted feeling of their dismal surroundings.

"Since you're going to see the place for yourself," he said, "you might as well know. You've probably got top-secret clearance, anyway." Tara squirmed. "From what Elliott told me, our spy satellites have uncovered suspiciously high levels of activity in an area where the Chinese claim to be building a simple power plant to electrify one of the poorest of their provinces."

"It's hard to conceive of any place poorer than this."

"The area we're going to isn't all that far from here. Back home we could cover the distance in half an hour by air."

"I don't understand. I thought those satellites of ours could pick out a wart on the hind end of a gnat."

"Just about. But that's a strange thing for an agent to say. Don't you people know all about satellites?"

"I told you. I'm a courier. Spy satellites aren't my department. Why does Elliott want ground-level photographs if he already has satellite pictures?"

"He didn't explain his reasons, he just gave me my orders. Sensitive, very high-tech machines like satellites are prone to glitches. Even with computer enhancement their photographs are subject to interpretation. And it looks as if the Chinese are actually hiding a good part of the installation inside a mountain. Elliott wants to know why."

"From what I've seen of him," Tara offered, "I don't think Mr. Elliott is entirely comfortable relying solely on high-tech information. I have the impression he's more the old-fashioned kind of intelligence officer who likes to buttress technology with live sources."

"Could be. In any case, he apparently saw my planned trip to Tibet as a godsend. What's more, I provided him with a two-fer."

"A two-fer? How's that?"

"Not only can I take his ground-level photos, I was trained as an engineer, so I should be able to tell a lot about the installation just by looking at it. Since he's your boss, you probably know Elliott well."

"I'm not sure if anyone really knows Roger Elliott. My family has been acquainted with him for a number of years. My dad's retired now, but he used to be an air force officer. He worked with Mr. Elliott on some project a few years back. They've kept in touch."

"I see. So that's how you got into the spy business. Well, Elliott's no dunce. He must consider you a particularly competent and sensible woman to have sent you, alone, into this kind of country."

Would a man undertaking a difficult mission, Tara wondered, want to know that the assistant he thought was a trained professional wouldn't know a coded message from a laundry list? Probably not. Besides, she had a more personal reason for maintaining the fiction of her supposed professionalism. The antipathy he'd evidenced about it from the moment she'd told him who she was might hold him back from any greater display of his interest in her as a readily available woman.

A blast of wind whipped around their little shelter and Tara pulled the blanket she'd thrown over her shoulders a little tighter. "I don't know how sensible it was to insist on coming along on this trip."

"I have to hand it to you. Frankly, I didn't think you'd be able to deal with the discomfort, but I guess you're well trained for this kind of thing."

Increasingly discomfited by her continuing deception, Tara just mumbled something about turning in.

"That blanket of yours doesn't look very warm," Kent observed. "It'll be tight, but there's room for two in my sleeping bag. Want to join me?"

"No!" Tara almost shouted out her quick refusal. She hadn't forgotten the comments he'd made while trying to convince her not to accompany him. "Thank you. I'll be fine."

She moved a few feet away where she lay down on a piece of ground that didn't seem to have quite as many rocks as elsewhere. Her hurried trip to the Barkhor hadn't provided her with the insulated sleeping bag she'd sought. A heavy woolen blanket was all she could find. "It's warm enough," she lied through her already chattering teeth.

The cold she could manage well enough. She wasn't at all sure of her ability to continue to refuse him. Not after two long days of unsuccessfully trying to disregard the sensations provoked by having his hard, lean body nestled so intimately between her thighs. Those sensations, unreasonably pleasurable, kept giving rise to thoughts she was striving mightily not to entertain.

"Suit yourself," Kent said as he reached up to click off the motorcycle headlight. With what little illumination they'd had gone, he disappeared into the darkness. The eerie cry of a wolf pierced the silence. Tara sat bolt upright.

"Don't worry," came Kent's reassuring voice. "Sound travels far in the mountains. I'm sure the wolves are farther away than you'd think. They won't bother us." Tara hoped he was right. "Unless they're really hungry." She chose to believe that the chuckle following his alarming comment meant he was only teasing her. "My offer about sharing my sleeping bag still stands. I'll leave the side open."

The wolf howl shivered once more through the night.

There was a place for stubbornness, Tara thought, a place for a woman to show her determination and independence. This wasn't it. She wanted to be sure that if a wolf decided to make a supper of her, she'd be near enough to Kent so that he wouldn't sleep through the whole thing. She crept closer to the man. His form was barely visible in the sparse light cast by the low-hung moon, but she felt better being able to hear the small sounds he made adjusting himself for the night. Hoping that Kent really did not have seduction on his mind—at least not at the moment—she lay back on her stony bed. Glancing up, she found herself wrapped in the black velvet beauty of a Tibetan night sky diamond-brilliant with stars.

Kent must have heard her gasp of wonder. "Quite a sight, isn't it?" His quiet voice came at her out of the darkness.

"Incredible," she breathed.

"I've seen the stars all over the world. But I don't think I've ever seen a sky any more spectacular than this. Good night, Tara."

In spite of the cold and her uncomfortable bed, in spite of their desolate surroundings and the fact that they were alone in miles of wilderness, Tara was aware of a growing feeling of contentment. She was also astonishingly aware that the suggestive remarks Kent had made a couple of days ago were beginning to seem much less a threat than a promise she almost hoped he would keep.

Kent woke at first light, his body slowly becoming alert to the soft, womany curves pressed tantalizingly against him. It was a wonder he'd gotten any sleep at all. Some time during the night Tara had wriggled over and slipped into his sleeping bag. He'd known she was more asleep than awake when she snuggled up against him for warmth, and he'd gently fitted his arm around her to pillow her head. Even though they were swathed in layers of bulky clothing, her closeness had propelled a hot tightness into his groin that had kept him awake listening to her soft, rhythmic breathing.

No woman should look that good after a night sleeping on the ground, he thought glumly. It wasn't fair to a man who was trying to keep his hormones in check and his mind on his work. He should have put his foot down with Songtsen about her. Then he wouldn't have had to put up with this nonsense from his body.

Maybe the Tibetans had something after all in thinking the beguiling Ms. Morgan a goddess, he conceded. The possibility wasn't too hard to imagine. Those dazzling eyes, delicately shaped face and luscious body looked sculpted in heaven. It was suddenly important to him to discover if her curly, copper-colored mass of hair felt crispy or soft. He touched her hair and marveled at the surprising silkiness of the crinkly strands sliding between his fingers.

She stirred, and the arousing movement of her body against his triggered a tremor through him that had nothing to do with the cold. More gruffly than he'd intended, he threw back their cover and ordered her to get up so they could get back on the road.

Hours later the BMW muscled through the last lung-torturing pass leading down from the lofty Tibetan plateaus to the high plains of Qinghai. Kent called a halt to consult the hand-drawn map Songtsen had furnished him with. "According to this, we cut off to the west at a ruined *chorten* maybe a couple of hours' drive down the road." He folded the paper and replaced it in a jacket pocket.

"Do you really know how to drive a motorcycle?" he asked as Tara was getting ready to climb back into the saddle.

"Sure. An old high-school boyfriend had a beat-up Honda. I thought the bike and the guy's black leather jacket were pretty cool. Of course the idea of their daughter tooling around on the back of a motorcycle gave my parents fits."

"I'm surprised they'd allow you to do it."

"The boy was the son of the base's commanding general. He wasn't quite as punk as his clothes advertised."

"Want to take her for a while?"

"You'll trust me to drive the Beemer?"

"Looks like we've a straight run on the road for a few miles, and the wind down here shouldn't be quite so bad."

The machine was built for a taller person. Her feet barely reached the foot pegs and the fairing angled the wind into her face. Still, Tara enjoyed piloting the elegantly responsive BMW for a couple of hours. She wasn't loathe to relinquish her position to Kent when they left the road to head cross-country toward the installation. Although the machine's knobby tires took to the flat, hard-packed dirt comfortably, she couldn't have managed the crude trail that meandered off toward the west. Farther inland, the increasing roughness of the terrain slowed their pace considerably until they found their way blocked completely by a deep river gorge slicing between them and their destination.

"No way we're going to make it down there," Kent said, eyeing the steep, rocky incline. "Must be some way to cross, maybe a bridge or a ford farther down."

There was. And Tara quaked at the sight of the rope-and-pulley bridge they'd have to use to get to the other side.

"Good heavens, Kent. That contraption looks like something from the Middle Ages. Do you think it's safe?"

The little man—apparently the winch operator—who'd been sitting inside a tiny wooden shack seemed to have no such worries as he laid down his bowl of tea and greeted his unusual customers with a grin.

Kent doffed his helmet and hung it over a handgrip. "Let me check out the anchoring of the cable at this end." He gave the iron column sunk into the earth a close inspection. "Seems okay. The rope cable is in good condition and that platform isn't as flimsy as it looks. The planks seem pretty solidly lashed together. I think it'll take the weight of the motorcycle. They probably haul all sorts of goods across on this thing."

While the bridge operator kept up a singsong babble exhorting them to get on with it, Kent tugged on one of the heavy ropes leading from the four corners of the dangling platform to the pulley connection, and seemed satisfied. "To tell the truth, Tara, I'm not all that eager to use this thing either, but there probably isn't anything better for miles. That's why they've gone to considerable trouble to build this. And our ferryman here seems to have no qualms about hauling us across."

Kent pressed his yuan into the old man's hand, wheeled the motorcycle onto the wooden platform—on which the machine barely fit—and set the centerstand to hold it firmly in place.

If an engineer proclaimed the contraption to be reasonably safe, Tara tried to reassure herself, then it probably was. She swallowed and stepped onto the platform, which swayed sickeningly beneath her feet. The toll taker closed the gate on them and pulled down the winch's lever. She locked her hands around one rough side railing and closed her eyes as the platform swung out over the churning river a hundred feet below. She'd faced ski lifts and cable cars strung between mountains with no problem. But on this swaying platform, she very much feared she was going to be sick.

As he'd done in the Potala, Kent locked his arms steadyingly around her. "Are you all right?"

"Can you help me get this helmet off, please?" When he lifted the helmet from her head and laid it by the machine, she gulped in a mouthful of air that carried the fresh scent of the water. She pulled her hands away from the railing to grab Kent's leather jacket and pressed her face into his chest. The warm steadiness of him helped, but still she dared not move. She scarcely dared to breathe.

"Heights don't usually bother me," she gritted out while keeping her eyes squeezed tightly shut. "At least not when I'm standing on something firm, which this thing definitely isn't."

"Can't say I'm getting much of a charge out of this myself," Kent admitted. She could hear the grimness in his voice. When the platform's rocking increased and it started to dip as it approached the middle of the cable, Tara moaned.

"Lift your head," Kent ordered.

Thinking he might need some assistance with holding the motorcycle upright, and wanting to help no matter how bad she felt, she did as he'd asked. Forcing her eyes open, she saw Kent's face descending toward hers, his lips only an inch away. Before she could react, his hot, hard mouth pressed firmly down on hers.

Chapter 4

Instantly Tara's body responded. A spark of fiery sweetness arced from her lips to her feminine core. The lovely sensation made her unclench her hands, spread them wide and slide them slowly over the supple leather covering Kent's chest. Though he'd taken her by surprise, the blissful feelings his kiss evoked banished any objections her mind was ready to make. Her heart was pounding furiously. Not from the sheer terror of a moment ago, but from the exciting currents of pleasure racing through her body. Kent's embrace was making her dizzy in a fashion not at all frightening. She felt as if she was spinning delightfully around on a carousel—the sound of its calliope music almost reached her ears.

She tried to press herself closer to the arousing warmth of Kent's body. On a little whimper of need, she parted her lips, and eagerly greeted the invasion of his tongue into the intimate recesses of her mouth. She'd tasted nothing more intoxicating in her life.

She felt the exciting pressure on her mouth lessen, and a soft moan of objection rose in her throat. She drew herself up on tiptoe to follow the retreating masculine mouth.

"We're here, Tara."

The words Kent had rasped out barely registered. Who cared where they were. She only wanted to resume the burning sweetness that had so tantalized her mouth and all the rest of her.

"We've crossed the river safely. We can get off this thing now."

River? Kent's unacceptable separation from her allowed his words to penetrate the mental fog generated by his mind-clouding kiss. River. Yes. She remembered, and her eyes popped open. The platform on which they stood no longer swayed. It had jogged onto the cliff on the opposite bank of the river. Kent released her. Without his support, her knees threatened to buckle under her. Attempting to gather her scattered wits, she grabbed for the railing.

"I . . . I . . . why did you do that?" she stammered as she stumbled onto the bank.

"Pretty obvious, wasn't it? That was a pretty scary experience. I was afraid you were freaking out and I wanted to take your mind off it."

Take her mind off it! His kiss had robbed her of any mind at all. "You had no right. You—"

"From where I sat," Kent interrupted dryly, "you didn't put up all that much of a fight."

Tara flushed; he was right. She was hardly in a position to complain about something she all too obviously had enjoyed. Better to simply put the incident out of her mind, as Kent evidently had already done.

"Let's get going," he said, wheeling the motorcycle onto land.

Kent was still shaken. He covered his lingering reaction to their kiss with an overly conscientious check of the fastenings on the bike's saddlebags. He'd used Tara's quite rational nervousness as the excuse for kissing her. But the truth was, he'd been aching to do that since the first moment he saw her. No matter how hard he tried, he'd been unable to keep his response to her unchecked.

He often traveled in territory which, though beautiful, was dangerously wild. Maintaining control of his physical and emotional reactions was necessary to keep from tumbling down a snow-covered precipice or falling into piranha-infested waters. That he was having difficulty holding that control in the face of such a simple problem as his physical attraction for a woman not only surprised but confused him.

On the motorcycle, Tara kept her hands curved safely around the padded leather sides of her seat instead of circling her arms around Kent's middle as she'd been doing. Thankfully, their situation kept conversation to a minimum. Her mind was still whirling from the arousing power of his kiss. Though it had thrilled her to her toes, she knew it couldn't really mean anything. Not anything serious, that is.

Most of her friends her age had already racked up several affairs, but she'd had only one short-lived intimate relationship with a man since her divorce five years ago. That must have been the reason for her reacting like a teenager to her first real kiss, she told herself. Believing that the promptings for her undeniable ardor had been purely physical was a whole lot less disturbing than the ridiculous idea that Kent Masterson might be coming to mean anything more significant to her.

Allowing that to happen would be a class A mistake.

She knew the kind of man he was. She'd met others like him, and in fact employed several as tour guides—strong, take-charge individuals who could shepherd a group of accountants, lawyers and teachers into the Andes, up the Amazon or across an African veld.

Such men could function beautifully in some of the wildest, most desolate spots on earth. They were often considerably less successful in normal, day-to-day environments. She'd noticed that women were often attracted to such masterful men—alpha males, the psychology books called them. She'd been attracted to a couple of them herself, but had kept to her rule about not becoming involved with an employee.

There was something erotic about courting danger—even when that danger was mainly illusion. She'd seen it happen time after time. Adventure travelers wanted to feel they were taking risks—although in reality the guides worked hard at minimizing any actual hazard. And for some, those risks included enjoying a romantic fling with an intriguing person they'd probably never see again. No harm done if the woman was smart enough to realize the relationship would necessarily be a short one.

Kent Masterson wasn't a tour guide, but he was, she guessed, the kind of man who wouldn't be content coming home every night to the little woman in the proverbial rose-covered cottage. To a certain extent, she was cut from the same kind of cloth.

Her gaze, which had been drifting vaguely over the barren scenery, was suddenly jolted into focus by a glimpse of movement in the distance. Man-made movement.

"Kent!" she shouted. "Look!"

"What?" he called back, slowing the machine to a stop.

"Over there." She pointed to a dust cloud evidently kicked up by moving vehicles. "Must be a road. Maybe the one leading to the construction site you're looking for."

Kent braced the machine and moved to one of the saddlebags where he withdrew a camera. He screwed on a telephoto lens and fitted the camera to his eye.

"You're right," he said excitedly. "There's a convoy of three trucks heading toward the mountains. That's got to be the road to the site. There are no others in this region." He angled the lens in the direction the trucks were heading. "I don't see any sign of the actual construction yet, but it can't be too far from here. Let's go." He hung the camera around his neck and remounted the motorcycle. "We don't want to risk being seen ourselves. Our best bet is to stay on this side of that ridge ahead and follow it west."

Every few minutes Kent stopped to climb the ridge and reconnoiter. At last he ducked back behind the ridgetop. "There she is," he called to her quietly. As excited as he, Tara scrambled up to him. He handed her the camera.

"Just look at the size of that place," he said with the outright admiration of an engineer.

Tara squinted through the viewfinder and gasped. A complex far larger than any town or village they'd passed rose from the valley floor. The tall chimneys that topped several of the nearly completed buildings pierced the thick pall of brown dust that hung in the air. She and Kent had seen scarcely a single human being the entire day, yet below them an army of workers swarmed over the enormous site.

Heavy construction machines common in the West were at a premium in the hinterlands. Only a couple of what looked like fairly old-fashioned cranes chugged puffs of blue smoke from their exhaust. What the country did have was plenty of human muscle power. Long lines of gray-clad people hacked at mountainous rocks with picks and shovels. Other lines snaked off through the choking dust with people carrying baskets of dirt and rocks balanced at the ends of long poles yoked over their shoulders. One by one, like cogs in a wheel, the workers climbed an immense pile of dirt to dump their burdens and turned around to march off and join the circle once again.

"Where did they all come from?" Tara wondered. "This is out in the middle of nowhere."

"Most likely they're prisoners. Probably political prisoners sent out here to work out their time slaving as unpaid labor for the state."

Unlike the military installation they'd passed a couple of days ago, this site wasn't surrounded by steel fencing. Probably because the vast size of the place would have demanded miles of fencing. Also, because the region was so deserted, building a wall to keep people out seemed unnecessary. A short distance away from the construction site ran rows of ugly gray barrackslike buildings. Housing and support buildings for the workers, Tara assumed. And those buildings were confined by a high metal fence. If the workers were the prisoners Kent suspected, the fence was designed to keep them in, not to keep people out.

"I see a group of marching men in uniform," she told Kent as she handed back their makeshift binoculars.

"Yeah. The People's Liberation Army must control the perimeter. I imagine they occasionally have to turn away wandering nomads and their yak herds."

"What next, Kent? It'll be dark soon. Shall we wait until tomorrow to get your photographs?"

"No. I'm going to do it now. I want you to stay hidden down there with the motorcycle."

Tara returned to the machine as Kent began taking his pictures. Accompanied by the constant *whirchink* of the camera's shutter, he darted along just below the crest of the ridge, quickly snapping one photo after another. After he'd used up a roll of film shooting with the telephoto lens, he replaced it with a wide-angle lens and took more exposures.

Tara was relieved when he finally ran down the ridge toward her. They'd been lucky so far, but prudence dictated that they get out of here as quickly as possible. They weren't that far from the site; eventually someone was bound to spot them.

With quick, decisive gestures, Kent emptied the cameras, slipped the rolls of film into their small plastic vials and handed them to her.

"These will give the experts a much clearer idea of the site, but I wasn't able to get decent shots of what's hidden inside the mountain."

"Are you crazy?" Tara burst out in horror. "You can't just walk into the place. There are hundreds, maybe thousands of people down there."

"Yes. But did you notice that most of the activity is centered on the far side of the complex? Looks like they've made completing that massive concrete building going up over there a priority. There's no one at all on this side of the cave entrance. It's safe enough. One thing's for sure. They're not building just a simple power plant down there. Oh, the site includes a power plant, all right, but it's not just to electrify a few villages. This area isn't too far from large uranium mines. And I've heard there are missile sites not far away. I know there's a nuclear weapons test site in the next province. Tell Elliott my guess is they're building a nuclear arms factory. I can't be sure until I get a look at the master control room they could be hiding in the cave."

A chill washed over her. "You mean...bombs?"

"I mean the same kinds of weapons we continue to manufacture. Nuclear missile warheads, bombs and atomic artillery. I don't blame Elliott for being concerned. If my assessment of its purpose is correct, this new plant will certainly throw a monkey wrench into softening relationships between the West and the Chinese. The Soviet Union sure as hell won't like it much, either. They're a lot closer to the Chinese than we are."

"Wait a minute," Tara blurted out. She'd been so caught up in Kent's recounting of his discovery that she'd let a few of his words slip by her. "What do you mean *I'm* to tell Elliott? You're going to tell him yourself."

"I plan to. But just in case something unforeseen happens to me, you'll have to pass that message to American authorities along with those roles of exposed film."

As Tara opened her mouth to register an alarmed objection, Kent thrust up a restraining hand.

"No time for argument, Tara. I've told you how it's going to be. I haven't come all this way to leave the job half done. That cave is impenetrable to our spy satellites. The main reason Elliott sent me here was for me to get inside and have a look around. Don't worry. I won't take any stupid chances." Kent folded her trembling hands in his. "But if anything happens to me, you're to take the motorcycle and get out fast. That's an order."

The worried frown on Tara's face deepened. This wasn't something she wanted to deal with.

"Do you hear me, Tara?" He hadn't raised his voice, but the command in it was unmistakable.

With great reluctance, she nodded. "I hear you."

"You've got the compass and the map." Kent fished a folded sheet of paper from an inside pocket of his jacket and handed it to her. "And here's the letter Songtsen gave me. If the situation here blows, get over to the nunnery he promised would give us shelter as quickly as you can. Ditch the machine and ask the nuns to help you link up with some Tibetans heading back to Lhasa. Stay clear of any Chinese."

Tara wanted to argue with him. She wanted to point out all the logical reasons he shouldn't do what he planned to do. But one look at the chiseled granite of his face told her any objections she might raise would be useless.

"I understand, Kent," she said around the constriction in her throat. "I don't like this. I don't want you to do it, but I understand."

The sexy grin once more began to play around his mouth.

"You're okay, Tara. I'm glad you came with me. These past few days together have taught me what a very special woman you are. I didn't think I could trust you at first. Now I hope I can."

The words made Tara squirm. He was talking about her trustworthiness when right from the word *go* she hadn't been truthful with him. She'd gone on letting him believe she was a professional when she wasn't.

"Because of that," Kent continued, "I'm going to take a chance and let you in on a secret I don't want you to pass along to your boss or anyone at State. Songtsen is helping me on this mission because I've promised to do something for him. I really came to Tibet to smuggle out of the country a sacred painting he calls the Light of Buddha. The monks don't want the Chinese to get their hands on it. I'd hate for the high lama's plan to fail. If anything happens to me, can I count on you to get the scroll out for them?"

"You mean that's what all that strange business between you and Songtsen was about? That's what he meant when he said you'd come at his request?"

"I was afraid you'd picked up on that."

"Of course I picked up on it. You say you didn't trust *me*. I didn't trust *you*. That's why I insisted on coming along on this trip."

His mouth twitched. "Was that the only reason you came?"

Tara dropped her gaze. "Of course. What other reason could there be?"

Kent placed his hands on her shoulders and turned her toward him. "Think about it while I'm gone. So, can I count on you to do that favor for Songtsen if the necessity arises?"

Right now the ultimate fate of a religious painting, no matter how revered, was much farther down Tara's scale of importance than Kent's safety. But she could lift that concern, at least, from his mind. "Yes. I'll take care of their painting. I guess we both owe the monks that. But I don't want it to be necessary." She filled her voice with warning. "You be careful. No intelligence photos are worth your life."

Kent chuckled. "Aren't you agents supposed to be more gung ho about this sort of thing? Keep an eye on me if you can, but it's more important that you stay hidden. Oh, and you'd better take this extra money." He fished his wallet from his back pocket and handed Tara a large amount of yuan. Then he turned to stride quickly to the slope. Tara rushed after him.

"Kent!"

When he turned to her, Tara flung her arms around his neck. "For luck," she whispered before pulling his head down and fitting her lips to his.

"Any more of this, woman," he rasped when she allowed him to come up for air, "and you'll make me forget my mission. Then you'll have some tall explaining to do when you see Elliott. He might fire you."

The thought of her continued deception ate at her. "Kent, I—"

"Later, honey. I've got to get down there while I've still got the light."

She clambered up the ridge after him. After a quick salute, Kent rolled over the top. In a crouch, half running, half sliding, he scurried down the slope toward the installation. The clatter of rockfall that accompanied him sounded so loud Tara was sure it would bring someone running. At the bottom Kent made a zigzag dash from one pile of rocks to another, and halted behind a small wooden shed.

One final spurt brought him to the mouth of the enormous cave, where he slipped inside and disappeared from Tara's view. She waited anxiously as evening shadows filled the valley and crept up the mountains, making the lights in the cave more noticeable. Why didn't Kent return? she worried. How long could it take to snap a few pictures? Had something happened to him in there?

Lights suddenly flashed on all over the complex and Tara's heart leaped into her throat. She was sure it meant Kent had been discovered. But the flurry of activity that followed the lighting of the site only seemed to portend the normal end of a work day or the changing of a shift.

After what seemed like hours a figure appeared by the cave's side wall. The relief that swept over her was quickly replaced by a new worry that Kent couldn't make it back up the slope without being seen. A short, quick run brought him to the safety of a rock pile, and the hope grew within her that he might make his escape after all.

Tara flicked her gaze back to Kent's surroundings and that hope froze in her heart. Only a few yards behind him, a soldier, rifle slung over his shoulder, strolled out of the cave toward Kent's hiding place. She knew that Kent, from his position behind the rocks, couldn't possibly see the guard approaching. With all her might, she threw a mental warning at Kent.

Stay there, Kent! Don't move. Danger. Danger. She couldn't shout a warning that would only alert the armed guard. For certain both she and Kent would be captured, maybe even shot. Her insides twisted in fear as Kent stood up and started from behind his hiding place. It was like watching a terrible accident about to happen. An accident she was powerless to prevent.

Before Kent had taken three steps, the guard saw him and snapped to full alert. He tossed away his cigarette and swung his rifle into position.

At the guard's shout, Kent froze. Slowly he turned toward his captor. Tara could see a tiny object flick from the hand Kent held behind him. The tube of film rolled down a gentle incline and out of her sight. Kent lifted his hands shoulder high and sauntered toward the Chinese soldier. Tara quickly deciphered the photographer's hunching of his shoulders and vague waves of his arms as the body language of a man about to be cited for something no more serious than a parking ticket. His stance seemed to denote embarrassment more than worry.

Lord. He was trying to play the part of a curious but stupid tourist, she realized. A brave and well-acted ploy, but no way could he get away with it. She couldn't hear the exchange between the two, but saw Kent begin to search his pockets for his papers. She transferred her attention to the young soldier who, strangely enough, looked much more nervous than his prisoner. He seemed loathe to get close to the intruder. Instead of simply taking the papers Kent held in his outstretched hand, the guard gestured to Kent to throw them down. Kent complied. With threatening motions of his rifle, the guard waved the prisoner back so that he could retrieve the identification papers.

It occurred to Tara that the soldier could be a young man from the provinces who may never have seen a Westerner before, let alone dealt with one. She was afraid that his nervousness could get Kent killed.

The soldier didn't carry a walkie-talkie. He was looking around as if seeking help in dealing with this unexpected break in his usual routine. From her bird's-eye view, Tara could see that he was far from any fellows who could render him assistance. The soldier forced Kent to fold his hands over the top of his head, and began prodding him with his rifle toward the hut a few yards away.

Kent, apparently at his guard's orders, opened the door of the construction shed. The soldier shoved his captive inside and fastened the padlock on the door. Tara watched the guard run off shouting excitedly in a language she couldn't understand.

She groaned and buried her face in her hands. Kent had been taken prisoner.

Chapter 5

Tara felt as if she'd had the wind knocked out of her. She slid a few feet down from the ridgetop and fought to hold back panic.

What should she do? The question kept chasing itself around in her mind. What *could* she do?

Get out fast! Kent's unequivocal order rang in her ears as she bolted down the slope toward the motorcycle.

Drawing in a deep, shaky breath she willed herself to calmness. Hysteria wouldn't help either of them. She had to think. But it was so hard to concentrate with the frightening picture of the guard's vicious-looking rifle pointed directly at Kent's heart crowding her mind. And there'd soon be a whole lot more weapons pointed at him.

Even as she recalled the exact intonation of his voice when he'd delivered the command for her to immediately escape if he was caught, she knew it would take a strength she didn't possess to carry it out. How could she possibly follow his orders to abandon him to the Chinese? Ever since the Tiananmen massacre, the authorities had been dealing harshly with rule-breaking foreigners. And being caught with a camera at a secret installation was no minor infraction of their multitudinous regulations. It was the kind of thing that could get a man shot. She thought it unlikely that Kent's ploy of being a harmless wandering tourist had held up even with an ignorant recruit. His photographic and travel permits surely wouldn't be enough to sustain that razor-thin cover under interrogation by a well-trained officer.

Delivering the film to Elliott was important, the only reason she was in Tibet. But in her personal value system saving a man's life was even more important. Was there any way to get Kent out? she wondered frantically. Could she run down there and try hacking at the padlock with a rock? No. That was a stupid idea. If it worked at all, it would take considerable time. And there was no time. In minutes they'd both be dragged off by a platoon of troops. Instead of one execution, there'd be two.

She'd been pacing furiously up and down in front of Kent's motorcycle, staring at the machine as if it were some kind of stand-in for its owner and could furnish a way out of the jumble of frightened and confused thoughts that threatened to overwhelm her. Suddenly the bright orange length of nylon rope sticking out of an open pack swam into focus, and an idea began to pick its way through the chaos in her mind.

Just before leaving on her trip to China, she'd sat down and watched a Western video with her dad. In the story the cowboy hero freed a jailed pal, doomed to be hanged, by tying a rope to the barred window, twisting it around the pommel of his saddle and urging his horse forward to yank out the bars. Kent's small prison had no window. At least none that she'd seen. But was there a chance she could accomplish something along the same lines?

Any chance whatever of freeing Kent was a chance worth taking. She pulled out the rope, but could find nowhere to attach it at the rear of the motorcycle. Hoping she wasn't setting things up so the strain would pull out some vital part, she tied the rope firmly around a steel tubing attached to the frame. As she hitched the remainder of the coiled rope over a shoulder, the thought of Kent's certain fury with her should her risky plan fail loomed almost as large in her mind as her fear of being caught by the Chinese. But she'd rather deal with his anger than with the shame she would always feel if she ran off and left him.

She put her helmet on, threw her leg over the driver's seat, twisted the key in the ignition and pushed the starter button.

With a roar the powerful machine leaped forward. The gathering dusk wasn't deep enough to hide her approach, but there was no time for stealth. She gunned the engine and raced on an angle up the ridge. At the top the BMW went airborne for a short distance, bounced to a landing and threatened to whip into a skid. Tara fought to keep command of the machine. If the BMW escaped her, it would be the end of two Americans. The struggle to hold on to the motorcycle almost tore her arms out of their sockets, but her frantic prayers were answered, and the machine remained upright.

An earsplitting Klaxon began shrieking its alert over the valley as her vehicle careened down the hill toward the hut. She hadn't judged her braking correctly and the rear of the motorcycle fishtailed into the bottom of the shed's wooden door, cracking it.

Tara's hands shook violently as she knotted the rope around the padlock's chain. "Kent!" she hollered. "It's me." A superfluous identification considering the noise of the motorcycle motor. "Get ready." She knew the siren would have sent everyone scrambling and even now platoons of troops had to be running toward them, but with great effort of will she kept herself from trying to watch for their approach. Right now she had to maintain a complete concentration on engineering Kent's escape.

Easing the machine forward, she paid out the rope behind her. The line went taut. She had to be careful not to pull away too quickly or the rope could simply snap under the tension. She gently gave the motor some gas. For a few agonizing seconds the motorcycle bucked and shuddered, restrained by its anchoring rope. Then with a crack the lock's metal hinges tore from the shattering wood and the door flew open.

Freed, Kent wasted no time in dashing to the BMW. Tara hastily pulled free the trailing rope and hurled herself onto the passenger seat.

She'd expected Kent to gun the motor and speed away. Instead of that he angled the motorcycle back toward the pile of rocks that had lent him a temporary hiding place. "What the heck are you doing?" she yelled.

"The film," he shouted back. "Maybe I can find it."

"Forget the damn film."

Evidently Kent had fixed in his mind the exact location where he'd been accosted by the guard. His gaze swept the area of the little incline next to the rocks. "There it is."

He slowed the machine only long enough to scoop up the small vial and shove it into a pocket. Then he sped back up the slope toward the nomad trail that led to the distant Golmud-Lhasa road. As soon as the rise hid them from sight, he braked hard, wheeled the machine around, cracked open the throttle and raced away in the opposite direction.

Tara locked her arms around him and hung on for dear life as Kent, demonstrating considerably more mastery over his vehicle than she had, piloted their wheels from one ravine into another. Frequently he had to stamp a boot onto the ground to hold the machine from a potentially disastrous lean. His helmet clunked against the handlebar where he'd hooked it before hitting the installation.

The rapidly dwindling light protected them from searching troops, but eventually slowed the motorcycle into little more than a crawl. It was one thing to travel at night on a paved road, quite another to ride cross-country without even the semblance of a track to point the way. Even in broad daylight the cheese-grater terrain threatened them with disaster. When complete darkness finally swallowed them up, their way became extremely treacherous.

Kent brought the machine to a halt and set the side-stand. "I have to get my bearings, Tara. Have to try to figure out where we are in relation to the nunnery."

When he got off the motorcycle to walk around the front and hold the pocket compass in the narrow shaft of light beaming from the front of the machine, Tara dragged her leg over the seat and gratefully stood on terra firma.

"The nunnery is to the south and west," Kent said. "My guess is the Chinese will assume we're heading in the opposite direction, toward the road. By the time they decide we haven't gone that way and institute a broader search, I hope we'll have thrown them off the track. Where's that bag of munchies?"

Eat? The man could eat when her whole body still twanged from the bouncing and jostling it had just been put through? When her nerves, newly freed from immediate concern about the BMW's passengers getting their brains dashed out on the rocks, were tightening up with the memory of how close Kent had come to being at the mercy of the Chinese.

She opened her mouth to express her indignation, but her lips refused to form coherent words. Kent glanced up at her, did a double take, and within a second had anchored her within his arms.

"Whoa, baby," he murmured. "Don't konk out on me now."

Tara clung to his solid strength. "Oh, K-Kent, I...I..."

"Hold it together." His lips pressed against her forehead. "You were great back there, but I still need you."

Tara drew in a deep breath. "I'll be all right."

"I know you will." He gave her bottom a couple of affectionate pats. "Now where's our dinner?"

Maybe he was just giving her something to do to keep her mind from lingering on their still-precarious situation, Tara considered, but it was working. She dug the plastic bag of trail mix out of the small compartment on top of the gas tank and offered it to him.

"Don't you ever have trouble eating?" she asked with a lightness she didn't really feel.

"Never," Kent answered unequivocally as he delved into the bag and came up with a fistful of raisins and nuts. "I've had to learn to eat anything, anywhere. Have some," he ordered. "Low blood sugar can result in foggy thinking and we've got to stay alert."

The nerve-racking events of the past couple of hours had completely robbed her of appetite, but she followed suit.

"Was it worth it?" she asked. "Did you find what you were looking for back there?"

"I got a quick look at the cave's master control room. I'm just about certain they're planning to manufacture nuclear weapons there. Elliott will need more information as the facility gears up to come on line. But that's his problem. Right now, we've got problems of our own." He tossed back another handful of trail mix.

"We can't make camp here. We're still much too close to the installation. The army will be swarming over these hills at first light. We're simply going to have to chance going on." He squinted into the darkness beyond the headlight's yellow cone and shook his head dubiously. "Heading cross-country into unknown territory in the dark is a dangerous proposition. I don't like it. But our only alternative is to abandon the machine, load as much of our equipment as possible on our backs and push on on foot. Frankly, I like that option even less. If we're discovered, at least the motorcycle gives us a fighting chance to outrun our pursuers."

"Maybe we have a third option, Kent," Tara offered. "Can you drive slowly enough so that I can walk ahead at the edge of the headlight's range and try to guide you away from large rocks and fissures? That way we can put a few more miles between us and the Chinese."

"That's a damn good idea. So far we've been very lucky. If our luck holds we might even stumble across the nunnery." His hand closed over Tara's shoulder and gave it an encouraging little squeeze. "Let's hope the monks are right about you being a goddess. Looks like we're going to need divine intervention to get us out of this."

After they'd downed the last of their hurried meal, Kent remounted the BMW. Holding its engine to a low purr, he followed slowly as Tara walked ahead as quickly as she dared, scouting out what she hoped would be a relatively safe passage. She tried to keep herself from thinking what a misstep into an unseen rock could do. Any injury could make her a burden for Kent to manage along with everything else he had to cope with. Much worse, a hidden crevice could trap a motorcycle wheel and send the vehicle and its driver crashing down.

Colonel Wu Chen of the People's Liberation Army replaced the black telephone receiver with the careful precision he gave to all his actions. No sign of the boiling rage rising within him showed on the man's heavy, square face. One would had to have been looking directly at him to notice that the coal-black eyes took on a cast even harder and flatter than usual.

He still could hardly believe the news from the excited base commander of the construction site in Qinghai. It was unthinkable that American imperialist spies had breached the security of the secret installation. Even more unthinkable that they'd actually done so and escaped capture.

How was such a calamity possible? the colonel asked himself. It was he who'd come up with the idea of hiding part of the site within the mountain, safe from the prying eyes of the damnable Western technology that outclassed anything his poor nation possessed. It was he who had successfully argued to the general that the site's remote location, marked only on classified military maps and deep within an area closed to their own people, let alone outsiders, would guarantee its secrets.

He'd lashed out at the base commander for the failure of his troops to patrol the site properly, but Wu Chen well knew that the general he served would fix responsibility for the disaster squarely on the colonel, who was his chief assistant in matters of security. The loss of face stung him to the core. Silently he swore by the graves of his ancestors that he'd make the Yankee running dogs, who'd brought such disgrace upon him, pay.

Most likely the damned American spy and the man who was his accomplice were headed back to Lhasa. He must be careful, the colonel reminded himself, not to underestimate the cleverness of the American, who had already proved himself a capable opponent. Was it possible the dog would try to confound his pursuers by plunging deeper into China, heading north to Golmud instead of south to Lhasa?

No matter. He'd already given orders to cover all roads, particularly those leading to Lhasa. The Friendship road to Kathmandu, the spies' most likely route out of China, was to be kept under constant patrol. All buses heading in either direction on the Golmud road, and out of Tibet, were to be scrupulously checked. All motorcycles were to be stopped and their drivers and passengers held. And for the foreseeable future no Westerner would board a flight from Lhasa airport without meticulous clearance.

He would have them, Wu Chen vowed. It was only a question of time until he would send them under heavy guard to Beijing. The colonel's thick lips curved into the barest hint of a smile as he contemplated the pleasure the capture of the Americans would bring him. He would prefer to shoot them both on sight, but that would anger his commanding general. It was enough that they could be used to make the imperialist American government—with its infuriating posture of moral superiority—look foolish in the world press.

In hindsight, he wished he hadn't fought so hard for the honor of being assigned the ultimate responsibility for the overall security of the construction site. It had added considerably to his already burdensome task of serving the military commander of the entire Xizang Zizhiqu, the Tibetan Autonomous Region. The general expected him to deal quickly and successfully with any unrest that might threaten their hold on a subject people. He was to make sure Tibetans held no demonstrations that would instigate negative headlines in the world press and cause tourists to take their desperately needed foreign currency elsewhere.

In a strange way, Wu considered, perhaps the Yankee agent named Masterson had done him a backhanded favor. Capturing the man would provide him with the means of ingratiating himself with superiors who'd been lashing him about his lack of progress on what had been until now his most important task. Wu Chen's big hands tightened into fists as the thought of his continued failure of that mission rose to rankle him.

Ever since the death of the old Gendun Lama, the lamas had been searching of the person who housed the revered lama's reincarnated soul. Wu Chen loathed all Tibetan monks and lamas. Who were they but superstitious-ridden exploiters of the peasants? Chinese ways would soon banish the ignorance that encouraged Tibetans to hold their priests and teachers in such high regard. In his view the day could not come soon enough when the only monks left in Xizang would be those used as scenery for the cameras of tourists with fat wallets.

The colonel's aide scurried in to place a pot of hot tea on his superior's desk, then beat a hasty retreat.

Absently Wu Chen poured a bowl of tea and lifted the steaming liquid to his lips. If the rumors that the reincarnated lama had been discovered were true, he had to track him down and bring him under the protection of the proper authorities. When he did find the reincarnative, the situation would be a delicate one to be managed carefully to avoid the mass rioting that had occurred when Chinese troops liberated Lhasa and attempted to bring the Dalai Lama under their control. The dolts had allowed the god-king to slip through their fingers into exile in India.

The colonel had no doubt that if he allowed any repeat of such an embarrassment, it would cost him his life. But he did not intend to fail. Not without feeling a twinge of guilt for the lingering superstition, he offered a silent prayer to his ancestors for their help in capturing both the new Gendun Lama and the American spies. Those accomplishments, he hoped, would finally give him entrée into the highest levels of the party and deliver him from exile in this backward land so far removed from the pleasures of Beijing.

"I think I see some lights up ahead, Kent," Tara called.

Kent pulled the motorcycle alongside her. She pointed to where a few dim lights glimmered through the night.

"Yes," Kent agreed. "Looks like a small village. It's got to be the place we're looking for, Tara. I don't think there's anything else out here."

"I don't see anything that looks big enough to be a nunnery."

"Songtsen said it was a minor shrine tended by only a few nuns—maybe on the other side of the village."

Skirting the village brought them to a single-storied whitewashed building marked with tattered streamers of colored prayer flags fluttering bravely in the wind. The place they took to be the nunnery was small and poor even by Tibetan standards.

"Look, Tara, there's a dharma wheel painted on that wall. This must be the place. If it isn't, we're going to have to get out of here in one hell of a hurry."

Nuns might be nervous about answering their door late at night, Kent considered. He took Songtsen's letter from Tara so he could quickly assuage the fears of whoever opened the red-painted door, and wheeled the motorcycle into the courtyard. Instantly, from around a corner of the building, two huge mongrel dogs flew toward them with fearsome growls and fangs bared.

Tara screamed and looked for a weapon to defend herself. Kent shouted a curse and kicked at the snarling beast trying to sink its teeth into his leg. Tara found the motorcycle repair kit and threw it at one of the attacking furies. The dog whined and scuttled away, only to turn a moment later and launch a second attack.

The red door swung open and a tiny old woman appeared in the doorway. Kent waved the letter at her. "Songtsen Rimpoche," he shouted over the din created by the barking dogs. "*Nga Amayriga nay ray.* I'm from

America." The nun bit out an order and the animals went slinking away.

"Are you all right, Tara?"

"Yes. The dogs didn't actually touch me. That vicious thing had your leg. Are you okay?"

"Yeah. Its jaws just grabbed the top of my boot."

The nun, her gray hair clipped close to her head, stared at the foreigners in wide-eyed wonder. She took one glance at Songtsen's letter and hurried them inside. Three other women wrapped in the burgundy robes of Buddhist nuns crowded around their unexpected guests.

The nuns didn't have to be told that the motorcycle had to be quickly brought in from the courtyard. Having someone notice that a foreign luxury motorcycle had appeared in front of their building would do them no good with the authorities. Before it was whisked from sight Kent pointed to the gas tank and tried to impress upon the nuns the necessity for obtaining some gasoline for the machine. He'd seen no other motorized vehicles in the village, and where the nuns might find the needed gas he had no idea. But without it, he and Tara faced a daunting journey of hundreds of miles on foot.

"Ngay ming Kent Masterson ray," Kent said, introducing himself. He gestured toward Tara. *"Korang ming Tara Morgan ray."*

On hearing Tara's name, the old lady broke into a smile and bestowed on Tara a flurry of cheerful nods. *"Ah... Tara. Ngay ming Lhamo ray."*

"The woman's name is Lhamo," Kent explained. "I gather she's the mother superior of the place. Evidently she feels you and she have something in common in both being named after goddesses."

Lhamo embarked on several rapid sentences with what looked like an expression of dismay on her face. Tara recognized the words *gonda* and *kyee* as meaning "sorry" and "dogs," and really didn't need Kent to explain that the nun was apologizing for their animals' attack.

"She wants to show us—mainly you, I think—their Tara shrine," Kent translated. "I have a feeling Songtsen's choice of this place wasn't entirely coincidental."

"I'd love to see it."

The small mural was old and the paint was flaking away. But there was enough left to see that the painting had been delicately rendered by a master. The artist had portrayed the goddess as a dancing girl, round breasted and voluptuous and very nearly nude.

"Tell Lhamo that I'm honored to bear the name of such a beautiful goddess."

"Lhamo says that ordinarily they'd put me out in the storeroom or the stable, but in deference to both the Rimpoche and you, they'll follow your wishes in the matter." He grinned. "What'll it be, Tara? Do I get to sleep inside with you, or outside with the goats?"

"You're getting a kick out of this, aren't you? I ought to send you out with the goats, but tell her I'd like us to stay together."

The superior led them to what was apparently the nunnery's single tiny guest room furnished only with rugs and a small knee-high table. Another nun entered with a tray of food.

"*Too-jay-chay,*" Tara murmured, "thank you" being among the few Tibetan words she'd learned.

At Kent's request the nuns provided them with a basin of water so they could at least wash their hands and faces.

It was after midnight, long past the nuns' bedtime, and the Tibetan women left their unforeseen guests to dine alone. The hunk of stale yak cheese challenged Tara's teeth, but she decided that *tsampa* tasted about the same as oatmeal. And thinking of the salty Tibetan tea as soup made it more palatable.

After they'd finished their meal, Tara moved the table to a corner. The long walk added to the day's frightening excitement had drained her. She had barely enough strength left to help Kent spread one of the blankets the nuns had given them over the rugs to serve as their bed.

Their chamber was far from being either luxurious or warm, but it provided them with a much more comfortable resting place than last night's freezing camp-out. At least the floor of hard-packed earth was free of rocks, and sturdy walls kept out the incessant wind. The August night was mild and the hot tea had warmed them enough to doff their jackets and indulge in the luxury of taking off their boots to sleep.

Tara sat on the blanket next to Kent. She made sure there was a good twelve inches of safe distance between herself and her bed partner. She was about to lie back and pull the blankets up when Kent stroked a finger gently over her cheek and turned her face toward him. At his electrifying touch, some of her tiredness fell away.

"Now, Ms. Morgan," he said in the manner of a displeased boss hauling up an employee for a lecture on the quality of her work. "It's time we had a talk. I thought I ordered you to get going if the Chinese discovered me."

Beneath Kent's threatening tone, Tara could detect a velvety rasp that stirred her weary body to interest. His face, stubbled with a three-day growth of beard, looked harsh and his dark eyes glinted black in the dim light of the butter lamp. Still, his gaze landed on her with an intriguing softness. And the purposeful way his eyes remained fastened on her face made breathing just a little more difficult than it had been a moment before.

She shrugged. "Maybe I'm not big on taking orders. So sue me."

"Sue you, huh?" Kent snaked his arm around her shoulders and pulled her closer to him. Her left arm was pressed against his chest from shoulder to elbow. Like a sensor it was picking up every little movement of his body and relaying the exciting sensations they produced throughout the rest of her. "I have a better idea of what to do with you." The light pressure of the firm masculine lips brushing hers immediately began to evoke the same pleasant dizziness that had overtaken her on the river crossing.

"Thank you, Tara," Kent murmured, "for getting me out of a tough situation. You're a brave woman. And a smart one." His mouth had pulled back barely a fraction of an inch from hers, and the words spoken against her lips were setting up the most delicious vibrations. "And you're very beautiful."

"Sure I am," she answered with a self-mocking little laugh. Coherent thoughts were becoming increasingly difficult to form, but as long as they kept talking she might be able to hold on to some degree of common sense. "My hair is dirty and full of tangles," she pointed out, lifting a knotted lock to prove her contention. When Kent didn't seem interested in shifting his attention from her mouth, she absently let the curly strand fall again. "I've been sleeping in my clothes and I haven't showered in three days. I probably don't smell like a spring bouquet."

Tara ardently hoped her joking words would push Kent away, since her hands, which had found their way to his chest, didn't seem to be able to do that of themselves. The deep red cashmere of his sweater was of a fineness that allowed her fingers to sense the shape and feel the heat of the hard muscles beneath them.

She could feel the vibrations of the chuckle that rumbled through his chest. "If you don't, I don't. So it doesn't matter, does it? You still look pretty wonderful to me."

Couldn't the man see that she really didn't want him to keep on stroking those stimulating little circles over the sensitive skin just behind her earlobe? If he didn't stop doing it soon, she'd have to order him to quit it.

"I owe you one, Tara. When I heard the BMW roaring toward my jail cell, I didn't know whether to be furious with you or kiss you." His mouth widened in the sexy grin she seemed unable to resist. "Kissing you seems like the better course of action."

Tara had to admit that it did to her, too, especially when the hard, intoxicating pressure of Kent's mouth brought a tingling warmth to her entire body.

"If we ever make it out of this mess we're in," he said softly, "I'm going to tell Elliott his agent deserves a gold star. I'm sure as hell glad I had a professional along to save my butt."

Tara dropped her eyes. The undeserved praise made her feel ashamed. She couldn't allow the charade about her real identity to go on any longer. It should never have begun.

"I have a confession to make, Kent. I'm a fraud. The only kind of agent I am is a travel agent. I'm no more a genuine intelligence officer than you are." She lifted her eyes to find his still riveted upon her face. "Maybe even less of one. You did your job well. You got out to that godforsaken place and took your pictures."

It felt strange confessing her deceit to a man whose face lingered only a few tantalizing inches away. In fact, as she tried to explain, most of her mind seemed to be rather purposefully engaged in studying the fascinating way the sensuous fullness of his lower lip dipped in the middle, and how his mouth was parted just enough to expose the edge of a line of straight white teeth. The tip of her tongue flicked out to moisten suddenly dry lips.

"My mission was a whole lot less dramatic than yours," she pressed on. "Anyone could have done it. Mr. Elliott must have heard I was in China through my father and decided to use me to get your film out. I've acted as courier for him a few times in the past. But that's all I am. A courier. No trained agent, just a person who occasionally carries the mail."

She'd expected her confession to make Kent pull away. Instead, if anything, his face was moving closer to hers. "You're telling me that the woman who risked her life to rescue me from a battalion of Chinese is really no more than a travel agent who works as an intelligence courier part-time?"

"I'm afraid so."

She wouldn't blame him for becoming angry at the deception. If she hadn't actually lied to him, she'd certainly been less than candid about her true identity. She'd just have to accept the tongue-lashing due her.

At first she thought the rasping in Kent's throat was the beginning of anger. Then she realized the man was chuckling. The chuckles escalated into an outright laugh.

"You mean we're *two* babes in the woods at this spy business? Some intelligence-gathering expedition we make."

"You mean you're not mad?"

"Mad? Why should I be mad at the woman who risked her life to set me free? I figured that kind of derring-do was all part of your job. Now you tell me you did it on just plain nerve. I'm not mad, Tara. My hat's off to you, but I do wish I hadn't gotten you into all this."

"I got myself into it, remember?"

"Thanks for the out. But it won't wash." He slid his hand under her hair to curve around the nape of her neck. She didn't resist his gentle pull. "If I'd really made up my mind not to take you with me, you wouldn't be here."

At the moment Tara almost wished she weren't here, in this tiny, quiet room, sitting so arousingly close to this big, fascinating man. If she hadn't come, she wouldn't have to deal with the compelling feelings he was able to produce in her with such embarrassing ease. She wouldn't have to face the fact that his kisses were making her want things she knew she shouldn't want.

"I've a confession to make, too, Tara. You're one hell of a fascinating woman. And God forgive me, though I couldn't admit it to myself at the time, I allowed you to come because I wanted to have you around for a few days."

The surge of satisfaction his words evoked was ridiculous, Tara quickly told herself. She didn't care whether or not he found her...desirable. But not even her intense wish that it were so could make her actually believe the truth of her mental protest. Not when every moment increased her body's urgings that it felt otherwise. Not when Kent's lips had moved to her temple to begin an exciting foray over her lidded eyes. And definitely not when his hand slipped beneath her heavy woolen sweater to stroke over the knitted silk of the undershirt covering her breast. He drew his thumb across her nipple and the stimulating caress hardened both nipples into supersensitive nubs.

Strange that the touch that tightened her lungs and abdomen could at the same time relax her into a comfortable slump against him. And the snug curve formed by the juncture of his shoulder and neck seemed specially made to cradle her head.

She'd been married to a good, caring man for almost a year. But no other man's touch had ever brought with it this extra dimension of rightness. The little shift of her body to allow him to reach more of her caused her fingers to encounter the tiny bud of a male nipple beneath the soft sweater. It seemed only fair to investigate its shape, since Kent's exploration of her was resulting in such lovely sensations.

She heard the swift intake of his breath before his mouth clamped over hers with a firmness that hadn't been present earlier.

He laid her back gently on the floor and swiveled himself over her to trap her beneath him. He had no need to push his leg between hers. One of her knees had already drawn up and fallen open of its own accord. She needed to feel the touch of his hand on her bare skin, and she tugged the shirt to her long johns out of their restraining pants. His hand stroked up to cup her breast, and her lips parted eagerly to allow the fiery invasion of his tongue.

Kent felt all his control slipping under this woman's electrifying responses to him. Her arousing softness, the silkiness of her skin, the hot moistness of her inviting mouth were banishing all thought of the danger that surrounded them. Everything about her felt so right. The way she fit into his arms. The way her mouth softened so beautifully under his. The way the satiny curve of her breast snuggled so perfectly into his hand.

He wanted her. And the way she was holding him so tightly, her tongue dancing provocatively around his, assured him she desired him no less. But a small residue of reason reminded him that at this moment the woman in his arms was very vulnerable. She'd just come through an exhausting, terrifying ordeal. Only a few days ago, when she'd had her wits about her, she'd refused him. How honorable would it be to take her now simply because all her defenses were down? For all her demonstrated courage and independence, he doubted that Tara Morgan was a woman to engage in meaningless affairs. And what else could there be between them, given their backgrounds?

Tara felt Kent's body tighten in a way that brought a sense of unease to feminine responses that had been reveling in the taste and feel of the man who until now had been holding her in such a close embrace. To make her longing clear to him she pressed herself tighter against the rock-hard thigh thrusting between hers.

Kent groaned and pulled his mouth from hers. The respite from his sweet assault upon her senses was slight, but it was enough to allow a tendril of reason to invade her clouded mind. She shouldn't want this, Tara's logic screamed. Surely she had enough sense not to want this.

"Kent," she gasped. "I don't—"

"I know." The hoarse croak of his voice and his grimace of determination told her what it cost him to lift his shuddering body from hers. Cold air rushed between them. "We need to get some sleep," he said grimly as he rolled to the very edge of their shared blanket.

Tara did the same. She knew that all it would take for him to resume their lovemaking would be for her to turn and touch him. Not even that. She need only whisper his name and he would be with her. She longed for his hard body to fill hers with its hot sweetness. The effort to keep that unwanted longing under control made her clench her fists and hold herself unmoving.

She was glad, her mind insisted, that Kent had stopped when he did. She'd been on the verge of giving herself to a man who would never make any kind of commitment to a woman. And no matter how powerful her body's yearnings, she refused to engage in an affair with a man for whom she'd never be any more than a handy female body to warm a temporary—very temporary—bed.

Chapter 6

Every few minutes, Tara or Kent returned to the window of their little room to scan the sky. To their relief, the day brought no evidence of an airborne search for the fugitives—at least not in this vicinity.

Since waking, she and Kent hadn't found a lot to say to each other. It was as if last night's intimacy had imposed a strain on their relationship. By tacit agreement, they'd both refrained from any unnecessary touching. When his fingers brushed hers—accidentally she was sure—as he passed a bowl of *tsampa,* no more than the flicker of her eyelids betrayed the quick jolt of electricity the action had given her.

That they'd sought each other's bodies immediately after the dangerous escapade in Qinghai wasn't surprising, Tara thought. Adventuring through a place that looked like a set for a science fiction movie, it was perfectly natural to add the requisite love interest. Flash Gordon and Dale Arden. What she and Kent had shared was no more real than a movie, she had to remember. Kent's wanderings were restricted to this planet. But at heart he wasn't all that different from Flash, for whom the challenge of Ming the Merciless would always loom larger and more exciting than settling down with poor Dale, who probably waited her whole life for him.

Tara had read in one of Kent's books that he could sit for hours waiting patiently for precisely the right moment to capture a special photograph. He was demonstrating no such patience during their enforced stay in the shrine. Since they could take no chances on being seen by visitors to the main part of the building, they were confined to their small room. Kent paced its short length and back again like a caged tiger.

"There's no point in holing up here, Tara," he finally said. "Sooner or later we're going to have to make our way back to Lhasa. I want you on a flight to Chengdu, then out of China, as quickly as possible. Chances are the authorities haven't yet identified you as my accomplice. But if you don't get out of the country soon, they might. Plus I've got to pick up Songtsen's *thangka* and start one hell of a long hike through the Himalayas to Kathmandu."

"I agree we'd better be on our way," Tara added. "We may be putting these women in jeopardy by staying here."

"Right. And I don't like that idea."

"You want to leave today."

Kent nodded. "Late in the afternoon so that we can get in a few hours' travel before dark, although we can't get far on the little gas we have left. I've asked Lhamo to search out any kind of motorized vehicle in the area. I promised her I'd rip off the gas myself. After all, I can't ask a nun to steal. I chose the BMW because its nine-gallon tank gives me well over three hundred miles on a fill-up, but I do have to feed it occasionally." A worried frown creased his brow. "If the nuns don't come up with the fuel, we'll have to abandon the motorcycle."

That possibility didn't thrill Tara any more than it did Kent. Distances that were manageable on wheels loomed ominously large to people on foot.

When her guests informed Lhamo of their decision to leave, the nun assured them that they were quite welcome to stay longer. All the Sisters held the rimpoche in high regard and were happy to do a favor for his friends. And they considered themselves singularly blessed, Kent translated, to be allowed to serve a namesake of their goddess. Kent thanked them profusely on behalf of Tara and himself, but insisted they had to get back on the road. Or more precisely, get back into the barren wastes where they'd be lucky to find anything as good as a trail.

When he asked Lhamo if she could direct him to Tibetans who might sell them a couple of the small, sturdy Mongolian ponies that many used, all four nuns erupted into giggles. They gestured for him to follow them to the storehouse where they'd hidden the BMW. To Kent's astonishment the fuel gauge read more than half full.

The nuns' giggles increased when Kent swept the diminutive superior off her feet and planted a loud kiss on her cheek.

A ragged, dirty-faced urchin they'd noticed running around the courtyard in defiance of the guard dogs marched into the room. His bright-eyed grin and puffed-out chest let it be known that the Westerners had him to thank for the gasoline. Kent rewarded the proud little thief with his last granola bar, and presented each of the suddenly somber nuns with a photograph of the Dalai Lama.

Later, when the travelers were pushing the motorcycle noiselessly past the outskirts of the village, they discovered the source of the miracle of the gas tank. A truck was parked on the dirt road just beyond the last of the houses. The driver, whose blue Mao suit and red-starred cap marked him as Chinese, gave a wheel a kick, then stalked around to bury his head under the propped-up hood, trying to find out why his vehicle wouldn't start.

Without the fear that Chinese troops were hot on their heels, it wasn't necessary to go on risking life and limb long after nightfall. The nuns' parting gift of a thermos of hot water allowed Tara and Kent to dine luxuriously on a packet of instant soup and Tibetan bread baked in the shape of a twisted rope.

"You know, Tara," Kent began, draining the last of his instant coffee, "we've spent every minute of several days together, but I still don't know much about you. For instance, where do you call home?"

Tara was about to answer Maryland when she gave the subject a second thought. "That's an interesting question, Kent. I have an apartment in a Maryland suburb of Washington, D.C., but I'm not sure I really think of that as home. My mom and dad live near my two sisters in a suburb of Chicago. I suppose wherever my parents are means home to me.

"Come right down to it, I guess that for me the idea of home means less a particular location on a map than it does the very close relationship that developed between the members of my family as a result of my dad's work. We had to rely mainly on each other to give our lives stability."

"You mentioned your father's in the military."

"He was. Dad's retired now, but as an air force officer he was posted in various places, not only around the United States, but around the world. Naturally we all traveled with him. In fact, my younger sister, Carole, was born in Germany."

"Sounds like your family life wasn't too different from mine." Kent got up to put away the small cooking pot and tiny camp stove. "You were a military brat. I was foreign service. In fact, I was born in London while my father was an attaché at the American embassy there. Did all that moving around bother you? For a youngster, constantly having to start over making new friends in a new school and a new neighborhood can get to be a drag."

Tara shook out the last drops of coffee from her lightweight plastic cup, added a handful of dry brown soil and swished it around in the cup to clean it. Funny. Back in the States she was downright finicky about cleanliness. Her apartment was spotless, her clothes always fresh and neatly pressed. Out in this no-man's-land, the American passion for cleanliness had to be jettisoned in favor of practicality.

"The rootlessness of military life certainly took its toll on my sisters. I guess our unsettled lives made them feel like outsiders through most of our growing-up years."

Having to move every couple of years did churn up her emotions when she had to leave friends, Tara admitted. But she'd been able to handle it. She'd always been supported by the solid underpinnings of her parents' love.

"Did it turn your sisters into travel nuts like you?" Kent asked.

Tara laughed. "No way. They reacted to all that moving around by marrying young and settling down in the Midwest. They're busy producing beautiful babies with very nice husbands who have no desire whatever to travel."

"How about you? No desire to get married again, have kids of your own?"

"I think about it sometimes. Especially when I'm visiting with the children. As a matter of fact, I was convinced that was what I wanted when I married a Virginian whose family had been rooted to the same spot for two hundred years. But in our case opposites definitely didn't attract for long. Edward is a fine man, but it just didn't work out between us."

"I'm sorry. The divorce was tough?"

Kent didn't sound too regretful, Tara noticed. "Not really. Our separation came as a relief to both of us. Edward has married again, to a Richmond girl who's perfect for him. We're still friends." Another attempt at marriage held no allure for her. Why compound a mistake by repeating it? Plenty of women were single by choice. Why not she?

She wasn't what a man, probably any man, wanted in a wife. She'd learned that with Edward. With all the best will in the world, they hadn't been able to make a go of it. And it had been mainly her fault. Staying home attempting to play the role of the dutiful wife wasn't enough for her. There was always the lure of the distant shore, the undiscovered island—Mars, if she could get it.

"How about you, Kent? You aren't wearing a ring, so I just assumed you aren't married." Good Lord. She should have made certain before she let the man kiss her. Fooling around with another woman's man definitely didn't fit into her value system. "Somehow you don't seem to be the marrying type."

"My ex-wife's sentiments exactly. Only I'm afraid our divorce wasn't quite as painless as yours." Kent still regretted that he hadn't been able to keep his breakup with Pamela from being messy and hurtful for both of them.

"I suppose your traveling so much was a problem."

"Not the traveling itself. It was my offbeat destinations Pamela didn't like. She came along with me to Paris, Hong Kong, Rio, any place with fine hotels and good shopping where she could enjoy herself while I did my thing. Destinations like Africa, the Middle East or Greenland were another story. Then there was that business you mentioned with the kidnapping." He dropped his gaze as if the subject were still painful to him. "For Pamela, that was the final straw."

Tara wondered if Kent realized that just now he'd clenched his hand just as he'd done at dinner the first day they'd met. It wouldn't be surprising, she thought, if he still carried some unresolved hatred for the men who'd abducted him.

"My wife couldn't handle it." He shrugged. "I couldn't blame her. It was a hell of a thing for her to go through."

Tara refrained from voicing the thought that the ordeal probably hadn't been too much fun for him, either. She also did not confess that if he'd been her husband, she'd have been so glad to have him back, she'd never have let him out of her sight again but would have traveled with him to the ends of the earth. Which, come to think of it, was pretty much what they were doing right now.

"My kidnapping was a shock to my family too, of course. But with our long foreign service background and the counterterrorist training we were all given, they were more prepared for that kind of thing. No—" Kent gave a decided shake of his head. "I've learned that marriage just isn't for me."

If there were times when his work and the challenge of discovering new places didn't seem enough, he consoled himself with the thought that he'd made his own choices, and at least he wasn't beholden to anyone other than himself. Most of the time remembering that helped. Not always. When it didn't, he'd swoop down on his brother and nephews and spoil the boys rotten for a few days.

"It's pretty obvious neither one of us is good marriage material," Tara said. "We simply aren't homebodies. If we were, we wouldn't be spending our lives roaming around the world."

"Right. You're a sensible woman, Tara." He raised his empty cup. "Here's to the single life. No strings. No—what do they call them these days? No *significant others* to hold us back from roaming where we will."

"I'm not too surprised at your lack of those significant others. But frankly I am surprised to find you so personally involved with Songtsen and his monks. I've noticed that professional photographers like you often survey life from behind the lens of a camera. Rather like some of my tour guides who prefer to live distanced from the real world. Are you like that?"

Startled, Kent looked up at Tara. "I've never thought of it before, Tara. I hope I'm not. I don't particularly want to be."

Her question disturbed him. Maybe Tara had put her finger on something that had been happening to him without his even noticing, Kent considered. In the years since his divorce, his life had become more solitary than he'd intended. Lately he'd found himself more detached from people than he liked. Somehow he'd simply drifted into a lonely life-style that brought him satisfying professional success but left him with an emotional void he hadn't really noticed until now.

An awkward silence descended on them, which neither sought to fill as they smoothed out the groundsheet then opened out the sleeping bag.

Tara convinced herself she was glad that tonight there was no silly banter between them about her sharing Kent's sleeping bag. She stretched out next to him as if their sleeping together meant no more than two travelers sharing a camp bed. Which, of course, it didn't.

Oh, the chemistry between them was undeniably there. They were alike in many ways, including their failed marriages. But the wanderlust they both shared was exactly what would preclude Kent from giving her what she needed from a man. Mother Nature had played a humorous trick on her—pairing her strong love of travel with an equally powerful need for the kind of permanent, loving relationship her parents had enjoyed for so long. Nurture in a loving family had developed in her a strong desire for fidelity and permanence in her relationships. And Kent Masterson certainly wasn't the man in whom she'd find those things.

What was it he'd said to her last night in the nunnery? The words had dropped from her mind, buried beneath the welter of sweet sensations his touch had evoked. They came back to her now. He'd allowed her to come with him only because he thought it would be fun to spend a few days with her.

Oddly enough, she felt more distant from Kent now, after lying in his arms and feeling his lips on hers, than when they'd been two virtual strangers forced to travel together. She wasn't seeking the total commitment of marriage any more than he was. He'd done the honorable thing and given her fair notice of where they'd stand with each other should they develop a more personal relationship. So why hadn't that cleared the way for them simply to take and enjoy what little each had to offer?

It should have been so. But it wasn't. Tonight, when she heard the howling of the distant wolves, she hardly noticed.

Kent could feel the womanly body back-to-back with his holding itself with as much stiffness as he himself was trying to maintain. He couldn't quite understand why their frank conversation hadn't led to more intimacy between them instead of less.

Buddhists preached that the root of all suffering was desire, he remembered, smiling ruefully into the darkness. Wanting and possessing, their priests maintained, kept a man from fixing his mind on more important spiritual matters. He still wanted Tara as much as ever. He was still aching to possess her. But in some crazy way, their talk about their similar opposition to any deep commitment had put a confusing damper on his continued pursuit of her.

Kent brought the BMW to a halt and planted his feet on the rocky ground to steady the machine. With a sigh he lifted the helmet from his head and drew his arm over his perspiring forehead. While Tara got off the motorcycle to stretch, he unfolded the map and spread it over the handlebars.

"It's no use, Tara," he said, squinting at the mountains off to their right and shaking his head. "I just can't find the nomad trail marked on this map. According to Songtsen it leads to another pass. At least it did. Maybe it's just faded with time since most of the nomads now probably use the paved road through the Tanglha Range."

"If I were a nomad, I'd do the same," Tara conceded. "The modern road surely must make the trek south a lot easier."

"It would do that for us, too, if we could take it. We can't just keep wandering around out here wasting gas." He folded up the map and took another swipe at his brow. "What I wouldn't give for a big, shiny American gas station."

"Yeah." Tara laughed. "One with a diner next door where we could pick up some nice cold soft drinks and a couple of cheeseburgers."

Kent gave a short chuckle and pointed upward with his thumb. "Don't mention food. I'm trying to forget about those two hopeful vultures up there." The large, ugly birds were ubiquitous in Tibet and in this region. "As I see it, Tara, we've got to head back to the road. If we don't we'll find ourselves stranded out here. The road means trucks and buses. And trucks and buses hold out the possibility of our getting some gas one way or another.''

"Maybe. But doesn't the road also hold out the probability of our running into Chinese patrols?''

A worried frown creased Kent's face. "It does. We're just going to have to keep a sharp lookout for authorities of any kind and try to avoid them. On our side is the fact that this is a huge area, and even the People's Liberation Army can't be everywhere at once. We haven't seen any signs that they've mounted an air search out here. I hope that means their resources are limited. But it would make sense to concentrate choppers and planes on a road where a motorcycle can be easily spotted from the air.''

"So how do we get around that, Kent?''

"I don't know yet.'' The dirt and grime smeared on his face didn't take anything away from the power of the sexy grin that cheered her. "Providing good luck is your department, remember? You're the reincarnated goddess. Get working on it, woman.''

Kent tried to keep the BMW at the bottom of ridges and dips in the terrain so that they could be less easily spotted from a distance. Suddenly he hit the brakes. In a flurry of dust and scattering pebbles, Tara was thrown against his back.

"Sorry, Tara. I need the telephoto lens.''

She reached down to the saddlebag behind her right leg and dug out the camera. "What do you see?''

"Looks like a small group of people have made camp over there at the mouth of a small cave maybe a quarter of a mile away.''

Tara angled her head around the broad shoulder in front of her. "Yes. I see them. D'you think they're nomads?'' she asked hopefully. "If they're Tibetans, we might be able to enlist their help.''

"I can't really tell.'' Kent lowered the camera. "They have several donkeys tethered nearby. But they don't have a tent or yaks, and I don't see any women among them. I'm sure they're not PLA, though. No uniforms.'' He handed Tara back the camera and she shoved it down into the case. "But I think we'd better just steer clear of them."

"Can we do that?"

"We're about to find out. They can't help but see us, but people out here tend to mind their own business."

"Do they have any dogs with them? I can do without any more run-ins with vicious Tibetan hounds."

"Didn't see any. We'll keep going. Whoever they are, they pose no real threat to us. We can outrun them if need be."

If the group camped on the slope noticed the motorcyclists passing by a little below them, they made no attempt at contact by shouting or waving. A mile or so beyond the camped travelers, the narrow valley took a jog to the left. Kent had barely swung the machine around the corner when he braked again, so quickly she could hear the gasoline slosh forward in the tank.

Tara almost lost her hold on Kent when he wheeled around and sped back full throttle in the direction from which they'd just come. She knew what had spooked him. She, too, had caught the flash. The slanting rays of the afternoon sun had glinted off a mirrored surface of some sort—like a piece of polished metal or an automobile's windshield. And the brief glare hadn't bounced off a vehicle on the still-distant Golmud-Lhasa road. The car or truck was heading down the valley floor directly toward them.

Kent knew that if they tried to top the ridge to make their escape, they'd be seen. Even without the binoculars the searchers probably had, a speeding motorcycle would show up against the landscape. The danger wasn't so much that the men in the vehicle would catch up to them, but that the soldiers—and who else would be traveling down a nomad trail in a wheeled vehicle—could relay the fugitives' location to their command post and bring in reinforcements. Once the Chinese knew where to look for them, it would be only a matter of time until he and Tara were captured.

He had to find a hiding place immediately. Behind them the army vehicle would soon be turning into this section of the valley and their motorcycle would be exposed to view. Ahead of them lay the camp of the unknown travelers, who could point out the Westerners to their pursuers. He and Tara could scramble into a ditch or simply throw themselves on the ground, where their dust-covered clothes might furnish a camouflage. But his frantic scan of the area disclosed no rock formations large enough to hide the machine.

He had only one choice left him. Ahead of him some of the camped group were running down the slope as they watched the motorcycle that had passed them earlier backtracking like a bat out of hell. Praying they were Tibetans, Kent veered the machine toward them.

His heart sank when they came close enough for him to make out their nationality. He heard Tara's gasp of fright, and with a groan he saw that their protective goddess had deserted them. The men ringing the motorcycle did not bear the smiling faces of the welcoming Tibetan nomads he'd hoped to see. These were tough, threatening characters who seemed all too ready to use the long, vicious-looking knives they carried.

They were Chinese.

Chapter 7

Tara stood within the protective circle of Kent's arms and tried to control her trembling. She had no idea what was going on. The sound of the BMW had scarcely died away when the noise of another vehicle reverberated through the hills. One moment it looked as if the scowling men would fall on them with those horrible long knives and turn them over to the authorities. The next moment Kent had bitten out a few words of Chinese and, to her amazement, four of the men hustled the machine and the two fugitives into the cave.

Inside, Kent had flattened himself along one damp wall of the cave and quickly pulled Tara into his arms. The limestone wall flared outward just enough to provide a small recess that might hide them from anyone standing at the entrance to the cavern and looking in. Only the mouth of the cave held any light. Tara and Kent huddled in near darkness, but their hiding place wasn't secure enough to conceal them completely. Anyone who took more than a couple of steps into the cave would surely discover them.

Tara could hear the loud conversation going on just outside the entrance. She couldn't understand the Chinese words, but the angry tone of the discussion made it clear that the travelers were not greeting their official visitors with any kind of respectful deference. In fact, the argument sounded like confrontations between cops and angry protesters in any American city.

Whoever these men were, Tara thought, they weren't behaving like average, understandably cautious Chinese citizens. It occurred to her that this clash of wills between travelers and officialdom might not be as one-sided as she'd first thought. There might not have been more than two or three soldiers or policemen in the vehicle. The government officials were surely armed, but they were out in a deserted countryside, and they faced seven bold men with knives who, from the sound of things, seemed not overly intimidated.

The argument went on. One voice grew louder than the rest and seemed to be getting closer to the cave entrance. Tara's cheek was pressed against Kent's chest. She could hear the thumping of his heart, remarkably slow and even—unlike hers.

Her gaze dropped to the floor of the cave near the entrance and she stiffened. She touched Kent's face to get his attention. "Look!" she mouthed silently. Kent's gaze followed hers to where the track of a motorcycle tire lay imprinted in the mud.

"We can't do anything about it now," he whispered. "Except pray."

After several minutes the argument outside seemed to be slackening off. Was it because the soldiers had begun a search of the area? she wondered. If that search brought them inside, there was no way she and Kent could escape. The cave ended only a few feet away and there was no other exit.

Tara's ears strained to decipher if the muffled sound echoing through the cave was an engine starting up, but she couldn't be sure. For what seemed a very long time she heard nothing but a few quiet words spoken by men near the entrance. Then came the sound of feet shuffling ever closer to their hiding place. Kent tensed. His arms tightened around her. She squeezed her eyes shut and held her breath.

"Okay," came a strongly accented voice from the dimness. "So'dier gone." Tara opened her eyes and turned her head to see the man who appeared to be the leader of the surly group who'd hidden the fugitives. She devoutly hoped he meant the bared teeth as a grin. Kent angled himself protectively in front of her.

"Booze pingteen," the man said loudly. At least that's what his words sounded like to her.

She heard the relief in Kent's low laugh. "Right, pal. Bruce Springsteen." He grasped the proffered Chinese hand and pumped it up and down. "Bruce Springsteen. The Boss."

"You know Boss?"

"Hey. Sure. Everybody knows the Boss."

"Mika' Jackso' "

"Yep. Michael Jackson, too. He's bad."

The man erupted in a flurry of encouraging nods. "Maygwo good."

"He thinks America is good, Tara. It wouldn't hurt if you could claim personal friendship with Michael Jackson."

To Tara, this conversation seemed straight out of *Alice in Wonderland,* but she was grateful for the universal appeal of American rock music. It looked as if she and Kent might owe their lives to a few smuggled-in music tapes.

"I once went to a Bruce Springsteen concert," she offered, bolstering her truthful claim with a little dance twist.

The man nodded approvingly. "Booze 'pingteen, okay. You okay! You come." He gestured for them to follow him outside.

"Be careful, Tara," Kent whispered. "We're not out of the woods yet. These guys could have saved us from the officials just so that they can pick us clean themselves."

"Who are they, Kent? Why did they hide us?"

"Did you notice the picks and shovels in their packs?"

She hadn't noticed anything but their knives.

"That's what made me take a chance on them. I'm pretty sure they're prospectors heading north to strike it rich in the newly discovered gold fields. We're dealing with the Chinese version of our forty-niners."

She'd already learned that China was full of surprises. This was just one more.

"These Springsteen fans," Kent continued, "are strong-minded men who have no love for the authorities. Ordinarily they'd have been hauled off by the cops and their goods confiscated. Then they'd have been sent back where they came from. The government is doing its damnedest to keep people out of the gold-mining area, but hordes of prospectors are trying to cut themselves in on the riches. In a way, we've already repaid the favor these guys have done us. Today the soldiers were more interested in hunting for us than in taking them into custody. That's probably what all the shouting was about. They were being ordered to go home, and apparently they weren't having any."

At the leader's invitation, Kent and Tara seated themselves on the ground within the group clustered around the camp fire. The men offered Kent a bottle of Chinese beer and pointed questioningly toward the pot of noodles simmering over the fire. "I think it would be wise for us to share their lunch, Tara. People we've broken bread with might be less inclined to hit us on the head before we can get away."

Kent's warnings to her weren't very reassuring, but to look at him glad-handing their hosts with noisy enthusiasm, he didn't have a care in the world. Tara tried to keep a smile on her face while munching her way through a bowl of noodles flavored with chicken broth, but the looks several of the men slanted her way worried her. Any woman would have recognized their implied threat. A tightening of Kent's face told her he hadn't missed their stomach-churning meaning, either. His one-man assault on the secret installation had proved his extraordinary bravery, but he couldn't be expected to battle seven armed men and win.

"It's time for us to try to get out of here," he said to her quietly after they'd put down their bowls. "These fellows want gold. I can give it to them." Kent stood up and slipped off the Rolex watch that until now had been covered by the sleeve of his jacket. With a good deal of formality, he presented it to the man who seemed to be the leader of the group.

"*Dzy-jen,*" Kent said. "*Shiay-shiay. Chong-woa ty-howla.* Thank you and goodbye. China is wonderful." The Chinese Springsteen fan knew gold when he saw it. His black eyes gleamed as he fitted the expensive watch over his own thin wrist and showed it off to the others.

While the chorus of appreciative comments was going on, Kent took firm hold of Tara's elbow and led her to the motorcycle. Two of the men, their eyes narrowed threateningly, sauntered over to stand in front of the machine.

"*Shiay-shiay.*" Kent firmly repeated his goodbye. He started the motor. The men blocking their way didn't budge. Kent gave every indication of being willing to drive right through them if he had to. As he was revving up the motor to do just that, the new owner of the Rolex barked out an order and his men reluctantly moved away.

Knowing that at least one patrol vehicle was still in the area, Kent continued the trip east driving carefully, alert to any repetition of their close encounter with Chinese officialdom. Even without his saying so, it was painfully clear to Tara that if they'd run into a search party this far out in the country, their chances of making it back to Lhasa without another confrontation were not good. She also was resigned to the fact that regardless of the danger, they really had little choice but to use the road. Cross-country travel was simply too time-consuming, ate up precious gasoline and apparently was not all that much safer.

At dusk they came upon what was clearly a Tibetan camp within sight of the modern road. A herd of yaks nosed the ground near where a flock of sheep and several goats were tied individually to a long rope—the Tibetan version of an animal pen. A large white canvas tent was set up on the rocky plain, and several nomad families crowded around it. Even from a distance it was clear these people wore ethnic dress, not the drab, styleless clothes of provincial Chinese. The bright color and Western fashion that had invaded Beijing was less evident this far away from the growing sophistication of the capital city.

The Tibetans greeted the Western visitors with infectious smiles and a certain amount of awe. Not many foreigners approached a nomad camp, and even fewer came out of the same wilderness they wandered. Tara and Kent accepted their invitations to join the group. Bowls of tea were brought out and passed around along with the ever-present *tsampa*.

To Kent's disappointment, no one carried gasoline. He still had enough to get the motorcycle up into the pass, but not much farther than that. He and Tara knew a few minutes of anxiety when a truck bounced over from the road, but the driver and his mate were both Tibetans seeking to join in the evening meal and socialize with their countrymen.

Dinner was a drawn-out affair and extremely informal. Accompanied, incongruously to Tara's ears although her hosts took no notice of it, by loud disco music from a portable radio. One woman brought out an unappetizing length of gray sausage that bore a distressing resemblance to its original incarnation as the insides of a sheep. Another placed a platter of boiled mutton on the communal table and everyone fell to, hacking off chunks with their all-purpose knives. Big bowls of sugar were laid out along with lumps of sticky, garishly colored candy. No forks appeared on the portable table made of planks and trestles. Nor did anyone but Tara seem unduly perturbed when a haunch of meat was accidentally dropped to the ground, then picked up and put back on the plate.

Tara was gratefully aware that these people were generously sharing what little they had with strangers. It was her place to practice the good manners expected from a guest whether at the elegance of the White House or in the simplicity of a nomad tent. Besides, she decided, if Kent could demolish a fairly large plate of sausage and greasy mutton with apparent enjoyment, she'd do the same—with a much smaller serving—if it killed her.

At dark a portable generator appeared to light a couple of naked bulbs hung from the tent poles. Though she and Kent had been given two of the few folding chairs at the table, he'd remained deep in conversation with the truckers standing behind him while they ate. She was able to pay little attention to their conversation because the women present were doing their best to engage her in a conversation of their own. One young woman who flaunted a gold-capped tooth gave Tara's hair a close inspection by combing her fingers through it. Their guest's green eyes were also the subject of much examination and comment.

Tara tried to express her admiration for the jewelry the women wore. Their long necklaces and dangling earrings of turquoise and coral beads strung on silver threads were much more beautiful than the cheap reproductions she'd seen in Lhasa's Chinese tourist shops. Kent got up to go over and huddle in a corner of the tent with the two newcomers. She saw him take out Songtsen's letter and show it to the truckers.

"The two truckers have come from Golmud," Kent informed Tara after he'd returned to sit by her. "They tell me there's no way we can avoid Chinese patrols on the road. They're out in force and are specifically questioning people about seeing any kind of motorcycle. The Tibetans don't think we'll get very far on the BMW."

That information didn't come as any great surprise to her. "What else can we do, Kent?"

"This group of nomads is heading back up onto the Tibetan plateau, and eventually some plan to keep on to Lhasa. We could travel with them, but they're in no hurry and the trip will take them at least a week. The truckers have no love for the Chinese, who make it rough for Tibetans to have any but the most menial jobs, and they've come up with an idea. They're willing to help us out by hiding us in the truck, only..." Kent trailed off, his expression extremely dubious.

"What's the problem? They don't want to take a woman?"

"Oh, no, you're included in the deal, all right. They plan to stay on the road all night, taking turns with the driving. If we go with them, we can be in Lhasa late tomorrow night."

"Sounds great," Tara said with enthusiasm. "Let's do it."

"It's just that . . . well, I have to warn you that our trip won't be at all pleasant."

"For goodness sake, Kent," Tara protested. "I've managed to survive days getting my bones bounced to mush on the back of a motorcycle, a bunch of cutthroat miners, going without washing, eating a sheep that was probably walking around only a few minutes before he showed up on a dinner plate, and all kinds of other things. What can be so bad about traveling in a truck?"

She found out. All the other ordeals she and Kent had shared seemed minor compared to what they were now going through. Huddled in virtually total darkness inside a large crate in a truck full of sheep being hauled to market was no way for a woman to maintain any dignity whatsoever. She prayed that the unbearable stench given off by a dozen filthy sheep only inches away from her nose would soon deaden her sense of smell.

Poor Kent was in even greater discomfort than she. At least she was short enough to sit upright in the packing case although her head did scrape its wooden slats. His height forced Kent to lie on the truck bed with his knees drawn up. Even after several hours in that cramped position, his only complaint had been a few muttered curses as he gritted his teeth and tried to shift his torturous position. Tara hunched out of her parka, rolled it up and slipped the makeshift pillow beneath his head.

It seemed that fate was always conspiring to throw them into embarrassingly close proximity for two people who weren't much more than strangers. Kent must have been thinking something along the same lines because his dry observation came out of the darkness. "I like being with you, Tara, but this situation gives a whole new meaning to the word *togetherness*. Thank God neither of us suffers from claustrophobia. We'd go nuts having to stay cooped up in here for twenty-four hours."

Whenever they came upon an official checkpoint, one of the Tibetan drivers would hang out the cab window and whack at the crate with a stick to warn them to be particularly quiet. So far no policeman had been brave enough to wade through the disgusting river of sheep droppings to inspect the large crate draped with a tarpaulin just behind the truck's cab. If one had ventured onto the truck, he'd have found not an entire crate of cabbages, but only a foot-deep layer on top of a false bottom.

"I don't think we're the first contraband these guys have smuggled into Tibet, Kent."

"No. They seemed well practiced at using those planks to convert a large crate of cabbages into a small load of cabbages and a hidey-hole. I'm sure they've a lucrative business going on over and above their legitimate hauling company. Maybe this was the route those decadent Western music tapes took into the countryside."

"Wouldn't that be a coincidence."

"The Chinese don't believe in coincidence. They do believe that a god in a good mood can shower good luck on a person."

"I'm glad we were able to repay our dinner hosts with a sudden windfall of cabbages," Tara said. Then she remembered the hard sacrifice Kent had made to increase their chances of reaching Lhasa safely. "I'm sorry you had to abandon the BMW." She laid a hand on his arm in sympathy. "I know how attached to it you were. Wasn't it incredible how fast those men were able to dismantle it?"

Kent groaned. "Don't remind me. I hated to give it up. It's seen me through many an off-road trek and brought me many a great photograph, but the thing had become a liability. I'm sure every motorcyclist in the country is finding himself in deep trouble today. And there was no way I could have used it to get out of Tibet with Song-tsen's *thangka*. Damn.''

Tara couldn't see the grimace of pain that must have flashed across Kent's face, but she could hear it in his voice. "I'm getting a cramp in my right calf."

"Let me try to massage it out."

Tara's hands searched for the cramped leg muscle and circled around it to begin working out its tightness. In a minute or two she could feel Kent start to relax a little. She kept her hands on his calf, rubbing it gently in case it should go into spasm again.

"Thanks, Tara."

When they ran out of the jokes they were telling each other in a vain attempt to keep their minds off the acute discomfort of their small, dark prison, they moved on to compare notes on good restaurants they'd visited all over the world. And although it was a kind of torture in itself, each insisted the other linger lovingly over every delicious detail of the menus.

They could tell night from day only by watching the slivers of light that entered the tiny cracks in the sides of the crate not entirely covered by the tarp. What with the incessant rumble of the motor, the outraged complaints of the sheep and the constant lurching of the truck, sleep proved impossible. The best they could manage were cat-naps. On the all too few occasions when the truck ground to a halt on deserted stretches of road or hidden behind a Tibetan village, they both heaved loud sighs of relief and groaned as they unfolded themselves from their painful positions.

"I hope that when all this is over I can still walk," Kent said, gingerly letting himself down from the truck.

Maybe their tight-fitting hiding place was making her hysterical, Tara worried. Maybe she'd just gotten to the point where she didn't care anymore. But as one of the drivers helped her over the side of the truck, she started to giggle. Kent and the Tibetans stared at her as if she were crazy, but she couldn't stop.

"I fail to see the humor of the situation," Kent observed as he pulled his aching body into a long stretch.

"I was just thinking," Tara said, trying to stifle her giggles with a hand, "of all the weird situations I've found myself in since meeting up with you." A new eruption of laughter nearly doubled her over. "One thing I can say for you, Kent Masterson. You sure know how to show a girl a good time."

A loud guffaw burst from his throat. "And one thing I can say for you, Tara Morgan. You're the only girl I'd ever choose to be cooped up with in a crate in the middle of a stinking flock of sheep."

"Thank you," Tara answered in mock solemnity. "That's the nicest thing anyone's ever said to me." Kent laid an arm around her shoulders and together they began a slow, wobbly jog, trying to work out the kinks before returning to their cage.

Tara thought it was neat the way the Tibetans used a blowtorch to heat the water for their tea. But even with such high-tech measures, the water never really reached a steaming-hot temperature.

The drivers had been overly optimistic about their traveling time. It was near dawn of the second night when they pulled up to the rear gate of Songtsen's monastery a few miles north of Lhasa. As the high lama had promised, a monk was waiting there to let them in.

The rimpoche's face broke into a broad smile when he saw them.

"My dear children, you've returned safely."

Kent wasted no time in getting to the item he and Tara had agreed was the most urgent right now. "Rimpoche, please, may we use the monastery's bathing facilities? Tara can't return to the hotel in this condition. And frankly, I can't stand my own awful smell anymore."

"You may, of course, my son. It is not customary for a woman...." He hesitated before waving away his own objections. "No matter. These are days of extreme circumstances which call for uncommon actions."

At Songtsen's order, an old monk led Tara to a small private room, which contained a large tin tub. Two other monks arrived to add a couple of bucketfuls of hot water to the cold water she'd drawn from the tap. Then all three bowed out, pulling the door's heavy drapes closed behind them.

The water was only tepid, but Tara didn't care. There was plenty of soap, and a bath was what she wanted most in the world. She sank down in the tub and washed herself from top to bottom several times before tackling her hair with the bar of harsh soap. The disgusting odor of sheep had so permeated her clothes that they were fit only for burning. Unfortunately she had to climb back into the dirty garments. The monks, of course, had no clothes for a Western female to wear and she could hardly return to the hotel wrapped in the robes of a Buddhist monk. Even the nylon tote that had seen her through the difficult trip bore an unpleasant odor.

Kent met her outside in the hallway. The remainder of his belongings had been here in the monastery during their trek north. Not only had he been able to change into a jogging suit of a rich blue color, he'd shaved for the first time in a week. She thought he'd looked just as good with the beginnings of a beard.

But the lack of the stubble she'd gotten used to seeing on Kent's face, and his clean clothes, brought home to her the incredibly disturbing idea that their shared adventure was over and she was about to leave him. They'd been forced into intimacy for what seemed like so long that she'd scarcely given any thought to the fact that once she left the monastery it would be a very long time before she'd see Kent Masterson again. And the possibility that she might never see him again was all too real and frightening. As unlikely as it might have seemed only a couple of hours ago, she suddenly wished herself back in the uncomfortable crate with him.

Kent took her hand. He apparently had the same trouble as she in finding something appropriate to say.

"Looks like this is goodbye, Tara. I hope you don't run into any trouble getting out of the country."

"I don't expect I will. There's no reason for the authorities to connect me with you. All bundled up the way I was, and wearing the helmet, I could have been a man. The only people who know your partner was a woman are Tibetans."

"And me." His voice held a deep, raspy undertone. "I know you as one very special woman, Tara." As if this was an avenue of discussion it wouldn't be wise to pursue, Kent cleared his throat. "What about the film? What are you going to do with that?"

"Elliott gave me a can of hair spray fitted with a false bottom to hide the film. I imagine security forces will be questioning everyone at the airport but I shouldn't run into any major problems. My papers are all in order, and the people at CITS want to keep us travel agents happy."

"You have your airline ticket?"

"Yes. It's for next Tuesday and they can get irritated with people who don't follow their appointed schedule, but I'm pretty sure they'll allow me on tomorrow's flight. Oh, and Kent? You don't have to worry. I won't say anything to anyone about the sacred scroll you'll be taking out of the country." Her concern about Kent getting himself out of China was a lot greater than any worry about the painting.

Everything they'd shared the past few days proved that her original instincts about him had been right, Tara reflected. Kent Masterson was an adventurer, his wanderlust deeply bred in the bone. It was just as well they were parting. Just as well she'd never given in to any dumb desire to have a romantic fling with him.

Still, it was proving to be a lot more difficult than she'd expected only a few days ago to walk away from the most extraordinary man she'd ever met. She couldn't think of anyone else who could have done the things he'd done to provide a service to his country. She'd already decided that this was *her* last job for Elliott. Out of a sense of patriotism instilled in her military family she'd agreed to do a few favors for her father's friend, but intelligence work wasn't something she wanted to get into any more deeply. She'd learned that getting scared out of her wits once was more than enough.

A monk appeared with the message that Songtsen wished to see them both. Tara was anxious to get back to the hotel, but she couldn't leave without saying goodbye to the high lama.

She was a little surprised when Songtsen received them not in the small chamber in which he'd met them earlier, but in a large formal reception room, its rows of square columns painted with swirls of blues, reds and greens. An immense golden shrine filled one end of the room. Songtsen was seated on a high, cushioned bench at the opposite end of the ornate chamber. The cushion was embroidered with gold swastikas—a hateful sign to Westerners, but to Buddhists an ancient symbol of good luck. Behind his thronelike seat hung a large, silken, exquisitely painted *thangka*.

Tara immediately sensed the greater formality of this audience. The lama wore a flowing cape of burgundy wool, and fitted on his head was a crescent-shaped hat of dark yellow felt. A thick upright fringe thrust forward over his forehead and ran back over the crown of the hat like the crest of some fantastic bird.

She and Kent bowed respectfully to the old man.

"Songtsen Rimpoche," Kent began, "your assistance allowed us to find the secret construction site and evade Chinese troops. For this we both thank you. Now I'm happy to repay your kindness by embarking on the task for which you summoned help from my grandfather. I'm sorry that it will take longer now for your *thangka* to reach safety because the authorities search for me. If I'd known the outcome of the mission to Qinghai, I might have refused it. Your request of the Masterson family is the reason I am here."

"There was no avoiding the journey to Qinghai, my son. It was your karma—your destiny."

"Perhaps, but now I must escape from Tibet by a long, hard trek through the Himalayas into Nepal or India."

The high lama, Tara noticed, seemed unperturbed by the change in plans. If she could achieve only a fraction of the old man's laid-back attitude, it would certainly alleviate the stress her work so often produced in her.

"We expected this," Songtsen said, "and are even now making ready for your journey."

"Good. I'll leave as soon as possible. Things are getting too hot for me here in Tibet. However, I must rest for a few hours. The trip from Qinghai was—" Kent glanced at Tara with a wry smile "—ah . . . rather uncomfortable. But your religious treasure, Rimpoche, the Light of Buddha, I'm anxious to see it. And I'm sure Tara would like to view the *thangka* before she leaves."

"I would, Rimpoche. I've learned something of your country the past few days, and I would very much like to see the religious painting."

"Yes. It is time to present the Light of Buddha."

When the old man indicated he would get down from his high seat, Kent offered an arm to help him. At the high lama's nod, a monk sounded a large bronze gong. Its deep reverberations still echoed from the high-ceilinged walls when a monk swinging a silver censer on the end of a chain walked slowly into the room. The censer's smoke wafted the pleasant odor of juniper to Tara's nose.

From the corridor outside the room came the sound of the low, melodic chant, *Om Mani Padme Hum*. The chant grew louder as a long, double row of monks filed into the audience chamber in solemn procession. Between them walked a small boy of five or six years whose bare feet peeped out from beneath the robes of a Buddhist monk.

When the phalanx of monks halted, the little boy walked forward and gravely returned Songtsen's respectful bow. Then, as if he could maintain a forced solemnity no longer, the child broke into a smile and slid a hand into that of the high lama. The rimpoche spoke to the boy in Tibetan and the grin on the little brown face grew wider.

Songtsen turned to Kent and Tara. "My children, I have the great honor of introducing the Light of Buddha, His Holiness the Gendun Lama."

Chapter 8

"**Y**our Holiness." Songtsen addressed the boy in English. "May I present Mr. Kent Masterson who has come from the far-off land of America."

Tara didn't understand. Kent had referred to a sacred scroll called the Light of Buddha, but Songtsen had called the child by that name. She glanced in confusion from one man to the other. Kent looked dumbfounded. "You mean this child is the Light of Buddha? The Light of Buddha is the new incarnation of the Gendun Lama?"

"Exactly so," Songtsen replied. "Such was the name given to the first Gendun Lama, who lived four hundred years ago. We use the name, hoping the Chinese, who know little of our culture, will not recognize it. This child is the seventh incarnation of the Gendun Lama."

At Songtsen's encouraging nod the little boy marched up to Kent and forthrightly thrust out his hand. "How do you do, Kent Ma...Ma..." The child thought for a second and tried again. "How do you do, Kent Massaton? My name is Jigme."

"Uh..." Kent floundered, accepting the boy's formal handshake. "I'm honored, Your Holiness."

"My name is Tara, Jigme." Tara repeated the child's pronunciation of "Jig-may." "I'm both honored and delighted to meet you." The dark-headed little boy gave her a shy, somewhat nervous smile and bowed deeply from the waist.

"Whoa." Kent backed away a step and threw up his hands in a gesture that plainly indicated he wished to call a halt to the proceedings. "Whoa, now. Hold everything. Rimpoche, you mean you expect me to take this child with me out of the country?"

"That is our hope."

"Now just let's wait a minute here. The way I see it, all bets are off. You led my grandfather to believe we'd be dealing with a sacred symbol, a treasured religious icon of some sort."

"The reincarnation of the Gendun Lama is one of Pö's—Tibet's—greatest treasures, both religious and political."

"I know that. But your letter didn't mention anything about a child. You must have known that we'd assume the Light of Buddha was a religious object."

"I must acknowledge that not revealing the complete truth was a form of deception." The high lama looked exceedingly contrite. "And for that I most humbly beg your forgiveness. But you must understand that the subterfuge was necessary. It would have been disastrous if I'd openly referred to the Gendun Lama in my letter to Randall and it fell into Chinese hands. They would give anything to get hold of any of our important incarnatives, especially this one."

"Are you not an incarnative yourself, Rimpoche? Why have they not arrested you?"

"I'm an old man. Perhaps they know that I would be of limited value to them. And this monastery has never been of the same importance as Gendun or some of the others. Nor has it played much of a political role in the past."

"But Songtsen," Kent pleaded, "surely you see that I can't take a child with me. The Himalayas remain as treacherous as they've ever been to a man on foot. There's no guarantee that I'll even make it through.''

Tara could hear a hint of growing desperation in Kent's voice. She wished he hadn't reminded her of the danger he faced getting out of the country. She didn't like to think about it.

"It's true the boy will face dangers on the trek,'' Songtsen conceded. "But if he remains here, he will face even greater danger. Do you know what happened to the old Gendun Lama?''

Kent winced as if Songtsen had scored a solid hit against him.

Well, Kent might know, Tara thought, but she didn't. "I must confess that I'm distressingly ignorant of events in your country, Rimpoche. I've never heard of the Gendun Lama. Please tell me what happened to him.''

"After the invasion, our Dalai Lama was able to escape. The Gendun Lama was not so fortunate. The Chinese took him away and held him prisoner for many years. When he would not accede to their wishes to become their puppet, he was tortured.''

Tara gasped. "They couldn't, Rimpoche. Not to a child.''

"Every Tibetan man, woman and child has already suffered under the harsh regime that rules our lives. When the old Gendun Lama's health could no longer bear the rigors of imprisonment, they sent him back to his monastery where he lived the last years of his life in complete seclusion.

"If the Chinese find this boy, they would surely take him away and allow him no contact with our teachers. Without any nourishing of his spirit in the ways of his people, what would become of him? Even if the Chinese treat him outwardly with every sign of respect, he would provide them with an effective means of control over our people. Tibetans would bear anything rather than allow harm to come to the Gendun Lama. Chinese domination of him would do much to eliminate embarrassing demonstrations in the streets against our tyrannical masters.''

The old man laid his hand gently on Kent's arm.

"The decision whether to take the boy to freedom must be yours to make, Kent Masterson," Songtsen said quietly. "I ask only that you allow me to explain further the reasons for our request, which I'm aware is a most serious one."

At Songtsen's gesture, a monk lifted the little boy onto the high bench that had been the high lama's seat. Songtsen waved Tara and Kent to low cushions before the throne and folded himself on another cushion. The attending monks arranged themselves in lines on either side of the chamber and sank onto the floor in the lotus position.

"Many years ago, just after Randall's last visit here, our State Oracle made some final prophecies before our enemies invaded and outlawed the rituals and practices which had stood us in good stead for centuries. For a long time we could not understand the oracle's words that seemed to suggest that the Light of Buddha was to fly over a great sea.

"Some interpreters thought the prophecy referred to a symbolic flight of the teachings of the Gendun Lama over the mountains you call the Himalayas. Before the Chinese came, the idea of a lama being forced to abandon the sacred ground of Pö was almost beyond imagining. But then His Holiness the Dalai Lama was forced to do so, and our conquerors taught us the true meaning of the prophecies. The young incarnate lama must be gotten to safety."

Kent nodded. His face remained grave. "I see that, of course, Rimpoche. But why me? Why not entrust the boy to one of your own people who surely knows the territory much better than I? Many Tibetans have already made their way over the mountains to India or Nepal."

"The prophecy suggested that a foreigner would accompany the lama. We chose to contact Randall because we wish much more for the new Gendun Lama than merely getting him to safety in another country. We want the reincarnation to have the protection of the United States government."

"I understand," Kent said. "That explains why you were so disappointed when I didn't turn out to be my brother, Andrew. You hoped that with his diplomatic immunity he could provide a greater degree of protection for the boy than I can."

"I admit I greeted your presence with an agitation unseemly in one who practices withdrawal from the passions of the world. It was a good lesson in humility." Kent returned the old man's gentle smile.

"Not only will the Gendun Lama study advanced Buddhist theology, he must learn Western thought and become familiar with the outside world in order to help guarantee Tibet's future place in it as a distinct cultural entity. We made a mistake by trying to live cut off from the rest of the world. Our failure to form ties with Western governments after World War II left us totally powerless to counter the Chinese takeover. Now we must make common cause with the West, with whose help we hope to regain some measure of independence."

Tara glanced up at the little boy who was the subject of these weighty matters and wondered how much of them he understood. She was sure he couldn't follow the English conversation because he seemed to be paying little attention to it. As fidgety as any American child laboring under enforced best behavior at Sunday service, he was playing with a cushion tassel and regarding her with the same nervous interest she'd sensed from the other monks at her first meeting with Songtsen.

Today the monks seated on the oiled clay floor were taking no such uncomfortable notice of her. Perhaps the high lama had given orders they were not to acknowledge the presence of the Western woman. Tara smiled at the boy and surreptitiously wiggled her fingers at him. Her action seemed to put him at ease and he grinned.

If Songtsen had caught the little byplay, he gave no indication of it. "Before the Chinese came," he continued, "it was not unknown in my country to send sons with exceptional ability to be educated in the West. We pray that under the protection of your powerful family, Kent, the boy will grow into a man who can take his place among world leaders and win for Tibetans by wisdom and diplomacy what we have not yet been able to accomplish. It is the boy's karma to dedicate his life to his nation."

Tara was about to interject that that was asking too much of any child, when she remembered that children born to be monarchs of England were expected to do pretty much the same thing. They too were locked into a life of regimentation from birth.

"Also," Songtsen continued, "I must be honest and tell you that we hope that passing the boy into the care of a famous Western family will give him a higher visibility with—what do you say?—ah, yes—with the media than if he were just another refugee."

"I think you hope for more than that, Rimpoche," Kent countered gently. "You could have simply sent the boy out of Tibet and then on to Randall without the personal involvement of any Masterson. By involving my brother in Jigme's escape, you were hoping to develop a close relationship between the two because Andrew has two boys around the young lama's age. You wish some kind of arrangement made to fit the child into Andrew's family, don't you?"

"I cannot deny it. Such an arrangement would make Jigme's transition into an alien culture easier. A child can learn from children. And I realize now that it was no accident that you were sent here in your brother's place. The wisdom of Buddha evidently means you to become one of Jigme's important teachers."

"Look, Songtsen," Kent protested. "I can't accept responsibility for any child's life, let alone that of a personage of such great importance. Let Tibetans get him to safety."

The little boy evidently could read enough of Kent's voice and body language to disturb him. With a worried expression on his face, the child hopped down from his high seat and said something to Songtsen in Tibetan.

"His Holiness has guessed that you are not enthusiastic about taking him with you, Kent," Songtsen translated. "He asks if it is because you do not like him."

Kent squirmed. As well he might, Tara thought. The disappointed look on the little guy's face made her want to go over and hug him. But she could hardly blame Kent for balking at the unexpected turn of events. This was no small thing the high lama was asking of him.

"Of course I like him," Kent asserted, reaching over to take the child's hand and smile at him. "The little fellow's cute as a button. Please inform Jigme, Rimpoche, that I recognized the great honor a person who ranks so high on the Tibetan social scale did an ordinary American by shaking hands with me. And tell him I was greatly impressed at how well he learned to greet us in English." Kent angled his head to the side to look around the boy at the high lama. "A nice touch that, Songtsen," he said in a lowered voice. "You must have coached him yourself."

"I saw no reason why His Holiness's lessons in Western language and customs shouldn't begin now. Unfortunately there was time only to commence his instruction in English. You must continue the lessons."

Tara knew Kent's tough, take-charge manner was no misleading advertising; their journey north had shown her that. But she knew also that it covered a kind and generous nature sensitive to those in need of his help. Like the poor nuns to whom he'd given a generous donation, or a woman suffering the effects of altitude sickness to whom he'd offered a strong arm. She doubted he could resist the pleas of a gentle old man and a bright, engaging little boy.

The glance the high lama threw Kent bore a surprising sharpness. "I know it is not necessary to remind you, my son, that your grandfather owes his life to a Tibetan monk. Now I am asking the grandson to save the spiritual life of a Tibetan monk."

Kent acknowledged the old man's subtle pressure with a wry smile. "You may be a mild Buddhist priest, Rimpoche, but you can play hardball with the best of 'em."

"I do not know this hard ball, but as a boy I was good at games."

"I'll bet." The wily old monk had him boxed in, Kent admitted. The mission on which Randall had sent him was turning out to be a whole lot more than he'd bargained for, but how could he refuse?

"All right, Rimpoche," Kent replied, despite his continuing deep misgivings about the situation. "I agree to try to get the boy out. But I'm not in any position to serve as his family. I'll take him to meet my brother and my nephews. Andrew will have to take it from there."

"We are most grateful, my son. You have a good heart. And to Tibetans a good heart is everything. Pö will be forever in your debt."

"For a long time the Mastersons were in your debt," Kent answered. "I'd say this makes us even. I planned to take my chances on the road from Lhasa to Kathmandu by hiking around Chinese checkpoints, but I don't dare risk taking the boy that way. Can you provide us with a guide to some other way through the mountains?"

"One of our monks will accompany you. I agree you cannot risk the road to Kathmandu. We have worked out a route which I'm afraid is much longer and more arduous, but we have no choice. To avoid your pursuers, your party must trek, not southward, but west to a place called Yonten-La. The monastery there is so remote and inaccessible that it escaped the almost universal destruction of the Cultural Revolution. It guards a secret and dangerous pass into Nepal."

"A trek into western Tibet. Doesn't that mean a trip of a good seven or eight hundred miles?" Kent looked down dubiously at the little boy. "And on foot."

"There will be horses, and yaks to carry the packs. But it will still be very hard."

Kent sighed. "Well, as you say, Rimpoche. We have no choice."

Tara leaned over to touch the large hand of the man sitting cross-legged beside her. "I'm glad you decided to do it, Kent. I don't think the boy could be in better hands."

This remarkable man wouldn't hesitate to match himself against the brute force of the most powerful mountains on the planet, she thought. The mountains might win, but Kent Masterson would never give in to them without a fight. She was beginning to wish she could be a part of that struggle. The monks were trusting Kent with their greatest treasure, and she had no doubt he would honor that trust to his utmost ability. And he'd do it because not only his mind but his emotions were involved in their cause. She doubted if any woman would ever engage his commitment in the same way. The thought spurred a little ache in her heart.

"The lady Tara speaks for me also, my son," the lama agreed. "I am confident that we are giving the boy into the care of precisely the right man."

Songtsen told the boy of Kent's agreement. Standing beside the seated Westerner, the child was on a level with him. Jigme threw his short arms around Kent's neck and blurted, "T'ank you, Missa Massaton."

The shower of compliments evidently was making Kent uncomfortable. "All right, folks. Knock it off. I'm just going to do what has to be done."

"Now, Tara," Songtsen said. "It is your turn to receive an explanation. Please. Come with me." Seeing that the old man was struggling to rise, Kent and the boy helped him to his feet.

The assembled monks stayed seated fingering their prayer beads while the rimpoche led Kent, Tara and the boy to the far end of the room where an exquisitely crafted gold-washed statue of a seated woman filled almost the entire wall. Massive bronze basins holding burning wicks floating in melted butter were set before the image elaborately clothed in robes of heavy red, green and gold brocade. The goddess held a representation of a golden lotus blossom in her right hand, and on her head was a golden tiara of stylized flames set with coral and rubies. Her wide eyes, their irises painted a brilliant green, gazed serenely into the room.

"An image of your namesake, Tara," the high lama explained. "For us, Tara personifies the female aspect of enlightenment. She is called the Green Tara and she embodies the active features of compassion. The oracle foretold that the Lady of Compassion would favor this monastery with her presence. All our monks know of this prophecy. When a woman appeared here with eyes the green of this Tara's eyes and hair the color of the rubies in her crown, she was recognized as an incarnation of the goddess. You have courage, my child, but perhaps our prostrations of devotion and respect due the goddess confused, even frightened you."

"I wasn't frightened, Rimpoche. I did wonder about it, but Kent explained to me about the unusual meaning of my name here in Tibet. My religious beliefs are different from yours and it is difficult for me to accept that your goddess has chosen to...uh, use me for some purpose. But I respect your beliefs, Rimpoche, and I recognize the very great honor those beliefs do me."

"I know that foreigners are not always as comfortable with things of the spirit as we are. East and West have different definitions of what is real."

"Perhaps not always as different as you might think. While Lhamo was showing me the nunnery's painting of Tara, I thought of my Celtic ancestors who probably held a view of the world not so different from that of your people, Songtsen. Long ago my people also worshipped the Great Goddess."

"Ah!" said Songtsen, as if he'd just added the last piece to a confusing puzzle. "Then perhaps that is why Tara has chosen to manifest herself in a woman not of our faith. But you need have no fear, my child. The goddess will do you no harm."

"I'm sure she won't, Rimpoche," Tara answered, nodding toward the statue. "The lovely, soft expression on the face of the image assures me of that."

Kent was standing next to Tara. He found her hand and gave it an encouraging squeeze. He was very proud of the graceful way she was responding to a situation for which no ordinary rules of etiquette could have prepared her. But then she'd handled with admirable aplomb everything both he and this land had thrown at her from the moment they'd met. Not only did Tara Morgan possess all the courage and strength of will of a goddess, even in dirty clothes she'd been wearing for almost a week she remained as beautiful as a goddess.

On the trip north she'd kept her hair tied back or hidden under the helmet. Now, after washing, it fell loose in a soft cloud of ringlets floating around her shoulders. As it dried, curly wisps of hair drifted a red-gold halo around her head. Her jeweled eyes, reflecting the golden flames of the lamps, looked lit from within.

Maybe because they'd spent so much time together the past few days, he kept forgetting that she was about to leave him. Every time he remembered, his chest tightened in a strange fashion.

"May I ask, Rimpoche?" Tara questioned. "What of the child's mother? Is she here? Will she be traveling with him?"

"Jigme's mother is a nomad with another child and elderly parents to take care of. It was difficult for her to part with the boy but she knew he was given the special blessing of Buddha, and his path to enlightenment lay in a different direction from hers. And of course, as the chosen one, the child brings great honor to the family."

"But he's so young. And the journey will be very hard. Kent will protect him, but don't you think he needs a mother, or at least a woman to take care of him?"

"That would be best, but we must make do with what the gods provide."

The little fellow tugged at Tara's sleeve to get her attention. "Jigme not afraid," he announced in a brave voice. "Tara come..." Evidently the boy's small command of the English language had run out because he finished his sentence in Tibetan.

"His Holiness says that he isn't afraid of making the long journey because he will travel under the protection of the goddess."

A flash of alarm shot through Kent. He could see where this conversation was leading. He had to derail any such idea before it could take root. "Tara must return to Chengdu on the evening plane, Rimpoche," he said in a tone that left no room for argument. "For her own protection she must get out of the country quickly." In a few short days, Tara had become important to him in a way he'd never expected. He refused to risk her life to the rugged Himalayas or her freedom to the Red Chinese.

Was Kent only concerned with her protection? Tara wondered. Or was some of that concern a result of worry that she might be entertaining unreasonable expectations about the temporary closeness that had grown between them? Maybe he was anxious to forestall any increase in that closeness that could lead to her pressing for a commitment he didn't want to make.

"I would go with Kent to help him with the little fellow if I could, Rimpoche," Tara said. "But I came to Tibet for a reason and that reason demands that I return to my government's embassy in Beijing."

The old man only gave her an enigmatic smile and bowed slightly. "It will be as Buddha wills."

"Tara no come?" The bright black eyes of a confused little boy looked up at her.

Tara knelt beside the child to talk to him face-to-face. "I'm sorry, Jigme. I'd like to go with you, but I can't. I think you understand very well the necessity for doing one's duty." Songtsen was translating her words as she spoke. "Well, I'm afraid that my duty lies somewhere else. But I'll see you in America. I promise." She looked up at Kent. "You'll contact me when you get home?"

"You can count on it. We—all three of us—will get together."

It really was a good thing she and Kent were parting, Tara told herself once more. She seemed to be thinking that a lot lately. The daring photographer was coming to mean much more to her than he should; much more than she wanted him to mean. The feelings he aroused in her were no good for either of them, and could only lead to heartache. Their parting had always been only a matter of time. Even without the current perilous situation, they would have had to go their separate ways.

Kent bent to help her to her feet. "Don't stay in Beijing any longer than you have to. Get the hell out of China immediately."

"I'm sure Elliott has given orders at the embassy to do that for me."

Kent's hands were clamped around her arms with almost painful tightness. His dark eyes were burning into hers with an intensity that seemed like a strange kind of anger.

"Well, goodbye, Kent." It was becoming difficult to talk around the lump building in her throat. "Good luck. I hope everything goes well for you and the boy." If he didn't kiss her farewell, she fully intended to give him what would be their final kiss.

Before she could do that, a monk came running into the room so fast he almost tripped. Without even the prescribed obeisance to his superior, he pointed back toward the outside hall and blurted out a message to Songtsen. The monks seated on the floor began an agitated murmur. At the high lama's gesture they fell silent.

"Quickly," the old man ordered. "Behind the shrine. Colonel Wu Chen comes."

Chapter 9

The tramp of marching feet was growing rapidly closer as Kent scooped up the boy. Tara followed quickly as he dashed into the small space between the wall and the massive altar. Kent placed the child on the floor and crouched into a stance as if ready to leap out. Although what good he could do should they be discovered, she didn't know. Tara sat on the floor and pulled the child into her arms. The little fellow's face bore a look of fear and he started to say something to her. She shook her head and held her finger to her mouth to indicate he must be silent.

Enraged that anyone could be so disgusting as to frighten a child—and even do worse—she tightened her hold on the trembling little body. The smoky haze from the candles had prevented her from noticing that the statue had not been positioned flush up against the wall. She prayed it would have the same effect on the PLA squad.

Before rushing behind the statue, she'd seen the high lama tuck his hands prayerfully under his robe and begin to walk slowly back toward the opposite end of the room. She hoped he would succeed in leading the military group's attention away from the Tara shrine.

A man barked an order in Chinese. His voice echoed incongruously loud in these quiet religious surroundings.

"You know I will not speak your language, Colonel," Tara heard Songtsen say. "And you cannot speak mine. Let us then converse in English, as we have done before."

"Chinese is your language, old man," the officer replied in English. When his comment provoked no reply from the lama, he continued. "What do you know of an American named Kent Masterson?"

"What should I know of him, Colonel?"

"Do not pretend, Songtsen. Masterson was seen entering your monastery several days ago, immediately before his sudden disappearance from Lhasa."

"Perhaps so, but we receive many visitors—even many Westerners, now that you allow them once more into our country because you need their money. They come to see the chapels and the murals. You cannot expect me to greet each of them personally. My time is taken up with trying to keep this monastery running in the face of your restrictive regulations. It is not easy, and it leaves very little time for socializing."

"Very well, let us speak then of something you do know about. Where is the reincarnation of the Gendun Lama? He has been found. Don't deny it."

"If you know so much, Colonel, why bother questioning me?"

Tara had the feeling this kind of confrontation between the two men wasn't anything new. She knew his religion forbade the rimpoche from uttering an outright falsehood, but it didn't seem to be preventing him from being cannily evasive. She wondered if Songtsen always got the better of the colonel, as he seemed to be doing now. The priest's voice retained a calm steadiness, while the officer's betrayed increasing irritation.

"Do not try my patience, lama," the colonel bit out. "Do you not know that we can crush you as we did the fools in Tiananmen Square?"

The high lama was silent for a moment. Tara wondered if he was offering a silent prayer. "Yes. It is true you crushed those unfortunate young people. But in your heart, Wu Chen, do you not fear that their spirit still lives?"

"Be careful, priest." The officer's voice throbbed with fury. "I can bring you in to my headquarters and force you to give me the answers I want."

Tara remembered what the high lama had told her about the way the Chinese had treated the former Gendun Lama, and shivered. Would the soldiers really drag the old man off and do the same to him? And what could any of them do about it if the colonel gave the order to do that? She glanced at the man beside her. Kent had set his mouth in a grim line and clenched his hands into tight fists. She hoped the child didn't comprehend enough English to understand the threat.

"You have the power to do that," Songtsen replied with admirable composure. "But not without provoking a repetition of the demonstrations in the streets of Lhasa."

"If you send your people into the streets, they will die. And their deaths will be on your head."

Songtsen spoke quietly in Tibetan. The indignant muttering of the monks died off. Evidently they were again seating themselves.

"I've just given orders," the high lama said, "that no monk of this monastery is to engage in demonstrations no matter what happens to me. I regret that my command will not prevent the people from taking to the streets should you arrest me. But you see, Colonel Wu, you cannot evade the real responsibility for any deaths which may occur."

"Enough of this. Listen to me, old man. If you learn anything about the American, Kent Masterson, or the new Gendun Lama—anything at all, do you hear me?—you will immediately inform me of it. Be warned, if you do not your entire monastery will pay."

Tara was from a military family. She had some understanding—if not sympathy—for the officer who, when it came right down to it, was only carrying out orders emanating from his superiors. It couldn't be easy to head up an occupying force in a country where the people hated you. But the colonel's last threatening words snatched away any softening in her feelings toward him.

On his order given in Chinese, the army contingent began marching out. A moment later Tara shot Kent a worried glance. Evidently he too had heard the sound of footsteps approaching the Tara shrine. Someone, most likely the commanding officer, since none of his men would dare, was evidently lingering before the statue.

"These harsh relations between us are unnecessary, Colonel," she heard Songtsen say placatingly. "All you need do is demonstrate some respect for our people, our customs."

"Your people are Chinese. Your old-fashioned customs have been replaced with better ones—true Chinese customs. Remember. Keep me informed."

Tara heard the sound of the man's boots clomping away into the distance, and breathed a sigh of relief. Still, no one in the audience chamber moved or spoke. After a few minutes a monk came and spoke to Songtsen.

"The PLA have gone," the high lama called. "It is safe to come out now."

The three fugitives crept from their hiding place. "None of us will be safe until we're out of Tibet," Kent bit out. "We must leave today."

"Yes. It grows ever more dangerous here for you and the little one. Our preparations will soon be ready."

"You have to get out of here, too, Tara," Kent told her. "I didn't like the sound of that Chinese colonel. I don't imagine he's the kind of man who'll rest until he tracks down both spies of Qinghai."

"Colonel Wu is a dangerous man," Songtsen acknowledged. "He believes in nothing but the power of the People's Liberation Army. He has posted sentries at the front and back gates. But Wu does not know everything. He is not the first to threaten us. Long ago our monks built other means of escape from this monastery." He gestured to a monk who approached, listened to his superior's command and nodded his understanding of it. "Go with my brother. He will lead you."

Tara turned to the old man. "Goodbye, Songtsen Rimpoche. I won't forget you and the others I met here in Tibet. And when I get back home I'll remember Tibet's cause and do what I can for it."

"We are most grateful for the goodwill you and Kent have already shown us, my child. The blessing of Buddha go with you."

She'd sensed the lama's disappointment when she'd told him she couldn't make the trek with Kent and the boy, but he hadn't tried to pressure her to do otherwise. "I'm aware that the Gendun Lama is an exalted person. But may I be permitted to kiss Jigme goodbye?"

"Tara is not subject to our rules," Songtsen replied with a smile. "And as I said, His Holiness's lessons in the customs of your country have already begun."

Tara wasn't sure whether the priest referred to her or to the spirit of the goddess that supposedly had taken up residence in her, but she knelt beside the boy. In only a few minutes the tyke had won her heart. She hated the thought of the long, hard journey that lay ahead for such a young child. She kissed the boy's chubby cheeks. "You know, Jigme," she said, trying to smooth down a cowlick that stood straight up on the top of his head, "there are many boys in America who have a name very similar to yours. They're called Jimmy."

"Jee-mee?" The little fellow grinned and tugged on the high lama's robes. "In Amayriga, my name Jee-mee, Rimpoche. I like." The little head bobbed up and down. "In Pö, I Jigme. In Amayriga, I Jee-mee."

The child didn't yet have a clear understanding of his own importance, Tara guessed as he threw his arms around the only woman he'd seen since leaving his mother. *"Tashi deleg, Tara."*

"Tashi deleg, Jigme." She slung her tote bag over her shoulder and stood up. "I'll see you in America." Hoping the goddess Tara wouldn't feel slighted, she offered a quick but heartfelt prayer to her own God that she would see the boy and Kent again.

She was grateful for the strong warm hand Kent slipped around hers. "Come, Tara," he said, and nodded to the guide that they were ready to follow him. With flaming torch in hand the monk led them down a twisting passageway hewn into the solid rock of the mountain. The passageway seemed miles long, but she was in no hurry to reach the end of it, and leave Kent behind. A narrow shaft of light showed the exit, only wide enough for one person at a time to slip through.

The monk stayed behind when Tara followed Kent into the sunlight.

"Walk down the mountainside to your left," Kent told her. "Within a couple of miles you should come upon the road. Make another left and it'll take you to Lhasa. I'm afraid it'll be a long walk back to the hotel."

"I can manage it."

"I'm sure you can."

He still held tightly to her hand. Soon she'd no longer have to deal with the muddled feelings dredged up by that exciting grip, that raspy baritone that so delighted her ears, the intelligent brown eyes that continually made her forget perfectly logical conclusions. Unaccountably she felt a lump rising in her throat. "Well, Kent, goodbye and good luck. Please be careful."

"I always am."

But he hadn't been careful enough, Kent thought ruefully, about keeping his feeling for Tara Morgan under control. She'd managed to reach him in a way no other woman ever had. Allowing her to do that had been stupid, but it seemed he'd had no choice in the matter. Just as right from the first he'd known they had no choice but to go their separate ways. She had her life to live, and he had his, and this time tomorrow she'd be on a plane winging her way to the opposite side of the world. Although he was relieved she'd soon be gone from China, the thought didn't cheer him.

Even after he'd handed her the bag he'd carried for her, the fingers of his other hand refused to unweave themselves from around hers.

They couldn't just stand here forever holding hands, Tara thought, but she couldn't seem to let go. The monk waiting just inside the cave murmured something. She didn't have to understand Tibetan to know that he was warning her to hurry up and leave. She twisted her unwilling fingers out of Kent's.

Suddenly his hands were burying themselves in her hair, steadying her head as his mouth sought hers. Nothing in the world could have kept her lips from lifting to his. No force of will could have prevented her arms from circling his neck one last time. His tongue invaded her mouth, plunging into every delicate recess as if to garner every last taste of her, which was exactly what she was trying to do with him. Then as quickly as it had begun, the searing kiss was over. When she opened her eyes, Kent was disappearing back into the monastery's hidden entrance.

After more than twenty-four hours spent in a cramped position, her legs rebelled at the long, tiring walk. It was near noon when she stumbled into the hotel lobby and retrieved her larger bag from the desk clerk.

"Did you enjoy your trip to Shigatse, Mrs. Morgan?" the Chinese clerk asked.

Tara mumbled something and took the key. "Please make a reservation for me on the bus to Gonggar Airport. I'll be leaving on this evening's flight to Chengdu." In her room, she pulled off her soiled clothes, donned her pajamas, threw her underwear into a basin of hot, soapy water, and was in bed within five minutes.

It felt as if her head had scarcely hit the pillow when a loud pounding on the door dragged her back from sleep. "What is it?" she croaked, raking her tumbled hair out of her eyes.

"You must come down, Mrs. Morgan. Colonel Wu Chen wishes to see you. All Westerners in the hotel are being questioned."

Lord! Wu Chen. The officer who'd been so threatening to Songtsen. It wouldn't do to antagonize him.

"Of course," she answered with a quick Chinese-style acknowledgment of authority. "Please tell the colonel that I must get dressed, then I'll be right down."

She splashed cold water on her face to clear the cobwebs from her brain and donned her woolen skirt and a clean white blouse.

When she entered the dining room where she'd been told the colonel waited, she hoped he wouldn't be able to tell that her heart was pounding in her chest like a triphammer. The PLA officer, whose khaki uniform bore bright red epaulets, didn't stand when she walked over to his table. That sharp black glance had landed on her before, Tara realized with a start. She was sure Colonel Wu had taken note of her the morning she'd first gone to Songtsen's monastery. He waved her to the chair opposite him.

"Your passport and papers please, Mrs. Morgan."

Tara handed him the documents she had ready in her hand and hoped that her vacant smile proclaimed her just another innocent tourist with nothing to hide.

"You've been gone from the hotel for several days," he said, his steely eyes glued to her. "Where have you been?"

Thank heavens Kent had insisted she study her guidebook while they were holed up in the nunnery, and work out details of the story she'd present to authorities should it become necessary. It had just become necessary.

"I did what most tourists to Tibet do, Colonel. I went to Gyantse, then on to Shigatse. My visa allows such travel."

"How did you get there?"

"I took the bus to Gyantse, spent a couple of days there, then took another bus to Shigatse."

"Most tourists don't usually spend so much time at those places."

"I'm a travel agent. It's my job to thoroughly investigate places to which I may send my clients." It wouldn't hurt to let him know that she had just a little more clout than the average one-time visitor to Lhasa. "CITS has been most helpful in allowing me to do that, and I've already worked out future tours to other parts of China."

Unfortunately the officer did not seem very much impressed.

"Where did you stay in Gyantse?" he demanded sharply. "What did you see?"

"I stayed at the Gyantse Hotel, the large truck stop on the left on the road from Lhasa." She then launched into a description of the gold-capped Kumbum *chorten,* the Temple of the Hundred Thousand Buddhas, one of the most colorful and most beautiful buildings in Tibet. She thought she was doing pretty well under the colonel's questioning, but she wished the expressionless black eyes would move away from her face. She tried to control her increasing nervousness.

"How much did the bus cost you?"

She quoted the latest numbers in the guidebook and hoped they hadn't changed.

"Please show me the ticket stubs from the buses and the bill from the hotel."

Tara hesitated. "I...I'm afraid I don't have them. I was saving the records of my expenses in an envelope in my bag. I forgot to close the zipper and the envelope must have fallen out somewhere along the way." Unseen in her lap, her hands were clutching each other. "Very stupid of me, I'm afraid."

"I see. Most inconvenient. Now I shall have to contact the bus drivers and people at the hotel to confirm your story. Also the guards at the checkpoints on the roads where you had to display your visa. Fortunately they should all remember seeing a Western woman with your unusual coloring."

Tara was growing more frightened of the man by the minute. She wasn't good at lying and was afraid the colonel would be able to see right through her. She'd no sooner wished Kent was here to give her courage when she was glad he wasn't.

"Do you know Kent Masterson?"

The question coming so closely on her thoughts of him gave Tara a jolt. Apparently she had to be careful not only about what she said but about what she thought, too. A cold sweat began to break out over her back. Should she just go ahead and admit it, she wondered frantically, or make some pretense about not knowing Kent at all?

The barest hint of a chilly smile played around her interrogator's mouth as he pointed over her shoulder with his ballpoint pen to the room's entrance. "Perhaps you hadn't noticed the video camera placed at the door for the protection of our visitors."

She hadn't, but she refused to give in to this man's attempts to cow her, without putting up some kind of a fight. She was an American, she thought proudly. And that counted for something, even in authoritarian China.

"Protection of your visitors, nothing," she shot back. "Police states always use that excuse to monitor people. Of course I know Kent Masterson. At least, I've met him. That isn't surprising. Two Americans staying at this hotel were bound to meet. We had dinner in this very room several evenings ago."

"I am told the two of you seemed very friendly."

"He was trying to get me to go to bed with him," Tara said bluntly.

The colonel gave a contemptuous sniff. "You Americans are all promiscuous."

"For your information," she countered hotly, "I refused the invitation." She leaned forward with a cajoling smile. "Look, Colonel, what's the point of our debating morality? I'll take the next flight to Chengdu, then I'll be out of your hair."

"I'm sure there'll be no problem about your flight, Mrs. Morgan," the officer said smoothly as he folded his hands over her passport. "Of course I must hold your passport and exit visa until a few minor details concerning your trip to Shigatse can be cleared up. A formality only. You understand."

She understood all too well. Colonel Wu Chen was holding her prisoner. Without her precious passport, she was trapped in China.

"You will oblige me by remaining in your room until such time as you are free to go."

"But I'm hungry. I wanted to go out to eat."

"I'll arrange for a tray to be sent to your room."

Tara forced a weak smile to her lips. "That...that's very kind of you, Colonel."

"Not at all. We Chinese are a hospitable people."

The hospitable colonel politely asked for her key, which he gave to the guard he sent to see her safely to her room. Without speaking a word, the soldier opened her door for her, stood there while she walked through, then closed it behind her. She wasn't at all surprised a moment later when she heard the loud click of the key turning in the lock.

She guessed that up until now the colonel had been only fishing. He couldn't possibly know she'd accompanied Kent to Qinghai. But a few telephone calls would convince him that during the past week she hadn't done what she'd claimed to have done. Perhaps even before then he'd call for a search of her things, and when Kent's film was discovered, she would exchange her hotel room jail for a real one with bars on it. No way was she going to stick around and meekly wait for that to happen.

She retrieved the rolls of film from the can of hairspray where she'd already hidden them and rushed into the bathroom to flush the film down the toilet. That would at least get rid of any hard evidence against her. But standing there holding the three rolls of film in her hand—the photographs Kent had worked so hard for—she hesitated. The main problem had changed from getting the film out of China to getting herself out. And if by some miracle she were able to accomplish that, she could also complete her mission as courier for Roger Elliott—which after all was why she had gotten into this jam in the first place. For now, she'd just hold on to the film.

Her only chance was to get back to Songtsen's monastery. She slipped off her skirt and pulled on a pair of pants that would allow easier movement, and traded her pumps for the sturdy walking shoes she'd worn to Qinghai. She fixed her hair in a thick braid and covered its telltale color with a scarf.

After dumping her large handbag out on the bed, she jammed back into it only the bare essentials. The film, of course. All the money she had left. A few toiletries. Her sunglasses, sunscreens and an extra pair of heavy socks. Plus the all-important guidebook. She jammed a sweater into the bag and retrieved the pink silk long underwear she'd likely need once again. They were still damp from their washing, but she rolled them up and added them to her bag. Unfortunately she had no choice but to don the smelly parka once again. She'd eventually need its warmth.

Ready to attempt her escape, she went to the window and looked out. In front, the white-painted hotel of modern design was cantilevered over the street. Here in back her room was a little closer to ground level, but it still looked like a good ten or twelve-foot drop. The safest way out would be to tie sheets together to use as a makeshift rope, but that would take time and she'd be in full view of possible watchers for at least a couple of minutes. She dared not take the chance. Slowly and quietly, holding her eyes nervously on the door, she slid open the window.

First she threw her bag down, angling it a little to the side so she wouldn't land on it. Then she hoisted her legs to the sill and worked herself over the ledge until she was hanging by her hands. Now her feet were closer to the ground, but it still seemed like a very long way to fall. She let go and landed with a hard jolt that rocked her off her feet. No one showed up to challenge her. She picked herself up and ran quickly away from the hotel toward the old Tibetan section of the city.

In the new part of the city, the Chinese had built ugly cinder-block houses for the thousands of people they'd moved into Lhasa from other parts of China. The trees they'd added to prettify the place for tourists gave Tara the feeling of not being entirely out in open streets visible to anyone watching from the hotel.

Reasoning that it was easier to hide in a crowd than on an empty street, she headed toward the old city, toward the Barkhor. The marketplace was crowded with shoppers both Tibetan and Chinese, not only on foot but on bicycles—apparently the favored mode of transportation throughout China. The area also felt crowded with uniformed men. Perhaps all the soldiers had been here the last time she visited the place, but then she'd had no reason to pay attention to them. Now, every time a security guard turned in her direction, her heart leaped into her throat.

Strangely enough, though her nerves throbbed with apprehension at her efforts to run from the Chinese colonel, she also felt a flicker of happiness that she was running toward Kent Masterson.

The shadows of late afternoon were growing deeper in the Barkhor. Tara glanced nervously at her watch. She still had a long way to go. If only Kent hadn't left the monastery yet. If he had, she'd be on her own in an unfamiliar country. She didn't like to think about that. The presence of all the bicyclers reminded Tara that the guidebook had cautioned tourists to lock up their bicycles or chance having them stolen. Which gave her an idea. As Songtsen had said, extreme circumstances called for extreme actions. She found an untended, unchained bicycle outside a shop, walked up to it as if it were her own and pedaled furiously into the crowd.

She had to leave the bike when she found the place in the road that she thought led up to the monastery's hidden entrance. Earlier, on the way to Lhasa, she'd noticed the *mani* wall—a heap of stones with prayers carved in the pointy, flowing Tibetan writing that looked nothing like Chinese writing. Although the Chinese had knocked down many of the prayer walls, there were still a few left standing. She only hoped this was the right one.

One brown hill looked the same as another, she was discovering. It felt as if she'd already covered much more than the distance of her walk down from the monastery.

She groaned at the thought of hiking back to the road and going the long way around to find the monastery's main entrance, which was sure to be guarded by soldiers. That would present problems of its own.

She was just turning away to do that when she caught sight of a patch of dark red against the dusty brown—a monk seated on the ground like a signpost waiting for her. Songtsen was wonderful, she thought as she hailed his sentry monk.

Kent did not seem at all happy to see her again. "Tara! What—? Why did you come back?"

Jigme, at least, was glad to see her. With a big grin the boy ran into her arms. "Tara, you come."

"I had to return, Kent. Colonel Wu Chen interrogated me then locked me in my room."

"But you can't come with us—" He turned toward the high lama. "She can't come with us, Songtsen. We face an incredibly difficult journey that will take weeks."

"As Buddha wills," the rimpoche answered prayerfully. Strangely enough, Songtsen didn't seem at all that surprised that she'd returned. What with stationing the monk outside, it was almost as if the old man had expected her back.

"I know it'll be hard, Kent," Tara said. "And that you'd obviously prefer to travel without me. But the colonel confiscated my passport. I can't get out through any of the normal channels." It hurt to realize that the man she'd just spent days with evidently hoped he'd seen the last of her.

"It'll be harder than you think," he said. "We won't have motorized transport this time out. I'm not entirely sure where this Yonten-La is, but we face a trek along the Himalayas of at least seven hundred miles. That's as the crow flies. And as we discovered on our last trip, in Tibet the crow doesn't fly, he walks up, down and around mountains—lots of mountains."

"I can do it," Tara insisted. "For heaven's sake don't look so put upon, Kent. I turned out to be of help on the trip to Qinghai, didn't I? I promise you I'll pull my weight on this one, too. I can help take care of the boy, perhaps make things a little easier for him—maybe even for you. Besides, what other choice do I have?''

The woman didn't understand at all, Kent thought. It wasn't that he feared she couldn't manage the trek or that she might prove to be a liability. His problem was much more personal. It had taken all the willpower he'd possessed to keep from making love to her on a trip that lasted mere days. How could he be expected to keep his hands off her when they'd be thrown into close proximity for weeks?

"I didn't mean to imply that you wouldn't be able to make it, Tara. And I know you'll be a big help. The little guy may possess a four-hundred-year-old soul, but in my books he's still a tyke who needs a stand-in mother to take care of him." Kent turned to Songtsen, who'd been quietly fingering his prayer beads while the two Westerners conversed. "Very well, Songtsen, it looks like there's to be another person in our party. You've already told me how you intend to turn me into a Tibetan. What can you do for red hair and green eyes?"

Quite a lot, as it turned out. Again, almost as if they'd been waiting for her, two young Tibetan women appeared to lead her back into the room in which she'd had her bath. They prepared an infusion of hot water and some sort of herb dye, then helped her off with her clothes. She insisted on retaining her lacy bra and panties, amid the women's giggles and what sounded like a little bit of envy over the pretty garments.

By sign language the women indicated Tara was to bend over the basin and wash her hair in the black brew. They soaked her hair in the dye for several minutes before toweling it dry. She was seated in a chair, and while one of her attendants dipped a rag in the dark liquid and carefully began applying it to her face, the other started expertly weaving her hair into the dozens of tiny, narrow braids she'd seen on nomad women. An unusual but attractive hairstyle, Tara thought, rather like the cornrows of a fashionable black woman.

After all visible parts of her body were painted a light golden brown, much like the skin color of the two young women, they dressed her in the loose-fitting black top and ankle-length skirt of a nomad. They also tied on an apron made of three bright bands of horizontal stripes sewn together. Black stockings and soft Tibetan boots with turned-up toes made of yak hide were slipped over her feet. The black fur *chuba*—a roomy, wraparound coat—they gave her to top off her costume was trimmed with a fringe of yak hair dyed a bright red.

The young women handed Tara a small mirror and waited anxiously for her reaction to their handiwork. Delighted with her expert transformation, Tara thanked her make-up artists profusely, both in English and Tibetan.

It took her a moment to recognize the long-legged gait of the nomad striding across the balcony opposite her window. Kent made an incredibly romantic picture in a heavy sheepskin *chuba* belted in a length of red silk. A black fox fur hat hid much of his hair, the requisite color though not as long as the average male nomad's. And his hand rested easily on the hilt of a dagger within the leather sheath swinging from his belt. His skin, too, had been darkened. His brown eyes weren't quite as dark as a Tibetan's but they were close enough.

She hurried to meet him in the corridor. "Those green eyes of yours are even more of a standout against dark skin, Tara," he said. "Back home you could be fitted with colored contact lenses, but here there's not much anyone can do about that."

The disguised Westerners were brought before Songtsen for his approval. Jigme, clad in a *chuba* that reached to his ankles, stood by the old man. Songtsen gave them the once-over and nodded a slightly dubious satisfaction.

"Under close inspection neither of you will pass for Drokpa—nomads," he admitted. "You do not have the proper oriental facial features. Few Tibetans are as tall as you, my son, and certainly no Tibetan woman possesses eyes like yours, Tara. The most we can hope for is that your garb will help you blend into the landscape like other nomads and make you less noticeable to the Chinese. People generally see what they expect to see. Let us hope the soldiers are no different.''

"About this old prophecy, Rimpoche,'' Kent said lightly. "Did the oracle say whether or not we'd make it?'' He'd made the remark jokingly, and wasn't much comforted by Songtsen's careful reply that interpreting the words of an oracle was always difficult.

"I have gifts for you both,'' the high lama said. A monk brought forth a beautifully carved wooden chest and opened the lid. Songtsen took out what looked like a small silver box about three inches square set with a circular pattern of turquoise and coral and hung by one corner on a heavy chain. "We call this a *gao*. The charm box is filled with tiny rolls of paper on which are written prayers,'' he told Tara as he fitted the heavy pendant over her head. "As long as you wear it those prayers begging the protection of Buddha will continually rise to heaven. I trust they will keep you safe.''

Tara lovingly fingered the exquisitely crafted religious object, obviously an antique. "Thank you, Rimpoche. It's beautiful.''

For Kent, Songtsen had a large round prayer box made of chased gold.

"Now it is time for us to leave. It is the custom in my country for friends to walk part of the way with those making a journey. Some of my brothers will accompany us to where the pack animals are waiting. We will carry our evening meal.''

Tara grinned at the little boy. "We're going to have a picnic, Jigme.''

"Peek-neek?'' piped up the child.

"Yes, Jigme. That's what we call carrying food to eat on an outing.''

"We have peek-neek,'' the boy announced to the assembled monks, who probably didn't understand what he was saying but nodded sagely anyway.

The monks who were to accompany them carried lanterns and flashlights along with their dinner and other

supplies. As the travelers began to file into the long corridor leading to the hidden exit, the monks left behind began a low, prayerful chant that echoed through the damp
stone walls of the passageway in an eerie fashion. Tara
wondered if it was only to her own ears that the chant
sounded very much like a dirge.

Chapter 10

They came out of the darkness of the passageway into dusk. Tara, who'd already spent most of the day walking, was glad to find they had to hike no more than a couple of miles. A small herd of yaks on their short, stumpy legs, a donkey and three sturdy Mongolian horses waited in the valley behind a neighboring mountain. The nomad herdsman tending the animals had already started a dung fire over which bubbled a pot of soup.

In honor of the departing guests—mainly, Tara suspected, in honor of the young incarnate lama—the monks had broadened their usual simple fare. The monks, who in Tibet had eliminated the usual Buddhist practice of traveling through the neighborhood with begging bowls, served up a mouth-watering feast of spicy *sabjij,* a ginger-flavored pancake made of ground potatoes, cauliflower, peas and green beans. The addition of raisins and dried apricots lifted the *tupa menda* from the level of ordinary rice, and the *jasha,* grilled chicken breast marinated in a mixture of honey, garlic and soy sauce proved to be absolutely delicious. Tara enjoyed the dessert of fresh pears as much as Jigme did.

After the meal the monks, including the little novice, began to chant their evening prayers.

"Let's check out what's going to serve as home for our intrepid little group for the next few weeks," Kent suggested, picking up a flashlight.

The traditional Tibetan tent was made of black yak wool, with an entrance flap of white-and-black appliqué in a spiral pattern that looked vaguely Irish. Only in the center of its pitched roof could Kent stand upright. All by himself he seemed to fill the space. The tent's only furnishings were a couple of rolled-up sleeping rugs, two small packs and Kent's and Tara's personal bags. Most of their supplies were already loaded on the pack animals. Much smaller than the usual family tent of thirty square feet, this tent would prove a pretty snug fit for the three of them and the guide.

At least the crowd would reinforce her resolve to make this trip with Kent different from the last, Tara thought. This time she'd make sure there'd be no romantic interludes with him that could short-circuit her brain and divest her of simple common sense. This wasn't a man with whom she wanted to develop a personal relationship. She'd be sleeping near him every night for weeks, but it would mean no more to her than would her sharing the space with Jigme. Forewarned now, she intended to keep close watch upon her heart.

Kent angled his chin toward the red-robed group outside. "I'll miss these men when they leave us."

His train of thought apparently had been much loftier than hers, Tara noted a little guiltily. "So will I. Especially Songtsen." The old man's gentleness and simplicity hid a strength of spirit she'd seldom encountered in anyone else. Just being in the company of a person of such simple human decency was a blessing in itself.

"Funny how much Songtsen reminds me of my grandfather," Kent mused. "They're such different men who've led lives about as unlike as any two lives can be, and yet they remain lifelong friends. They both have adventurous spirits which I doubt they'll ever lose. And they're both kind persons who've always thought more of the well-being of others than of themselves.''

"I'd like to meet your grandfather someday, Kent."

"I hope you will." Kent realized that he'd like Tara Morgan to meet all his family. That he'd like to get her reaction to Andrew's boys and the big old house that he loved so much in Philadelphia. What that meant, he didn't know. But Songtsen wasn't the only one he'd miss when all this was over. He wouldn't soon forget Tara Morgan, either.

"Just in case I haven't mentioned it, Kent. I think the high lama made a smart move in choosing you for this operation."

"He didn't exactly choose me, remember? He chose my grandfather and expected my older brother to show up."

"But I'm sure he's glad now that you turned up instead."

"Thank you, ma'am. It's always nice to know the troops have confidence in you."

Tara ducked under the tent flap Kent was holding open for her to follow him outside. The quiet singsong prayers of the monks seemed perfectly suited to the setting.

"Kent?" Tara ventured. "Something still puzzles me. The monks obviously had everything ready for me—the ethnic clothes, the make-up women. How could they possibly know I'd have to return to the monastery? For that matter, how could they have known I'd show up there in the first place? That first day I just decided to go to Songtsen's monastery at the last minute. I mean, come on, you don't really believe in oracles." She threw him a sidelong glance. "Do you?"

"Can't say that I do. On the other hand, this trip has tested my belief and nonbelief in a lot of things." For starters, his up-until-now firm conviction that a serious relationship with a woman simply wasn't in the cards for him. "Two weeks ago would you have believed you could be turned into a Tibetan nomad?"

Tara looked down at her striped apron. "I still don't quite believe it."

"I think even Randall would have a hard time accepting all this. But despite Chinese efforts to wipe out the native culture, Tibet is still a land of mystery."

To Tara, the central mystery remained Kent Masterson and the strong hold he'd fastened on her feelings despite her best efforts to throw it off.

"But to answer your question about the oracle, Tara, I'm sure the monks would reply that nothing happens without the knowledge of Buddha. In their minds, Buddha simply granted to the oracle the power to view this little scene a few years in advance." Kent glanced over to the circle of chanting monks and smiled. "I've seen how Songtsen operates, and I'd put nothing past him. Don't you have the feeling that our lama is on excellent terms with the Buddha?"

"I sure hope so. Seems to me his personal clout with Buddha and all those Tibetan gods is the only way we can get away with this incredible scheme of his." She noticed that the men were rising to their feet and assembling the things they intended to carry back to the monastery with them. "Looks like the monks are leaving."

Songtsen and the child walked over to the Americans. "My brothers must return to the monastery," the lama said. "We will spend the night here and begin our journey in the morning."

"We—?"

"We—?" Both Tara and Kent had picked up on the word at the same time. Tara let Kent finish the thought for both of them.

"Rimpoche," Kent protested. "You don't really plan to come with us?"

"Ah, but I do, my son. You will need a guide. Yonten-La is well hidden. You would never find it alone, but I have visited there once before."

Kent nodded toward the herdsman who was tending to the horses. "But I thought he—"

"Dorje will stay with us until the first ford of the Tsang Po. Then he will go north to return to his people. We will go south."

"But Songtsen..." Tara shared Kent's concern for the elderly man. "You seem in very good health, but you're...well, you're not young. Everything I've read about traveling to western Tibet even in a good four-wheel drive says the trip will be extremely difficult. How can you...?" Tara didn't like to come right out and say the man was too old to stand the rigors of the trip, but she was worried about him. "I mean..."

Kent was ready to be a little more candid. "Rimpoche, my grandfather is over eighty. You must be at least that age." He could remember Randall saying the lama was several years older than he, but that seemed hard to believe. "We definitely would like to see you leave Tibet. It's not safe for you here. I don't think the colonel was just making idle threats earlier, and I'm sure you don't think so, either. But you're evidently a thorn in his side, and I believe he'd be glad to get rid of you. If you asked, he might readily give you permission to leave. If not, couldn't you get out through a route easier than the one we must take?"

"It's true I'm an old man." Songtsen seemed unperturbed by their worry about his ability to make the trip. "But perhaps I'm stronger than you think. Only two years ago I made a pilgrimage to the sacred mountain. It is true that I did not walk all the way, only the last hundred miles. But I did make the circumlocution."

Kent was astonished. "You walked all the way around Mount Kailas?"

The old man's black eyes twinkled. "Three times. So you see, riding on a horse to Yonten-La will seem quite a luxury. If my presence causes any problems for you on the road, I assure you that I will simply leave and return to my monastery. Any Tibetan will be glad to assist me along the way."

Kent and Tara looked at each other helplessly. How could they refuse to allow a man who'd made the long, difficult circuit of a mountain to come with them, even if he was heading into his nineties? Tara's gaze dropped to the boy by his side. There was another reason, she'd noticed, to include Songtsen in their party. The child was obviously disturbed that the monks who'd been his protectors were about to leave. A worried look on his little face, Jigme was clutching the high lama's hand in a death grip.

Evidently Kent hadn't missed the little fellow's dismay either. After all, how would any six-year-old like to be forced to leave everyone familiar to him and go off with virtual strangers, even if one of them was a goddess?

Kent bowed to the old man. "Your presence on the journey will be most welcome, Rimpoche, and I'm certain, most helpful." From the look on Songtsen's face, the outcome of the disagreement had been a foregone conclusion. One by one the monks approached and prostrated themselves before their superior and the exalted child.

Tara's eyes grew misty as she saw the deep reverence and affection in which both were held. These men would spend their lives studying how to distance themselves from human attachments. But when it came to this particular old man and this special little boy, it was evident that few of them had yet reached that nirvana. Jigme was trying very hard to be brave, but the firelight glinted off the tears pooling in the little boy's bright black eyes. The Westerners, too, came in for their share of farewells and thanks.

As it turned out their tent wasn't crowded—at least not for this first night. Tibetan nomads—and Jigme was one—were always happy to sleep out under the stars. And apparently the old man was also quite comfortable doing so.

Tara lay staring into the blackness of the tent's roof. Kent's tossing and irregular breathing told her he was as wakeful as she.

"Kent?" she whispered into the darkness. "Do you really think we'll make it?"

"We're sure as hell going to try." His hesitation before giving her an answer wasn't exactly encouraging.

In a chill dawn, the Drokpa herdsman taught Kent and Tara how to take down the tent, fold it and pack it onto one of the yaks. Songtsen helped Jigme load the last packs on the donkey, who demonstrated he wasn't very interested in the idea by taking off every time someone approached him. Between them, Dorje and Jigme managed to corral the beast and hold him steady. The Tibetans already knew how to balance the weight on either side of the animals so the packs wouldn't slip down, or fall off. Tara understood the principle of the thing, but she discovered that actually accomplishing it wasn't all that easy.

Jigme scampered off with Dorje to drive the yaks and lead the donkey. Tara was glad to see that a night's sleep had restored the child's natural good humor. Before his life took such a dramatic turn, he'd been destined to grow up to be a herdsman like Dorje. He'd already begun to learn the trade of yak-boy and was fearless around the huge black animals with the long, coarse hair.

Tara watched as Kent helped the old man onto his horse. Songtsen sat the animal well enough, but obviously his mounting and dismounting were more difficult. So far she'd been reticent about touching the high lama. Some Buddhists had rules about a woman doing that. Songtsen didn't seem a blind follower of rules and regulations, she'd noticed, and strict rules of etiquette were going to have to be relaxed on this trip. Not only concerning the boy, but also about Songtsen. When Dorje left, Kent would have enough to do looking after the animals and the equipment that meant survival in the sparsely settled territory into which they were headed. She intended to do everything she could to help him. And her natural role seemed to lie in looking after the old man and the child.

She would be the one to help Songtsen dismount. If he protested, she'd simply remind him that he himself had claimed she was harboring the spirit of a goddess. And after all, didn't a goddess rank at least as high as a lama? But when the time came, Songtsen accepted her help without discussion.

"Aren't we moving awfully slowly?" she asked Kent as they made camp after almost a week on the trail. "We haven't even reached Shigatse yet."

"Spoken like a woman who's used to hopping on a jet and getting to anywhere in the world in just a few hours." He laughed. "Don't worry, you'll adjust to this slower pace. Until thirty or forty years ago, everybody in this country traveled just the way we're doing. So far, at least, our trip is turning out to be a lot easier than I thought it would be. I fully expected that I'd have to hike out of Tibet, remember? Hey, we're traveling in style. We don't have to carry our own packs. And we've got horses."

Horses that needed to be looked after, saddled and unsaddled, which took time. It wasn't yet necessary to break out the feed of dried peas they'd brought along with them. Here in an area of fertile valleys the animals could forage on the tough grass. It would be much different later on.

"I'd give anything for a hot bath," Tara said to Kent with a sigh after a day that had seemed particularly long. "I'm sorry. I know I shouldn't keep saying that."

"Go ahead, if it makes you feel any better. It's the only complaint I've ever heard you make."

The lack of bathing facilities bothered her most. But after the first try, she couldn't bring herself to full immersion in the freezing river whose waters were fed by runoff from icebound mountains. A quick sponge bath was the most she could stand. Kent shaved almost every day. She'd seen Tibetans with mustaches and wispy chin beards, but none with the kind of heavy beard he had developed on their first trip.

"We will take the southern route west," Songtsen told them over their usual dinner of tea, soup and *tsampa*. "It is more direct, but also more difficult than the northern road. However, it is much less traveled than the main route, which suits our purposes."

"It suits our purposes, all right," Kent agreed. "But the northern route is more popular for good reason, isn't it, Rimpoche? I just hope we don't run into floods and washed-out trails on the way."

"As the gods decree," the priest replied calmly. "The season of heaviest rains is over. Perhaps the river crossing will not be too bad. My concern now is for snow. The snows can come early to the high passes." The old man peered worriedly off to the west. "I pray we will arrive at Yonten-La before the end of September. Any later than that..."

Kent covered the lama's hand with his own. "Remember, Rimpoche," he said, nodding toward Tara who was putting away the cloth bag of roasted barley flour. "We travel with a goddess."

The high lama's narrow-eyed glance fell on Kent. "An interesting point, my son," he said with a glint of amusement in his eyes. "To Tibetans, the lady is a manifestation of a goddess. I wonder... what is she to you?"

Jigme had picked the perfect time, Kent thought, to come running over to show them the prettily colored stone he'd just found.

Dorje left them just beyond Lhatse to take the road's north fork to Ngari, his possessions loaded on one of the yaks. Tara wondered what the man, who spoke no English, made of the curious party for whom he'd supplied horses and pack animals and which he'd guided to this point. It was clear that Dorje held the high lama in great esteem. But the way the Drokpa man treated Jigme like just another child, hollering good-naturedly at him when needed, indicated he had no knowledge of the boy's true identity. Which was a good thing, she thought. The fewer people who knew of the Gendun Lama, the better.

"Unfortunately, we dare not take the ferry across the Tsang Po," Songtsen observed as the group stood on a hillside and watched the huge platform jammed with people and animals being towed across the river. "The crossing would be so much easier, but permits are needed and there is a Chinese checkpoint down there. We will have to go on to a ford and hope the river isn't still too deep from the rains."

"There are more nomads out here than I expected," Kent observed.

"This is one of the three times a year that nomads move into their winter encampments," Songtsen explained. Nomads did not usually pack up and move every day as

Kent's party was doing. They'd pitch their tents in one spot and stay there until the grass for their grazing herds ran out.

"It keeps us from being noticed among all the others," Kent allowed. "But it also means we can hardly avoid running into people."

"We need have no fear of Tibetans, my son."

"Maybe not. But they're bound to notice that Tara and I are more than just a little different. Without meaning to harm anyone, they might talk."

At the point where Songtsen instructed them to cross, the river looked ominously broad. Kent stood squinting into the distance and trying to judge the force of the current. He shook his head dubiously. "That's got to be almost a hundred yards wide. I'd better find out how deep it is before we risk taking the animals across."

"Maybe we should wait for a few days," Tara suggested. "The water level might go down."

"We can't wait, Tara." Kent took off his *chuba* and boots and tied them firmly on the back of his horse, which also carried his precious cameras wrapped in plastic. Nervously, Tara watched him wade into the river. Slowly and carefully he walked out into the middle, prodding the depth of the water ahead of him with Songtsen's walking stick. The water rose to his thighs before he turned around and slogged back.

"Damn! That water's cold," he said as he hauled himself up on the bank. "The current doesn't seem to be too strong and the water seems to be no more than three feet deep. I think the animals can make it. We have to go ahead and chance it. All of you stay here while I lead the donkey and the yaks across."

No one was surprised when the donkey dug in his hooves and refused to cross. From the first, the animal had given them more trouble than all the others combined. Kent whacked the recalcitrant beast on the nose and yanked on the reins. The donkey's sheer orneriness had forced Kent to give up any compunctions he'd had about treating an animal so forcefully. Now, apparently, the donkey decided he'd met his match in the big man who refused to take no for an answer, and reluctantly splashed into the water.

Kent hobbled the beast on the other side and came back for the dull-witted yaks, which looked to Tara like a cross between a furry cow and an American bison. She wondered if the large, slow-moving beasts could raise their heads above the water, since she'd never seen them lift their noses from the ground. They did.

Kent's teeth were chattering when he waded the broad expanse of the flooded river a fourth time to lift the boy onto his horse—the largest of the three—with instructions, repeated by Songtsen in Tibetan, for him to hold on tight. A shock of cold water lashed Tara's legs when she urged her horse forward after them. Positioning herself just downstream of the old man, she watched him carefully in case he should need her assistance.

The fording of the river had taken hours. To everyone's relief, Kent gave the order to make camp early, and Tara was quite content to lie in the sun waiting for her clothes to dry.

Every day Songtsen tried to find the time for Jigme's lessons. Now the two were sitting cross-legged side by side on a dry spot near the riverbank. In front of them lay a Tibetan book the lama had brought along carefully wrapped in cloth. The book's unbound pages were almost two feet wide, but only four or five inches long. Songtsen was teaching the boy to read. When the child stumbled over the words, the priest would gently encourage him. Never had she seen the old man express the slightest bit of annoyance with the boy, for whom he'd evidently become a grandfather figure. The love and trust between the two was evident in the way the child leaned comfortably against the lama's knee and looked up at him with a question.

Kent, clad in only the loose trousers of a nomad, sat next to her. "Those two are something, aren't they?" he said.

"I wonder how they're going to take to the outside world. I mean...look at all this." To the north lay the low, rounded mountains of the Tibetan plateau ranging off to far horizons. To the south the magnificent snow-shrouded peaks of the Himalayas scraped the sky. "It's so quiet and beautiful here. So serene."

"Not exactly like New York at rush hour," Kent agreed.

"No, not much. You know, Kent, when I first came to Tibet, all I saw was the poverty, the few possessions almost everyone, but particularly the nomads have. Now I wonder if people like Dorje, living in complete harmony with nature and his gods, are really worse off than we. He roams the world as he wishes, content with his butter tea and *tsampa*. He's never suffered from any sort of identity crisis—except when the Chinese tried to force him into a communal farm, which didn't work. He knows his world and his place in it."

"That's something I've thought about, too. And living in such a powerfully beautiful country, is it any wonder that their lives are centered around religion?"

Kent himself was really something, Tara thought. Born to a life of luxury and ease, well able to afford any comfort, he'd chosen to endure these hardships out of his sense of commitment to his grandfather and his concern for the safety of a special child.

She sat up. For two weeks they'd spent every minute of every day together, but without any real intimacy. Among people who lived in tents out in open country privacy was at a premium. And despite Kent's upbeat comment that their flight to freedom wasn't as difficult as he'd expected, it was hard work, especially after Dorje left.

Unpacking the tent and setting it up every evening, only to take it down the next morning and repack it on the yak, not only got to be too much work, it took up too much time. The days were mild, even hot, except in the passes where fierce winds sweeping down from ice-covered peaks made the temperature plunge. So unless it rained and they all had to crowd into the tent, the Americans had taken to sleeping under the stars like the natives. This was one of the few times she and Kent had even been able to sit alone together and talk.

Kent leaned forward to rest an arm over a pulled-up knee, and the muscles rippled across the hard planes of his back. Knowing it was exactly the wrong thing to do, Tara couldn't prevent her hand from reaching out and flattening itself against the firm, warm skin. An immediate tremor ran through him. She should break the touch, but right now that seemed impossible to do. Kent turned his head. His eyes speared into hers over the hard, smooth curve of his shoulder. "That feels nice," he growled. "Very nice."

It did to her, too. So nice that she slid her hand up the hard column of his spine. Her fingers began a slow massage of the muscle at the top of his shoulder. A low rumble of pleasure sounded in his throat. His darkened eyes told her that what she was doing to him was dangerous, but she couldn't bring herself to stop. He caught her hand and lifted it to brush his lips over the inside of her wrist. Tara's pulse raced. It had been so long since she'd felt those lips on hers. And although she'd often told herself she wanted it that way, it wasn't true.

"Tara." Kent's voice was husky. "I—"

"Ama," a child's voice piped up. Evidently Jigme's lesson was over. "Come, *Ama.* Play *chibi* with Jee-mee."

With obvious reluctance, Kent dropped her hand. "Do you know that the boy just called you mother?" he asked quietly.

"Yes. He started that a couple of days ago. But he usually calls me that only when I kiss him good-night or when he's overtired. I guess the idea of a makeshift mother is a little easier for him to grasp than the concept of an incarnate goddess. I don't think there's any harm in it, do you?"

"I guess that would be up to Songtsen to say."

"He hasn't mentioned it, although I think he must have heard the child use the word."

Tara stood up and Jigme kicked a small ball stuck with buzzard feathers into the air. Tara thought the toy looked a little like the shuttlecock batted back and forth in a game of badminton. In *chibi* the object was to keep the feathered ball in the air as long as possible. Jigme told her she was getting good at it, but he could always keep the *chibi* in play longer than she.

Day after day they pushed on. They'd long ago left behind the checkerboard patterns of tilled fields and trees, towns and shops of any kind. Here were wide expanses of grassland, nibbled to the ground now and turning brown after a season of grazing sheep and goats. Sometimes they followed low stone fences that ran straight as an arrow for miles.

Upriver they crossed again, their route paralleling the road on which they never ventured, although they kept the telephone poles marching along its edge always in sight. Fortunately, this time of year, because of washouts and avalanche, most vehicles heading west used the alternative route. But occasionally a couple of trucks, driving in tandem in order to pull each other out of mud holes, did appear, and raised their anxiety level.

Jigme's young eyes spotted the red-starred military convoy first. He didn't need to be told to run to Kent, who hoisted the child up in front of him on the horse. Silence gripped the little party. Even Jigme's usually high spirits waned until the trucks, the first sign of Chinese military presence they'd seen, drove out of sight.

The party's slow progression up into the zigzag passes gave Tara few recurrences of the headache that had sometimes gripped her on the rapidly moving motorcycle. Altitude posed no problems whatever for Songtsen and Jigme, born to the high country, but the Westerners had to be careful not to be trapped in a high pass overnight. For them, sleeping above twelve thousand feet could trigger severe altitude sickness.

Even though the gales and blizzards of winter were weeks away, the fierce winds of the higher altitudes now forced the travelers into the tent every night. In the cold, setting up the tent became not only a slow but a painful task. Tara folded down her *chuba*'s overlong sleeves to cover her hands and keep her fingers warm.

They discovered where the army vehicles had been heading when they passed a dingy-looking military camp, which they kept as far away from as possible. Several hours distant from the PLA garrison, Kent rode on ahead to scout out places to make camp. He soon came galloping back and pulled up his horse next to Tara's. "Remember that hot bath you said you'd give anything for?" he asked, a huge grin on his face. "What will you give me if I can provide it for you?"

"A hot bath?" Tara laughed. Her chances of indulging in that luxury seemed as remote as the possibility of sleeping in a real bed and enjoying a nice fresh salad anytime soon. "What are you asking for it? My firstborn child?"

"I might want that, too. But I'm hoping to get something from you a little sooner than that."

Tara had no trouble interpreting the glance delivered from under Kent's half-lowered lids. Ever since their interrupted interlude at the ford, she'd often felt his eyes on her. Just as often, hers had sought him out. And their hands seemed to be accidentally touching more and more often as they set up the tent or passed things to each other.

From quite a distance away they could see the steam rising from the hot springs. Jigme let out a whoop and dashed toward the pool.

Wide-eyed, Tara stared at Kent. "I thought you were only kidding."

"Who would dare kid a goddess?" Kent's dark eyes suggested he would dare much more than that.

Ever the hard taskmaster, Kent ordered his troops to set up camp before indulging in the luxury of a hot bath. When he dismissed them, Jigme was the first to throw off his *chuba* and shoes and jump into a small pool with a great splash. Songtsen doffed his maroon robe, but kept on the lightweight saffron shift he wore underneath.

Tara decided that her pink long johns wouldn't really serve as a swimsuit and waded into the blessedly warm water in skirt and top. A way to clean her clothes and take a bath at the same time.

Kent had warned that the water would be scalding hot near its bubbling center, but it cooled as it trickled over pink-and-white limestone terraces to their pool. She sank into the water and closed her eyes, luxuriating in the wonderful feel of being warm all over. Perhaps because of the relaxing bath, she found herself wishing strongly that she and Kent could be alone for just a little while. Knowing she shouldn't indulge in these kinds of thoughts, she climbed out of the pool and headed for the tent.

Intending to wrap herself in a blanket and hang the garments outside for the wind to dry, she slipped off skirt and top and wrung them out. She was bending over, drying her hair with a towel, when her glance fell on a pair of bare feet.

She couldn't say she was surprised that Kent had entered the tent after her. Nor could she pretend her pulse hadn't just taken a jog.

Her gaze traveled upward. The weight of Kent's wet trousers pulled them low on his lean hips. The wet fabric clung to his thighs and so clearly delineated his maleness that her mouth went dry. A feeling very much like what she'd felt dipping herself in the hot pool slowly mantled her.

A sprinkle of water droplets nestled in the band of curly black hair that showed above the low-slung drawstring waistband. All her nerve endings leaped to life as her gaze followed the line of black hair narrowing upward to his navel. Long days of rigorous exercise on the trek had hardened even further the squared-off muscles of his chest.

When her gaze finally moved up to his face, she saw that he was contemplating her body in much the same way she'd been drinking in his. She held fast to his smoldering gaze as she allowed her towel to slip to the floor. The purpose of her long underwear was to fit her like a second skin. And it did. Damp, the silky garments clung to her body even more tightly, so that she stood before him looking next to naked.

Despite her continuing apprehension of Kent Masterson as a man she didn't want to tangle with, despite her best efforts to break free of the attraction he held for her, she continued to be irresistibly drawn to him. As she was now. Her whole body ached to have him close.

Before she'd completed her first step toward him, Kent reached for her. It was so good to feel his hands smoothing over her once more. So good to feel his strong arms enclosing her, pressing her to the warm, solid wall of his naked chest. She made no pretense of not liking it. Flattened against him, she could feel his heartbeat thumping against his rib cage no less wildly than hers.

His lips moved slowly over her forehead, her eyelids, her mouth, where they lingered lovingly at each corner. Her head fell back of its own accord to allow him free access to her neck. When his foraging mouth moved lower to range even more arousingly over her breasts, she managed to gasp out a caution. "No, Kent. What of the boy...the priest...."

"Songtsen is teaching him a new prayer." Kent spoke thickly, his words muffled against her breast. "He understands. He'll give us the time we need."

Slowly, like a man unwrapping a precious gift, he peeled back the top of her underwear and uncovered her breasts, touching them with gentle, almost reverent fingers. Their soft pink crests hardened instantly into tight, sensitive little nubs. As if touching her had unleashed within him an excitement he could no longer control, he began showering her bare breasts with kisses. His hands slid down over her silk-covered bottom to press her against the hardness she could feel against her abdomen. His mouth closed hotly over a straining nipple.

She moaned. Logic lost any relevance under Kent's inflaming nearness, his burning touch, the exquisite pleasure his mouth was bringing her.

They both froze into immobility at the sound of the short, loud burst of machine-gun fire.

Chapter 11

The loud staccato series of rapid, sharp cracks again echoed down the valley. Tara had immediately recognized the sound for what it was. She'd grown up on military bases. She knew automatic weapons fire when she heard it.

From the look of shock on Kent's face, he was experiencing the same fear that was shooting through her. They'd been discovered. The army was about to take them into custody, maybe even gun them down. In an instant he was on his feet, thrusting his arms into his *chuba*.

"Stay here!" he commanded, jamming the concealing fur hat on his head.

Tara hurriedly yanked on her damp blouse and skirt and grabbed for her sunglasses to hide her telltale eyes. She wanted to run out after Kent to check on the boy, to face their captors with the others if necessary, but she restrained herself. Of all the members of the party that wasn't what it seemed, her looks could most quickly give them away.

Desperate to find out what was going on, she knelt at the tent flap, pulled it aside a little and peered out cautiously.

Kent raced toward Songtsen and the child, while the lama furiously waved the boy, who could run much faster than he, toward the photographer.

"Into the tent," Kent called to Jigme while continuing toward the old man. Behind Kent, the little boy tripped and fell. Tara was about to rush to him when another burst of gunfire sounded very close. Why were the soldiers firing at them before they were even in sight?

Suddenly an animal with tawny fur and dark, saberlike horns broke from the rocks nearby. Running for its life, the antelope, blood streaking its flank, shot past them.

The animal had no sooner sprinted by when an open, four-wheel-drive vehicle careened around a hill, narrowly missing Kent and the priest. The two soldiers in the vehicle ignored the nomads they'd almost run over and sped away, laughing and shouting, after their prey.

It had all happened so quickly. All four travelers just gazed dazedly at the dust cloud settling behind the Chinese army vehicle. Then Jigme, sprawled on the ground, started to cry. As much from the unsettling sight of a bleeding animal, Tara guessed, as from fear of the soldiers. She left the tent to comfort the child, but Kent reached him first and picked him up.

"It's all right, son," Kent murmured. "They weren't after us. They were only hunting the antelope." The little fellow's tears kept flowing as he clung to the tall man. "Hey, Jimmy." Kent shushed the boy gently. "Come on now, fella. Us guys have got to be brave, right? I need you. You've got to herd the yaks so we can get out of here." Kent's thumb gently brushed the tears from the little face. "Can you do that for us, Your Holiness?"

Tara knew that Kent had deliberately used the frightened child's formal title to encourage him to dry his eyes. Songtsen was adding his comforting pats on the boy's back and talking to Jigme in his own language, pretty much repeating what Kent had said, she imagined.

The child's sniffles trailed off. He wiped his eyes with a grimy hand. "Jee-mee okay," he said, although his lower lip still trembled.

"Darn right Jimmy's okay," Kent agreed heartily. "Jimmy's more than okay. Jimmy's one heck of a great yak-boy."

A wobbly smile appeared on the child's face. Kent put him down, and the boy ran to complete the task the trek leader had set him. "I know it's late in the afternoon," Kent said to Tara and Songtsen. "But we've got to get out of here in case those soldiers decide to come back and investigate."

They rode on, putting as much distance as possible between themselves and the military camp. Night had long fallen by the time the four huddled around the small cookstove in the tent and shared another meal of tea, *tsampa* and soup.

Tara handed Jigme his bowl of soup. *"Thupa,"* she said with forced cheerfulness.

"Zoop," the boy responded listlessly. Tonight neither of them had much heart for playing the language game they usually enjoyed. Jigme, learning English a lot faster than she and Kent were picking up Tibetan, usually loved the mutual lessons. But their frightening meeting with the Chinese hunters had cast a pall over everyone's spirits.

In the morning they pushed on through a gray curtain of mist. For Tara, the days became one long blur of riding, walking, setting up camp, falling into an exhausted sleep and in the morning starting all over again.

She'd never again be able to refer to her business as organizing adventure tours without feeling silly. She and her guides worked hard to make sure the paying customers experienced no more than the illusion of danger when in fact the risks were minimal. As was the illusion of being totally cut off from the outside world, as the four of them truly were now. And those treks and safaris with clients always included porters or supply vans, a staff to set up camp and cook decent meals. Best of all, at the end of the day, her trekkers could relax in a warm bath, or at least were provided with enough hot water to sponge off.

Here they had to hoard their precious hot water, because at these altitudes, even with the blowtorch Dorje had left them, it took so long to heat. And on this long, hard journey, the risks were real, not illusory.

After weeks of heading west, Songtsen again directed them south. The Himalayas begin where other mountains leave off. That was the reminder the Himalayan Rescue Association gave trekkers attempting even the easiest of its trails. Here, on the north-facing side of the world's highest mountains, jagged, snow-topped peaks dwarfed them on every side and untamed nature ruled. And they were still only among the lower mountains. The main towering white wall of the Himalayas still lay a forbidding distance away. So strong, so impregnable that travelers could penetrate its rockbound, icy fastness only through a few perilous high passes. Here the forces of nature could prove to be an even more implacable enemy than the Chinese colonel.

And each day the mountains tested her strength and endurance, she remained agonizingly conscious of the fact that being with Kent was testing her heart. It had been so much easier in the beginning when she simply thought the man was no more than an inveterate rolling stone with a chronically adolescent sex life. It had been a long time since she'd been able to dismiss him so easily. Who was she kidding? She'd never been able to dismiss him.

She saw how much each of them relied on his quiet unflagging strength. Kent was always there. To lift a heavy pack when her tired muscles rebelled. To call a short halt when the old man's face became drawn. To notice when the little boy's spirits drooped and cajole him into joining in for yet another painfully off-key rendition of "Ninety-nine bottles of *chang* on a wall."

But Buddha, or the goddess Tara, or God must have been mindful of them, after all. After a particularly long, trying passage, they rode into a valley and every one of the weary travelers stopped dead, mesmerized by the spectacular sight spread out before them. Rising between the wide V of the valley slopes shone a snow-veiled mountain majestically outlined against a sky impossibly blue. The calm, crystal lake at its base reflected the mountain's breathtaking, perfectly symmetrical beauty. They needed no discussion to stop right there and pitch camp.

"Our people say this mountain is a goddess," Songtsen told them. Tara could almost believe it herself. The place had the feel of a church. "That craggy black peak to the west is her consort, who visits her at night. If you listen well tonight, you will hear him moving his ponderous body toward his lover."

Kent had kept his cameras close to hand on the journey and took photographs whenever he could along the way. He was setting up his tripod to record the spectacular scene when Jigme excitedly came running up to show them the rock with curious spiral markings that he'd found.

"That's a fossil," Kent explained with the help of Songtsen's translation. "Some sea creature which lived a very long time ago left an imprint of its shape in that rock, Jigme. That's quite a find. I've seen photographs of those fossilized remains, but I've never seen the real thing before."

"A living creature in a rock?" The boy's eyes grew large at the idea of such a miracle.

"Yes. Because there was a time when that rock wasn't rock at all, but land under water at the bottom of an ocean."

Tara noticed that the rimpoche was allowing Kent to be the boy's teacher when the lama could have explained the fossil himself. He'd done this often during the trek, weaning the child away from himself to the man who was to be his new protector.

"Water?" the child repeated, puzzled. "Like in that stream?"

"Nothing like that stream. A great sea." The boy looked totally lost. Tara could see how the young inhabitant of a country that lay far from any ocean would find the concept difficult to grasp.

"Have you seen Nam Tso?" Kent asked. Jigme nodded. "Nam Tso is a very large lake, but it's tiny compared to the size of the ocean that once covered the whole of these mountains. Even the highest peak, which you call

Chomolungma the Great Goddess and we call Everest, once lay at the bottom of a sea."

The boy looked dubiously at the lama for confirmation of Kent's fantastic story. "It is so, little one," Songtsen agreed. "Our own scholars teach that the mountains were thrust from the floor of an ancient sea. It is said that the highest rocks bear the imprints of waves washing against a shore." He pointed to the stone the boy held. "And strange sea creatures like this that disappeared when the gods lifted this land to make their abode."

"I didn't know all this, Kent," Tara confessed. "I'm just as dumbfounded as Jigme looks right now."

It was cool but not cold in this protected valley and the wind was less strong here. The lama and the boy chose to curl up outside for the night, as did Kent. Tara opted for the privacy of the tent where she could take off her skirt and top.

They'd oriented the tent so that its opening framed a view of the mountain. The dense night that had descended on them in other places couldn't totally claim this valley. The sharp white outline of the beautiful peak faded as the sky changed from cerulean to midnight blue, but never really disappeared. The moon bathed the snow-covered hills and mirrored lake in a wash of silver.

The crack and clatter of rockfall rolled down the valley. Tara smiled. She'd heard the sound before, of course. Rockfall was common in any mountainous area. But this was the sound of a god visiting his goddess.

The memory of their so frighteningly interrupted love-making had come often to torment her with lovely thoughts of Kent's mouth on her breast. It was sensible of him to sleep outside, of course, to prevent any resumption of that unwanted intimacy. But she wished he hadn't. Tonight, all by herself in the tent, she felt particularly lonely.

Kent lay on the hard ground a short distance away from the gently snoring Songtsen and Jigme. The sound of slipping shale reminded him of Songtsen's little folklore story—which shot his musings back to Tara. The question the lama had posed him a few days into their journey had never been long from his mind. What was Tara Morgan to him? It was a question he still was unable to answer.

That she continued to hold him in the grip of a fascination growing stronger by the moment couldn't be denied. That every night he lay little more than arm's length from her, aching with wanting, was painfully true. At least the rigors of the journey allowed him to keep his desire for her under control during the day.

Whether she was with them now only because of Colonel Wu Chen, or by decree of a goddess, every day on the trail made him more and more grateful for her presence.

He'd noted and appreciated both the careful nurturing the woman gave the child, and her mindfulness of an old man's dignity as she helped him off his horse or settled him in their tent. It was largely Tara's special presence, he decided, that was molding a party that had started out as virtual strangers into a kind of family. A family he would miss a great deal, he realized, when their journey was over.

Until that journey was over, he couldn't let arousing thoughts of Tara Morgan interfere with his doing his part on the flight on which all their lives depended. The incident at the hot springs had taught him the folly of giving in to his desire for her. That time they'd been lucky, but he had to be careful not to let down his guard again. On their first mission against the Chinese military, they'd had the advantage of surprise. Now he couldn't allow himself to forget for a moment that the whole damn Chinese occupation army was out after their hides. And as if that weren't enough, the unforgiving mountains demanded that he remain ever alert to the dangers they posed.

Shoving away the tantalizing mental picture of her standing before him, her pink underwear skimming her luscious curves, he heaved himself to his other side. He had to get the lovely redhead out of his mind. He needed his sleep.

Another crash of rockfall reverberated through the valley.

Tara sensed Kent's presence even before she felt the light brush of his lips against hers. Her heart leaped. Her eyes flew wide to see him kneeling beside her. The upper half of his body was hidden in darkness, but the slant of moonlight pouring in through the open tent flap etched the shape of his naked thigh. Her throat tightened and a swift hot shaft of desire lanced through her.

Her mind may have lulled her into believing her response to his lovemaking at the hot springs was only a temporary, regrettable lapse of control. But the way she felt now, as if her body had been strung tight awaiting only the release of his kiss to spring to pulsing life, belied all those mental excuses. She *needed* to be with him. Helpless to do anything else, she opened her arms to him.

Kent folded back the single blanket that covered her and stretched the long, hard length of his body next to hers. The urgency of her desire needed no long, slow period of arousal. Already her breath came in rapid gasps. As did his. Already she could feel his hot male hardness pressed demandingly against her thigh. And already a heated moistness slicked her pulsing feminine core.

She reached for the hem of her undershirt, but Kent caught her hands. "No," he said in a gravelly whisper. "Let me. The thought of undressing you has been making me crazy for a long time."

He pulled the pink undershirt over her arms and pushed it aside. Cupping his hands over her breasts, he pressed his lips to the sensitive valley between them. She buried her hands in the thick dark waves of his hair and guided him to her aching nipples. The touch of his tongue lit a flame of pleasure that licked along every nerve of her body.

He stripped the silk from her legs, and his ragged sigh told of his gratification at seeing her clothed only in shadows. The chill breeze that invaded the tent and played over her naked and fevered body did nothing to cool her. Incongruously, her burning skin demanded, not the relief of a cold wind, but to feel the satisfying heat of Kent's body.

"Touch me!" she pleaded.

His searching fingers began to map in electrifying detail the curves and hollows his eyes had spent moments devouring. The tremors sweeping through his body spoke of his fight to control his own desire as he caressed her gently, lovingly, bringing a sweet liquid fire to all her soft and secret places.

Was the roar filling her ears caused by the wind surging down from the peaks and plunging into every crevice in the upthrust earth? Or was it the sound of her own pounding pulse? She didn't know. Didn't care. Her body arced shivering toward him, seeking to experience all there was of every igniting stroke of his hands and fiery touch of his lips.

His rapid breath pulsed warm against her ear as he gasped out the mindless, timeless words that lovers have always used to utter their passion. And she, just as mindlessly, returned them.

"I want you, Tara," he rasped. "Lord! How I want you."

As she wanted him. Her whole body cried out to be engulfed by his. The ache to feel him part of her was overwhelming. She moaned her need and locked her thighs around him. He drove himself into her—hot and deep— flooding her with a sense of completion she'd never known before. He crested with a deep shuddering groan and she lost herself in him.

Somewhere in the mountains an avalanche thundered to earth. Neither of them heard.

The first rays of the rising sun poured a dazzling spill of liquid gold over the summit. The light flashed from the mountaintop onto the glassy surface of the lake at its base. After the spellbinding night spent in Kent's arms, Tara was ready to concede that the place of such spectacular beauty was truly the abode of the gods.

The four rode from the valley with many regretful backward glances, but they hadn't the time to linger.

They'd already safely forded several small rivers and mountain streams, but the rampaging waters that faced them now looked fiercer than anything they'd yet encountered. Steep rock walls hemmed them in on almost every side. Either they crossed here or they'd be forced to backtrack into yet another miles-long detour.

Kent didn't need to caution them to take special care with the fording. The grim set of his mouth and the nervousness of the horses and donkey warned them they faced danger.

"The stream is only three or four yards wide," Kent said. "But I'm going to set up a safety line, just in case." He dug into one of the packs for the rope they'd already had to use once or twice. "If your horses start to flounder, let them go, grab the line and hold on. I'll come in for you." He looped one end of the rope around a jagged spur of rock near the stream bank and climbed onto the shoulders of the lead yak. "You come up here with me, Jigme."

Nothing bothered the evil-smelling yaks, nor hindered their incessant grazing even on apparently bare ground. They plowed through snow and rockfall and rushing mountain streams like four-footed tanks. If anything could make it across, these heavy, hairy bovines would. Reaching the opposite side, Kent gave the yaks into Jigme's care and tied the rope to another solidly planted rock. He kept his hands firmly closed around the guide rope as he returned. The water wasn't all that deep, barely up to his knees, but the force of the current and the slippery rocks on the riverbed made it difficult for him to keep his footing. He mounted his horse and wrapped the donkey's leads around a hand. "After I get back on the other side, you two come over one at a time."

Tara gestured for Songtsen to go first. The lama urged his animal into the foaming water. His horse seemed to be making it across without too much difficulty when suddenly the animal stumbled. Losing its footing completely, it went down, throwing Songtsen into the water. The old man grabbed for the rope, but missed, and the swiftly flowing current kept him from regaining his feet. In seconds, the icy flow swept away both man and animal.

As soon as Tara had seen Songtsen's horse stumble, she'd wheeled her own mount and galloped downstream along the narrow bank. Her instincts on automatic pilot, she urged her horse into the water toward the drowning man whirling through the current.

The lama slapped up against her horse's legs. Tara grabbed for his robe, but it just came away from his body. She caught a flailing wrist and held on. The commotion around her horse's legs frightened the animal into a nervous prance. Tara was afraid her horse would fall, too, or that one of its hooves would land disastrously on the helpless lama.

Kent, who'd raced down the opposite bank, waded into the churning water. He hooked his arms beneath Songtsen's and dragged him to shore, the robe's dark length trailing out in the water behind him. Tara's horse lost no time in making it back to dry land.

Jigme, knowing what was needed, ran up with a blanket and Kent's *chuba*. The old man's chest heaved as he gasped for breath. He had the strength neither to move nor to utter a word as Kent removed the sodden robe and wrapped the blanket around the lama's thin, shivering body.

Kent carried the priest back to where the animals waited and gently laid him down on a sleeping rug. His examination uncovered no broken bones. Apparently utter exhaustion and cold were Songtsen's biggest problems. Aside from a bump already starting to swell on the side of his head, and several cuts from the stream's sharp rocks, he'd suffered no serious damage. While Jigme held a cup of tepid tea from the thermos flask to Songtsen's lips, Tara and Kent quickly set up the tent to get the injured man into shelter.

"The horse?" Songtsen whispered as soon as he could manage the words.

"Gone, I'm afraid," Kent answered. "But I saw him come up on the opposite bank downstream. I guess he'd had enough swimming because he galloped off the way we'd come. He'll probably wander down to graze in the lower valleys. The gods might smile on a lucky nomad and present him with the gift of a new horse."

"My book?" the high lama gasped out hopefully. They all knew how much his treasured book meant to him. He'd taken good care of it, continually checking the fastenings of the long box fixed to the high back of his saddle.

"I'm sorry, Rimpoche. The book and the rest of your belongings on the horse have gone, too."

The old man sighed. "I thought as much. I had the book very long time. But Buddha teaches me a lesson. It is not good to become attached to things, not even a book of holy words."

Kent drew the blanket up to Songtsen's chin. "Don't talk anymore, my friend. Just rest. Try to get some sleep. We'll spend a day or two here."

The old man closed his eyes painfully. "I hoped I would not become a burden to you, my son."

"You're no burden, Songtsen," Kent protested softly. "We can all use the rest."

Kent was a lot more worried than he sounded. Only the lama knew the way to Yonten-La. If anything should happen to the old man, they'd be trapped here in the killing wilderness without knowing which way to turn. Even figuring out the way down wasn't always easy when they had to go up and over so many hills and passes. And even if he were able to lead them back to the main road alone, they were many, many miles from any kind of settlement, Tibetan or Chinese.

Leaving the boy to sit with the lama, Kent left the tent. He saw Tara standing a few yards away, her shoulders hunched, her arms folded tightly in front of her, and walked over to stand behind her.

"Songtsen's a tough old bird," he said, wrapping his arms about her. "Don't worry. He'll make it."

Tara allowed herself to relax a little against him. "I'm sure he will. It's just that . . ." She turned within his arm and dropped her head against his chest. "Oh, Kent. I thought we were going to lose him."

He pressed his lips to her forehead. "But we didn't."

"No. Thank God for that."

He was content to stand and hold her for as long as she needed it. After a while the woman's natural optimism asserted itself.

"I guess in a way it's not so bad we lost one of the horses," she said. "We're running low on feed for them and the donkey."

"I know."

"Our own provisions worry me, too. We don't have an awful lot of *tsampa* left, although we still have a number of instant soup packets."

"Then we'll all just have to get along on short rations. Horses included. I hope it won't be for too much longer."

"Kent?" Tara looked up at him hesitantly. "I really hate to bring this up, but are you sure Songtsen is leading us in the right direction? I mean, he said himself he'd only been to the monastery once. There must be a reason why they call Yonten-La the Hidden Place. And he made the trip a very long time ago. The terrain can change, can't it? Through avalanche, or flood?"

That same disquiet had risen in him over the past few days, Kent admitted, especially when the lama didn't seem quite certain of his way. But he'd carefully kept from voicing his own increasing concern. His charges didn't need any more worries to add to their already lengthy list. But if they didn't soon come upon some evidence, like a road, a *mani* wall or prayer flags that might indicate the presence of a monastery or anything else in the vicinity, he'd have to make a decision about continuing on this way.

"I'll still bet my money on the high lama getting up there," he said with more conviction than he really felt. "We have to stay here a couple of days to let him recuperate. I'll talk to him tomorrow."

But by the time Tara opened her eyes the next morning,
ongtsen was sitting up in his usual cross-legged posture of
editation. He absolutely insisted on their resuming their
ourney immediately.

The donkey apparently differed with that opinion. All
ie way, the beast's loud hee-haws and flailing hooves had
t them know it was an unwilling participant in this forced
arch. Jigme more or less dragged the donkey along bend the yaks while Kent led the party under the lama's
rections as navigator.

Those directions led them into a glacier-sealed valley.
heir sunglasses weren't enough to fend off the sun's rays
ouncing from every direction off the dazzling whiteness
  snow and ice that surrounded them. Songtsen's col-
ed glasses had been lost in the river along with the rest
  his things. With his eyes unprotected, the old man could
ffer snow blindness—a threat hanging over all of them,
nglasses or no. Tara fashioned a makeshift eyescreen for
e lama by tying around his head a folded length of cloth
to which she'd cut two narrow eyeslits.

Kent pulled the broad brim of his fur hat down over his
rehead to shade his eyes, and she made Jigme do the
me with the front flap of his woolen helmet. She herself
as wrapped up like an Arab, leaving only a narrow slit in
r headscarf. Their precautions still didn't prevent the
inful glare from knifing into their eyes. Often they had
  bury their eyes in their hands to rest them from the
inding sun.

On this leg of the journey, no more bottles of *chang* fell
f the walls. It took all their efforts just to keep going.
ongtsen steadfastly maintained they were getting closer to
onten-La. The lama's assurance didn't cheer Tara as
uch as it had the first time he'd made it—several days
o.

A light snow began to fall as they followed the trail to a
iturally formed path of sorts up a mountainside.

"I don't trust the boy's footing on the track, Song-
:n," Kent said, eyeing the narrow ledge that would force
em into single file. "Let's put him up there on my horse

with you." He turned to Tara. "Will you take charge of t|
donkey? If you hold his reins, he should follow witho|
too much problem, especially sandwiched in between yo|
horse and Songtsen's."

Halfway up the hill they found themselves picking the|
way over a ledge that grew so narrow their legs scraped |
against the vertical wall of solid rock on their left. On t|
right, the slope fell away to a distance as deep as the riv|
gorge that had made her so nervous in Qinghai. The hors|
had difficulty maintaining their footing on ground th|
grew increasingly slippery in the wet snow. The donk|
disliked it so much it tried to pull away by continual|
yanking on the reins Tara held.

"Can you manage, Tara?" called a worried-looki|
Kent from his position in the lead. "Wait there. I'll co|
back to you."

Tara didn't want him to try. There was too little room |
which to edge past the pack animals.

"It's okay," she assured him, brushing away the flak|
of snow sticking to her eyelashes. "I've let go the rein|
The stupid beast can't go anywhere but up with the rest |
us."

Apparently in a hurry to do just that, the donkey bu|
ted into the hindquarters of Tara's horse. The animal shi|
away. She struggled to control it. Under the heavy poun|
ing of the horse's hooves the wet ground began to give wa|
Fighting for solid footing, the animal reared up, throwi|
her from the saddle. She landed on her stomach, half o|
half over the side of the ledge, and let out a cry of pain.|

She had to get up, her dazed brain told her. Through t|
falling snow she could see that Kent had squeezed past t|
yaks and was making his way toward her. She was reliev|
to see that her horse and the donkey seemed to be all rig|
and had kept on going. Setting her hands on either side |
her body, she tried to push herself to a sitting position. T|
ground broke away under her.

Tara screamed Kent's name and frantically tried to st|
her slide. She grabbed a small shrub a few feet beneath t|
path. The bush held for a moment as her legs flailed f|

upport, but her weight was too great and her tenuous feline ripped out by the roots. She tumbled down the ope, jagged rocks tearing at her body and flying stones igging at her face.

To Kent's agonized gaze, Tara's terrible slide down the mountain seemed to go on forever. Songtsen had pulled up is horse just before the break in the trail where she'd allen. Jigme clung whimpering to the old man. The lama ointed downward. "A ledge stopped the Tara's fall."

Kent knelt on the edge of the path and stared at the oman sprawled like a rag doll on a small outcropping wenty or thirty feet down the mountainside. "Tara!" he alled. "Tara, can you hear me?"

She made no answer, and the hand splayed out above er head didn't move. Utter terror clutched at his heart as ie snow continued to drift down, lightly but inexorably overing the body of the woman lying so dreadfully still elow.

Chapter 12

Colonel Wu Chen still smarted from the general's late tongue-lashing. The general had never been able to see tha the escape of the American woman wasn't Wu's fault. Th moment the report had reached him that the operator of cable crossing in Qinghai had seen the Yankee imperiali spy Masterson, and that his accomplice wasn't a man all, but a woman with red hair, he'd rushed to Tara Mo gan's hotel room. Too late.

He'd consigned her to her room only because he sensed a nervousness about her, an evasiveness that ofte meant guilt. Although at the time he hadn't connected he with the breach of security at the installation. Now, course, he could guess that even as she'd sat across fro him and lied so poorly, she'd had possession of the inte ligence film and meant to fly out of Xizang with it. B Tara Morgan had not boarded a plane to Chengdu, or anywhere else. He'd seen to that. She still must be trapped along with Masterson, within Chinese borders. If she Masterson had made it out, he'd know it. The foreign pre had begun to carry articles about the well-known ph

ographer and a beautiful travel agent lost somewhere on
tour of China.

He didn't understand it. He'd sent out full descriptions
f both spies to checkpoints all over Xizang. The wom-
n's dramatic coloring would make them easy to spot, even
mong Westerners. He was sure the two Americans were
aveling together. To whom else would the woman have
one after her escape? She could hardly make her way out
f China alone. Masterson must have remained in the
hasa area waiting to see if his accomplice would make her
scape. For a while he'd had the man within his grasp. Wu
hen's hand closed into a fist. The Americans were mak-
g him look foolish. And for that they would pay. Sooner
r later they'd have to come up through a final pass where
uards armed to the teeth waited for them.

He needed a victory. And soon. Or he would find
imself among the prisoners and peasants conscripted
o labor at the construction site. Beijing was issuing un-
asonable demands for the capture of the reincarnative
endun Lama. This time he was sure the rumors that the
oy had been found were true.

Damn Songtsen, Wu cursed. Damn his monastery and
ll the monks in it. His troops descended on the place every
ay to search for the boy and the old man, but found
othing. The high lama was on pilgrimage to a holy shrine,
e monks maintained. Who knew when he planned to re-
rn? But the priest could just as well be hiding some-
here within that rabbit warren of a monastery where a
undred men could never search him out.

Without a doubt, if the child had been found he'd have
een taken to Songtsen for safekeeping. The monks might
e ignorant, but they knew as well as he did what the cen-
al government planned to do with the boy. To prevent
at, they'd very likely try to get him out of the country.
et them try. PLA troops covered all known passes. Wu
hen stopped and considered. Troops covered all the
nown passes. But might there be passes unknown to him?
ight the traitorous monks try to spirit the child out
rough one of those damnable secret passes whose exis-

tence was no more than legend—at least to Chinese lik
himself?

He had to find out if such passes were fact or fantasy
And quickly. Songtsen's monks were religious fanatics wh
would accept death before revealing anything. Despite h
threat to the high lama, he saw little point in wasting tim
and useless effort on them. But ordinary Tibetans—no
mads—were another matter. The colonel reached for th
telephone and briskly gave the order to pick up the lead
ers of nomad groups roaming the southern edge of th
Chang Tang—particularly any older men who might b
expected to know of any secret passes. He had no diff
culty adding the order to use any methods necessary t
obtain from them the information he wanted.

A knife twisted in Kent's gut as he looked at the sti
figure of the woman lying below him, the snow swirlin
around her. He had to get down there. Somehow he had t
get down to her. Songtsen called to him. Kent looked bac
and saw that the old man was preparing to dismount.

"No, Rimpoche," Kent shouted. "It's too dangerou
Keep going. Get yourself and the boy to safety. The end o
the track isn't much farther. I saw it from the bend u
ahead."

"You will need help getting the Tara back, my son."

That was exactly what he'd do, Kent vowed. Or d
trying. But he could guess what Tara would think of hi
endangering other lives into the bargain, and what sh
would say right now if she could speak. "I won't risk any
one else's life on this ledge," he told the lama.

"The responsibility will be mine." The old man bore
look of determination. "We will help."

"But the child . . ."

"The child is learning something of value."

Kent knew that the lama's assistance might well mak
the difference for Tara's life. He steadfastly refused to a
low his mind to form the awful, final word lurking there

"Very well, Rimpoche." Tara's fall had gouged a cou
ple of feet out of the edge of the trail, but the hole wasn

 big the horse couldn't step around it. "Bring your horse
ver here. The track is more solid on this side and there's
ore room." Tara's luck had deserted her at the single
ost treacherous spot on the trail.

Kent reached over to grasp the horse's harness and led
e animal and its riders across. "There's a rope in that
ght saddlebag behind you, Rimpoche. Can you tie it
ound the pommel of your saddle?"

The lama did so, and handed the rope to Kent. Kent
lged himself over the side and began slowly and pain-
lly working himself down to the ledge where Tara lay
nmoving. If he slipped, they were both gone. The old
an and the boy would be unable to help them. Stretch-
g to his utmost length for rocks and small clefts to use as
otholds and handholds, he struggled down to her.

Already small white drifts were accumulating in the
ack folds of her *chuba* and in her hair's dark braids. She
as lying prone, one arm twisted under her and her head
rned to the side. Kneeling beside her, Kent brushed the
now from her face. Her cheek was cold, but he thought
e could detect some warmth in it. He sought the pulse
int in her neck. An overwhelming sense of relief stung
ars into his eyes. Her pulse was there! Feeble and un-
eady beneath his fingers, but there.

He turned and waved to the two waiting anxiously at the
p of the cliff. "She's alive," he yelled. "She's alive," he
peated gratefully to himself as he leaned over her. He
oved her gently onto her back. There was an ominous
oody gash on her forehead, and the long rip in the pink
k of her underwear was tinged with blood from the tear
 her thigh. The unnatural dent in the front of her leg—
st above the boot—indicated that her fall might have
apped the tibia. Whatever her injuries, there was noth-
g anyone could do for her here. There was very little
om to work on the ledge, and he didn't know how solid
was. He wanted to get both of them off the lifesaving
lge of earth quickly.

One wasn't supposed to move an accident victim who
ight be suffering from spinal or internal injuries, but he

had no choice. He had to get her up the slope. He loope
the rope under her arms. If he lost his footing while he wa
carrying her, she'd at least have some chance of bein
pulled up by Songtsen.

He hefted Tara's limp body over his shoulder, her hea
hanging down his back to protect it from contact with th
slope, and looked up. It seemed a very long way to the to
Snowflakes continually fell into his eyes and he had to kee
blinking them away. Songtsen picked up the slack in th
rope as he climbed, twisting it around the pommel of h
saddle.

Maintaining his balance with the woman's dead weig
on one side wasn't easy, and his grip on the slope was pr
carious. It took every ounce of strength he possessed
pull himself from one rocky handhold to another. H
progress up the cliff was agonizingly slow, and he had
stop often to drag air into his gasping lungs, but finally
was able to roll Tara onto the path and heave himself u
alongside her.

"We will put her on this horse," Songtsen said. "Th
boy and I can walk."

Kent shook his head. "Her horse will be waiting at th
top of the pass. I've carried her this far. I can manage th
rest of the way. Go on ahead, Rimpoche."

At the top of the pass Songtsen and the boy hurried
help him. "Rimpoche, do you know of any kind of med
ical facility around here, a rural clinic, or a nurse, even
Chinese one?" Tara needed immediate medical attentio
Kent was ready to take her to anyone who could help.
thousand times better that they should both become pri
oners of the Chinese than that she should die.

"There is nothing, my son. Yonten-La is our on
hope."

Kent had expected the lama's regretful shake of his hea
Songtsen was right. They had to make it to the warmth an
shelter of the monastery. Out here in a storm, even insi
a tent, without heat, without even the most rudimenta
attention, Tara wouldn't make it through the night. H
survival now depended on an old man's possibly faili

memory and his ability to lead them to their destination through a blizzard growing heavier by the minute.

They didn't dare let the boy down off the horse to herd the animals. Either the yaks and the donkey followed along in the wake of the humans or they went off on their own. In either case the yaks would probably be all right. And the truth was he didn't care what happened to the donkey whose antics had nearly killed Tara.

Kent sat Tara's horse, holding her unconscious form in front of him, a blanket wrapped around her and draped over her face to protect her from the snow. He almost wished that, just once, he could hear her groan with pain. She'd made no sound at all since he'd found her. In a way, it was a blessing she'd remained out of it during the dangerous climb, but he didn't like to think that she'd sunk into such a deep state of unconsciousness that she could feel nothing at all, not even pain.

Blindly he followed the lama's horse, his hope fading with every hour they plowed on through the desolate white wilderness searching for the hidden valley. He was desperately aware that not only Tara but all of them could perish in the snow that had almost claimed the life of his grandfather so many years ago.

For the first time since coming to Tibet he considered that he might fail the people who depended on him. The child given into his care might never live to fulfill the promise he held for his people. The old man's efforts to complete a prophecy might end in a silent death out here in the middle of nowhere. Kent grimly resolved that if the others, all weaker than he, disappeared in the fastness of the Himalayas, he would, too. He didn't intend to stumble all alone out of these cruel, endless mountains.

The afternoon faded into deepening gray and then into swirling patterns of white against black. As if they'd accepted that now it was the haven of Yonten-La or death for all of them, no one suggested stopping to make camp.

Songtsen's cry over the howling wind jolted Kent out of his lethargy. He drew his horse up abreast of the lama's and followed the direction of his pointing arm. At first he

saw nothing. Then for a moment a gust of wind whipped
away the curtain of snow. Ahead of them lay a high, oval
cleft in the rock face. Beyond it Kent could make out several pinpoints of light beckoning through the swirling
snow.

"Yonten-La," the lama cried.

As if the animals, too, sensed the end of their exhausting journey, all made for the opening in the mountainside. Once through, the valley's protective rim of steep-
sided cliffs shut out the worst of the storm. They'd come
into the valley halfway up a mountain. Down to the right
on the valley floor, a cluster of lights marked a village.
Only a short distance farther up the mountain two huge
lanterns illuminated the monastery entrance.

At Kent's loud shout, a door swung open on the courtyard, then another. Monks began calling to each other and
hurrying out into the snow. Some quickly lifted the boy
and Songtsen down from their horse, while others relieved Kent of his precious burden and tended to the animals. He followed them inside.

A man as old as Songtsen, the abbot of the place, Kent
assumed, bowed a welcome to his unexpected guests.
Songtsen spoke a few words in Tibetan and the monks
around them fell to the floor and prostrated themselves
before the boy, who was rubbing his sleepy eyes.

"Rimpoche," Kent interrupted. He had no time for the
niceties of Tibetan protocol right now. "Please ask them
if there's anyone here with medical training. And ask them
to bring me hot water and bandages, antiseptic, whatever
first aid items they may have."

Tara's bearers carried her into a small room where they
laid her on a couch. Songtsen bade everyone but himself
and Kent leave the room. As gently as possible so as not to
do her any more injury Kent removed her fur coat and
boots, then took off her torn clothing. The heavy charm
box around her neck had slipped over her shoulder to the
couch. He left it there. The *gao* hadn't averted her fall, but
he wasn't about to give up on anything at all that might
offer her some protection.

A tightness gripped his throat as he looked at her. Lying there in tattered long johns smeared with blood, she looked as terrifyingly vulnerable, as fragile as an injured child.

A monk carrying a long wooden box on a leather thong looped over his shoulder hurried into the room and knelt beside her. The expertise with which he ran his hands over her body relieved some of Kent's fears. The man obviously knew something about treating injuries. Kent assisted him in splinting Tara's leg and tending to the slash in her thigh and her other cuts and abrasions with a mixture of herbs and hot water. The doctor monk rubbed medicated oils on her nostrils and temples, then cleansed the wound on her forehead and wrapped a bandage tightly around her head.

"The physician is worried that the Tara's head injury is more serious than he's able to treat," Songtsen interpreted. That bloody head wound worried Kent, too. It could indicate a fractured skull and concussion. Moreover, he feared that her ghastly fall must have resulted in internal injuries that needed the care of a hospital and medical specialists. He and the monk had done what they could for her, and made her as comfortable as possible under several soft blankets, but her breathing remained low and ragged.

The boy had been taken away, fed and put to bed long before. And despite Kent's urging that Songtsen also retire to get some rest, the high lama, too, remained by Tara's side. Kent, of course, didn't intend to leave her. He couldn't eat the food they'd been given, but sipped at the bowl of hot tea. The room's old kerosene heater wasn't really keeping the place hot, but it did furnish some extra warmth for the injured woman.

The oil lamp the monks had left behind threw a weak pool of yellow light over Tara's face, deepening the hollows of her eyes.

"This is all my fault." Kent's low, anguished admission brought Songtsen out of his meditations.

"Ah!" The lama's voice came softly from the shadows in a corner of the room. "It was your fault a donkey shied

resulting in the Tara's fall down the mountain." Songtser
poured himself a little more tea from the small brass ur
on the tray by his side, and curled his hands around the
bowl. "How is that, my son?"

"If I hadn't let her come with me to Qinghai, the
Chinese would never have suspected her, and she'd have
gotten out of the country. Right now she could have been
lying safely in her own bed in Maryland instead of..." He
squeezed his eyes shut. "Instead of this."

"You cannot order the whole world, Kent Masterson."
The high lama spoke with gentle firmness. "Nor its gods
And no man can alter the will of Buddha."

Kent wasn't a religious man. At least not in the same
sense as the rimpoche, who lived intimately with the spir
itual world. But though he seldom practiced any forma
religion, sometimes, in places of spirit-lifting beauty like
the goddess mountain where he and Tara had made love
he became strongly conscious of a higher power. He
prayed now to that life source, to that Being greater than
all of them, to spare Tara's life.

He sat by the couch and clung to her cold little hand a
if that connection could hold her back from the eterna
dark that so obviously threatened her. Sometime during
the night he'd noticed that it had stopped snowing, but the
wind still rattled the small, square-paned window and cold
drafts blew across the floor. The lama, Kent saw, had gone
back to his meditations. For himself, there was nothing to
do but wait through the long hours of the night. Some
how he'd gotten it into his head that if Tara could only
survive to open her eyes on morning light, she'd be al
right. Exhaustion forced him to rest his forehead on the
couch where she lay. Slowly, his eyes drifted shut.

Suddenly he jerked up his head and searched Tara'
face. Even half asleep, he'd registered the change in her
breathing. He'd prayed for that ugly, raspy sound to lift
and it had, but now her breathing had become even more
disturbingly quiet and shallow. The blanket over her breas
rose and fell scarcely at all. And her lips had taken on a

ickly blue cast against the brown dye on her face. A heavy
ear engulfed him. She was slipping away from them.

"Tara!" he cried. "Tara?"

Kent's anxious call pulled Songtsen out of his prayerful
attitude. The old man came over to the couch. He bent
over the unconscious woman, his calm, wizened face
breaking into the weak circle of light around her bed. As
Kent, too, got to his feet, the *chuba* draped around his
shoulders like a cape dropped unnoticed to the floor. He
could read the lama's sorrowful conclusion on his face.
The words he'd been trying so hard to resist forced themselves to his lips.

"She's dying, isn't she, Rimpoche?" Kent's voice
cracked. "Tara's dying."

The lama said nothing, only touched Kent's shoulder.

Everything in him rebelled against the thought of a
world without Tara Morgan. "No," he gritted out in anger. "No. She can't die. I won't let her die." Even as he
spoke, he knew he was utterly helpless to do anything
about the useless promise.

He'd felt just this same powerless, futile rage when his
grandfather lay fighting for life in the hospital after his
heart attack last year. But Randall had been saved by the
best doctors and the finest of medical technology. Tara had
no such miracle cures available to her. She had only a
helpless American and a prayerful Tibetan monk.

Then Kent remembered. Slowly, he lifted his head. This
monk had once been instrumental in saving his grandfather's life. His childhood had been filled with Randall's
exciting stories of his trip to Tibet. They now came flooding back to him.

"Rimpoche, my grandfather often told me how you
found him in the snow and brought him to a lama who
saved his life through some means he still swears was
nothing short of miraculous—*Qi*, he called it." As a boy
he'd readily believed in a thing so excitingly mysterious,
but as a pragmatic adult he found it difficult to accept the
idea of some kind of magical healing. But whether or not
he really believed in *Qi* didn't matter. He didn't believe in

the charm box, either, but he was ready to grasp at an straw, however slight, that might offer Tara life.

"The lama who saved your grandfather," Songtsen re plied, "was one of our wisest teachers—a noted *Qi* mas ter. He has since passed on to another life."

"Your teacher. Yes." Kent stooped to peruse the shorte man's face. "Did he also teach you of *Qi*, Rimpoche?" Realizing that he had grasped Songtsen's left arm, bare by rule within the confines of the monastery even on th coldest days, in too strong a grip, Kent released it. "Rim poche." He pondered. "That's a title given not only to in carnates but to very special teachers, isn't it? Very specia teachers—like you, Songtsen. Have you, too, become sucl an adept? Do you know the mysteries of *Qi?*"

The high lama seemed to be growing very uncomfort able under Kent's close questioning, as if he could se where it was leading and wanted no part of it. The pries turned and walked to the darkened, shuttered window. " have studied the discipline. But you must understand, m son. *Qi* is meant primarily as a means of gaining master over one's own body."

"I know. In Beijing I saw a man who called himself a *Q* master use his power of bodily control to prevent a sharp edged sword from hacking into his neck."

"No, no." The old man vigorously waved away such a unpleasant idea. "Such people misuse the power in orde to make a few yuan as entertainers."

"I don't care about others, Rimpoche. I only want t know if you're a hands-on healer like the man who save Randall. I only want to know if there is the slightest chanc that you could save Tara's life."

"I . . ." Songtsen had accepted the loss of his preciou book with less agitation than he was now demonstrating "Sometimes . . . with my brothers . . . I have been able to hel a little. But I have not the gifts of my teacher," he adde quickly. "And our powers seldom work on unbelievers.'

"They worked on Randall Masterson."

"Randall was an unusual Westerner. A man open t other ways of thinking, other levels of seeing. And yo

ust remember that there were few foreigners who braved
trance to our country at that time. Now we are more
ivate about using those powers and techniques our
inese masters claim are no more than superstition.''

"Since when does Songtsen Rimpoche allow the Chinese
dictate his personal religious practices?'' Kent's voice
s controlled but resonant. "And besides, Tara may be
unbeliever, but apparently that didn't stop the goddess
om choosing to manifest herself within her.''

"Yes. Do you not see, Kent? That is exactly it. Tara. I
ow our concept of a deity taking up residence in a wor-
y human is foreign to you. But I believe this woman *is*
e Tara. For some reason Tara allowed her vessel to fall
wn the mountain. I cannot presume to seek to change
e will of the goddess.''

"How can you be so sure you know the will of the god-
ss?'' Kent pressed. "Maybe it was she who saved her
ssel—as you call it—from death. Maybe your Tara
shes you to use your talents to keep my Tara alive.''

The lama nodded reluctantly. "Perhaps you are right,
y son. That is something I had not considered. It is true
at one can never be certain of the will of the gods. One
n only try to discern it through prayer and meditation.''

When the high lama had successfully tried to convince
m to accept the boy, Kent remembered, the priest hadn't
sitated to use considerable emotional pressure on him.
save Tara's life, he wasn't above using the same kind of
essure on Songtsen.

"The responsibility for this woman being here with us
ght now lies not only with me, Rimpoche. You also
ayed a part in her fate. Do you remember how strongly
u encouraged her to go with me on the trip to the north?
didn't understand why at the time. Now I know that your
ophecies hinted of her presence on this journey and you
nted to keep us together. Don't you perhaps owe Tara
organ something for that?''

The lama's silence lasted so long Kent was coming to the
nclusion the old man had simply abandoned the discus-
n. His heart sank. He had presented all the arguments

he could think of, but he couldn't force Songtsen to something he didn't wish to do. Finally the lama sighed

"Very well, my son. Perhaps I do have a duty to t young woman." The priest walked back over to the cou where Tara lay and stood looking down at her. "I will ne your help. Your attachment to the woman is very stron Your young energies will support mine."

"Of course, Rimpoche." Kent was eager to help. "B what can I do?"

"Sit at the top of the couch and hold her head gently your hands while I prepare myself."

"Is that all? I mean, just hold her head?"

"That is all." The wrinkles etched into the dry, pape skin at the corners of the almond-shaped eyes deepened those eyes narrowed in wry amusement. "If you a expecting something more dramatic from me, I'm afra you will be disappointed. What I will attempt to do will n possess the drama of an operating room in a prestigio American hospital. Our ways are much quieter."

Kent did as the lama had asked, and Songtsen sank the floor by Tara's bed in his usual lotus position. "Foc your thoughts on the woman, Kent. Call her name sof from time to time."

Songtsen sat very still, centering in with his eyes close his breathing controlled. Kent hadn't the lama's yogic e pertise, but he tried to do something of the same. Focus thoughts on Tara, the rimpoche had instructed. But rig now his head was a jumble of fears, of frighteni impressions of how she'd looked sprawled on the ledg Better to start at the beginning, he thought. That first d at the Potala when he'd glanced down the steps to see a g whose fiery hair floated around her like a cloud, a whose loveliness took his breath away.

Tara felt as if she were floating in a soundless, botto less void. She knew vaguely that something bad had ha pened to her, but it took too much effort to rememb what. Just as it took too much effort to listen to the voi that came and went ever more faintly in the deepening

ace. One of the voices spoke a name that dimly regis-
ed as hers.

The void cleared a little and it seemed as if she were
vering near the ceiling of a small room. She looked
wn. A woman—herself, she recognized distantly—was
ng on a bed. Two seated men were bending over her.
though she couldn't see their faces, she sensed that
e—the man with the dark hair—was very upset. She
nted to tell him he shouldn't be, that she was all right,
t doing that would take more energy than she pos-
ssed. So much easier to drift off into the tunnel of cool,
lming light starting to surround her.

The man's voice penetrated the light, disturbing the
aceful sleep into which she was ready to sink. She wished
would stop repeating her name. His incessant voice
turbed her, made her conscious of pain. Pain that kept
r from sinking deeper into the cold but unthreatening
ht waiting to claim her. The growing pain brought an
age of the man's face to her mind. She knew the dark-
ired man angrily drumming her name into her ears. She
uldn't quite remember his name, but she knew him. She
ew, too, that she was leaving him.

The nebulous thought rippled across her tranquillity.
guely she realized that she didn't really want to leave
m. But the pain was growing stronger now, and if she left
n it would stop. Beneath the cold creeping over her, she
uld feel the warmth of his hands at her head, his touch
lding back the chill. She didn't like the pain, but the
rmth he was giving her was good. Maybe she'd stay in
e warmth of his hands for just a little while before let-
g the cold light carry her away.

No. That wasn't enough, she realized fuzzily. She had to
lly want to stay in Kent's warm world. Kent. That was
e man's name. She discovered that if she gathered her
attering thoughts, she could see him more clearly. His
oulders and arms were bare. A memory tugged at her
nd. She could almost remember how the long, corded
uscles of his back would feel beneath her hands.

The tunnel of light offered ease and peace and no mo
hurting. And that ending, or beginning—she wasn't su
which—was still drawing her toward it. But what s
wanted more, she decided, was to stay with the man ur
ing her so desperately not to leave.

The cold white light still hovered around her, but it w
growing fainter. She pushed the last of it away, and a r
laxing heat spread through her body.

Kent was exhausted. He didn't know how long he a
Songtsen had been kneeling over Tara's unconscious bod
but now morning light was beginning to lift the shadov
from the room. A healthier pink had banished the bl
from her lips. And her breathing sounded natural ar
regular. Hope burst over him, and Kent looked to Son
tsen for confirmation. The old man seemed total
drained, but he managed a weak smile and a small no
Kent helped him to a corner of the room where he slipp
to the floor into the Tibetan sleeping position, with I
knees drawn up under him like a baby's and his forehes
resting on the floor.

Kent retrieved his *chuba* and pulled it over his shov
ders. He folded his arms over the side of the couch ar
rested his head on them. Now he wasn't afraid to sleep.

Chapter 13

ara sat propped up on a pile of cushions on her bed.
How do you feel?" Kent asked.

"You've asked me that a hundred times over the past
e days, Kent. Honestly, I feel fine. I'm still just a little
ak, that's all. You don't have to worry about me any-
re."

"You don't have any pain? Your head? Your leg?" Kent
shed the skirt of the long, green silk gown the monks
d given her up to her knee and ran his hand over her
ver leg.

"I wish you'd stop that," Tara said, which wasn't ex-
ly true. She just wished that his touch didn't still dis-
b her as much as it had always done. Any replay of what
d happened between them at the goddess mountain
uldn't be smart. A regrettable weakness—and the ro-
ntic atmosphere—had caused her to succumb to Kent's
using lovemaking once. She didn't intend to do so
ain. Not that she could have done much about it had she
nted to. When she'd awakened after a sleep lasting two
ys, she'd barely had the strength to lift an arm. Only
w was she beginning to feel normal.

"It's the doctor's opinion that my leg is fine." Kent h[a] been there when the physician monk had made that p[ro]nouncement, and he didn't look any more convinced o[f] now than he had then. He still insisted on treating her li[ke] a delicate porcelain doll that might break under anythi[ng] but the most careful handling. "The bruise still loo[ks] pretty bad, but that will clear up in a few days."

"I still think we should have left the splint on as a p[re]caution."

"I stood on that leg this morning and took a few ste[ps] I was a little wobbly, but it didn't give me any real pr[ob]lems."

"And he took the bandage off your head. I was afr[aid] you might have a fractured skull. Thank God you didn't[.]"

Tara gently probed the healing cut on her forehead. "I[t's] still a little tender, but it doesn't really hurt." Her injur[ies] weren't posing any great problems right now, but the roo[m] she lay in was. The walls were covered with pictures [of] various gods practicing esoteric sexual acts. "I wish the[y'd] left me in that quiet little room downstairs where I fi[rst] woke up."

"That room was too near the main entrance to t[he] monastery. The monks were afraid a visitor from the v[il]lage might see you, so they moved you up here. This who[le] wing has been closed for years, like most of the oth[er] rooms in the monastery. Because of who you are, they['ve] given you this place of honor. I suppose they figured th[at] being more or less a divinity yourself, you'd feel right [at] home in a room dedicated to a goddess."

She didn't feel right at home. It felt strange to be livi[ng] in a chapel, especially this one. Apparently all the deit[ies] represented on the walls of the room were gods and go[d]desses of fertility. Any Western churchgoer would [be] shocked at the examples of tantric eroticism exuberan[tly] portrayed in this shrine. But many equally religious H[in]dus and Buddhists saw the energy and human male-fema[le] wholeness of sex in all its aspects as something to be ce[le]brated and worshiped.

Equally as disturbing as the intimate touch of Kent's warm hand on her leg was the effect his presence had on the room. When she was here alone the psychedelic frescoes writhing over every inch of the walls and ceiling scarcely seemed erotic. There was such a wealth of color and detail in the pictures that it wasn't always easy to decipher their subject matter. In fact, she'd lain on her bed for several hours puzzling them out.

But when Kent walked into the room the sexual nature of the paintings just seemed to jump out at her. She saw clearly that those red designs at the bottom of one of the pictures weren't funny-looking erupting volcanoes at all, but enthusiastically rendered depictions of spurting male organs.

She could look right over Kent's dark head now to the wall behind him, which carried a mural of a wild-eyed god whose blue-painted consort had her legs wrapped around his middle. And in painting the goddess with her head thrown back and her mouth open, the artist had done a realistic job of depicting orgasmic frenzy. Not exactly the kind of decor soothing to an invalid.

To wake up in such an overwrought room and learn that Kent had been her nurse, spooning soup into her mouth, stripping off her torn and dirty underwear and dressing her in the gown was disconcerting enough. But she vaguely remembered someone gently sponging her off all over with warm water and soap. That someone had to have been Kent. The thought of him performing such an intimate act while she lay semiconscious was even more embarrassing. Of course, there were no other women here in the monastery.

Another thing about the room made her uncomfortable. After spending weeks with Kent on the trail, it didn't feel right that he should be anywhere but a few feet away. Close enough to call, if she wanted to. Close enough to reach out and touch, instead of far away in the small cell the monks had given him at the far end of the hallway.

Tara lowered her eyes from both the mural and from the sight of Kent's long, strong fingers on her leg, and leaned over to flip down her skirt, indicating he was to remove his hand.

"I'd like to go out on the terrace, Kent." She needed air and the room had no windows. "This place is too gloomy."

The only light in the room came from a small battery operated lamp and the natural light entering from the windowed gallery that led to the shrine. The Chinese electrification of some parts of Tibet hadn't reached this remote valley. Given the virtual inaccessibility of the monastery, she thought it would be a long time—if ever— before it enjoyed more modern conveniences. That very inaccessibility had saved it from complete destruction by the Red Guards, although its facade had been damaged and the twenty-foot-high Buddha in the courtyard had lost great chunks from its stone body.

"Hold on," Kent said as Tara started to swing her leg to the floor. "I'll carry you. I don't want you doing too much walking on that leg just yet." He slid his arm around her and hefted her from the bed.

"Honestly, Kent," Tara protested as he carried her down the hall to a doorway leading out to a small terrace formed by the roof of the rooms below. "Sometimes I think you'd be happier if I were still lying there moaning and groaning." She tried not to notice how lovely it felt to be resting once more against his strong chest, with his pleasant masculine scent teasing her nostrils.

"Of course I wouldn't. I'm very glad you feel so well. It's just that when I brought you here, you were one sick lady. And there's no point in taking any unnecessary chances that you might fall and reinjure yourself."

"Why can't you just accept the fact that my injuries weren't as bad as you thought, or I wouldn't have recovered so quickly?"

That's what she told herself whenever she remembered the strange, disturbing dream that remained so vivid in her mind. She really wasn't yet up to examining the meaning of the dream—it if had any meaning, that is. She hesitated to mention the dream to Kent, only to have him dismiss it as the delirium she knew it must be. After all, how did a person go about explaining to a man that she thinks he . . . well . . . died for a little while, and only returned to the land of the living because she couldn't bear to leave him? He'd think her crazy. And maybe she was. Would anyone with a properly functioning brain consider such a thing?

Still, the very idea that even in a dream her feelings for Kent might be so strong they could anchor her to life was powerfully unsettling. Whether true or not, it indicated she hadn't been able to keep him from laying claim to her heart. And that worried her.

Kent carried her toward the padded bench placed there specifically for her use. The monks evidently shared Songtsen's conviction in her identity as *the Tara*, as he kept referring to her now. Apparently the lama thought she'd had enough time to get used to the idea that the spirit of a goddess was living within her, and wasn't making any more concessions to her delicate Western sensibilities. She'd decided that if it made the monks of Yonten-La happy to bow and do reverence to the other Tara, their goddess, this Tara shouldn't complain.

Even though the buildings of Yonten-La remained, many in dire need of repair, over the years most of the monks had been scattered. Taken away, killed, or moved forcibly onto communes. The monks who remained went to great lengths to serve their honored guest. For her enjoyment they'd turned the terrace into a private garden by hauling up dozens of potted plants culled from all parts of the monastery and setting them out around the edge of the roof. This late in the season the bright red geraniums, yellow and purple chrysanthemums and small blue alpine flowers she'd never seen before were growing leggy and dropping their blossoms. Still, she loved the color and the perfume they provided.

"I'd like to stand near the edge of the terrace, please, Kent, so I can look down into the valley."

Kent stood her on her feet just in back of the raised roof edge and wrapped his arm around her waist to hold her steady. In the day's warmth, he wore his *chuba* Tibetan style, with only one arm shoved through a sleeve, the other bare. The tightness of his grip encouraged her to lean against him, so she did. The heated strength of his body made her feel safe, protected.

Resting her head on his uncovered shoulder, she gazed at a view so magnificent it almost brought tears to her eyes. In every direction, range after range of dazzling white peaks rolled away to the horizon.

The purity of the thin, crystal-clear air played tricks on the eyes. The nearest majestic icebound cone, thrusting impossibly high through its cloaking clouds, looked close, although it was miles away. Yonten-La itself was perched on top of a mountain. Here one didn't need to look up to see clouds. The white wisps drifting below her feet made her feel as if she and Kent were standing in the sky.

On the valley floor below, several monks were bringing in the last of the year's harvest of barley. Another burgundy-robed man stooped to gather vegetables from a small square plot, which still showed green. Only a few white patches remained in areas of deepest shadow.

"I wish . . . I wish . . ." Tara's throat tightened.

"You wish we could stay here in this beautiful place," Kent finished for her. She nodded. "I wish so, too, Tara. But as soon as you're strong enough to travel, we've got to get back on the road."

"I know." The beauty and tranquillity of the secluded valley masked the reality of fear and destruction that now gripped the whole of Tibet. "This might look like the paradise of Shangri-La, but it's in China, and China is dangerous for us and for Jigme."

"China's dangerous for a lot of people right now," Kent agreed grimly. "For the sake of the Chinese people, we've got to hope it won't always be so. But let's try to forget all that for a little while. Let's try to pretend that for these few days we're in Yonten-La on holiday. I'm just here to take pictures of all this." The sweep of his arm encompassed the splendid panorama before them.

"And I'm looking the place over to bring a tour group here next year." She laughed. "Can I sign you up?"

"You can put me at the head of the list."

With Kent so close, how easy it was to fantasize about things that would never be. She had to remember that pretending their togetherness would last beyond the time it would take to make their escape was only that—fantasy. His fingers brushed lightly down her cheek. She looked up as he slid his hand under her chin and gently tipped her face to his. His kiss, tender and very sweet, did a lot to banish the melancholy mood creeping over her.

Kent reveled in the warmth of Tara's lips beneath his. Throughout that interminable night he'd feared he might never feel their velvety softness again. He wanted to agree with her frequently voiced belief that she couldn't have been that badly injured. No other conclusion made any real sense.

His own eyes showed him the woman growing stronger each day in a recovery that seemed nothing less than miraculous. He considered himself a knowledgeable and sophisticated man. He'd traveled the world over and witnessed many strange and inexplicable sights. But none had been so foreign and puzzling as the experience he'd undergone that night with Tara and Songtsen. Never before had he felt so spiritually close, so emotionally bonded to another person as when he'd held her head in his hands and tried to will death away from her.

No sensible person believed in wizardry. It still seemed impossible that the old priest's healing touch had somehow mended torn flesh and damaged muscles. There had to be a more reasonable explanation for the success of the rimpoche's unconventional treatment. Even Western doctors were beginning to concede the mystifying powers of the human mind. Perhaps what Songtsen had done wasn't really as mysterious as it seemed. When his nephew had broken a leg, Kent remembered, the doctors had used low-voltage electric pulses to speed the bone's healing. Maybe the high lama had somehow learned to harness his own natural electrical energy to do something of the same thing.

The easiest explanation to accept, of course, was Tara's opinion that her leg hadn't been broken at all. And her state of unconsciousness, which had so worried him, hadn't necessarily been due to a fractured skull or the presence of severe internal injuries.

Whatever the truth of it—and Kent suspected they would never know the truth—the way he'd felt about her that night had affected him deeply. So deeply, he was almost afraid to consider what it might mean. That is, if the confusing incident meant anything at all. The mind can play funny tricks on a man as exhausted as he'd been that night. And his fear for her had no doubt kept him from thinking clearly.

He'd expected that making love to her would tamp down his desire for her, straighten out his head. It hadn't. But he could handle the idea that his desire for a woman could flare out of control. That was still within the parameters of an allowable relationship. Anything more was worrisome, and unfair to a woman who deserved more from a man than being relegated to a few days' break in his travels.

The truly ironic part of this was that the bonding with her he'd felt so strongly that night had been all one-sided. Tara knew nothing of it. She'd been out cold at the time.

A child's shout interrupted Kent's musings.

"Ama! Ama!" Jigme came running across the roof.

The little boy had spent much of his time here studying with Songtsen and the monks. Because, Kent guessed, the high lama wanted the men of Yonten-La to remember that they'd once met the Gendun Lama. He was sure Songtsen recognized the psychological importance of impressing upon them that the boy was real, and that someday, as a man, he would return to the land of his birth. The monks' awareness of the child's identity posed no threat to the boy. They took their religion so seriously that every one of them would sooner die than betray the Gendun Lama.

"*Ama.*" The child held out a piece of candy. "For you." Tara wasn't all that keen on eating the sticky, yellow sweet offered from a small, none-too-clean hand, but she wasn't about to hurt the boy's feelings.

"Thank you, Jigme," she said, popping the treat into her mouth. "It's delicious."

Jigme, no doubt in concert with the cook, often brought her special treats from the kitchen to tempt her appetite. Quite unnecessarily, since she'd awakened from her long sleep with a voracious hunger.

Songtsen appeared at the entrance to the terrace and walked slowly over to one of the stools placed near Tara's bench. The effort of climbing two flights of stairs had evidently tired him, but he didn't sit down. He waited until Kent had helped Tara to the bench. Only then did the high lama bow to her and lower himself to the stool. Kent remained standing, while Jigme scampered off to inspect the flowers.

Songtsen's kind old face crinkled in a smile. "You are better today, Tara?"

"Yes, Rimpoche. I'm making good progress."

"The warm sun will speed your recovery. And tomorrow will bring a special pleasure to all of us. It is a festival day. A time for young people like you and Kent to enjoy yourselves. The villagers will be coming for a celebration of worship to Kali."

"Kali!" Tara said. "But I thought she was a terrifying goddess. In the old days, weren't some of her devotees killers?"

"It is so. In India, Kali is a fearsome, death-dealing deity, but here in Tibet Kali shows her most benevolent side. In Yonten-La we venerate her as the goddess of lovers. You must stay hidden, of course, but if you wish you can watch the ceremonies from the screened gallery near your rooms."

Yonten-La blazed with lights. Thousands of twinkling butter lamps dotted the surrounding hills. Strange musical horns, so long they had to be supported on wooden stands, droned deep, sustained notes into the valley. The ritual in the chamber two stories below them had been going on for hours. On a flower-strewn platform, a six-foot-tall painted statue of Kali ingeniously carved from butter had been ceremoniously carried into the center of the room. The powerful, multiarmed goddess, depicted with flexed knee and bent foot frozen in one moment of her eternal dance, rested amid huge urns of burning incense and juniper boughs.

A line of priests in colorful antique costumes of appliquéd silk, and wearing ornate painted headmasks portraying their old gods, snaked around the divine image. Their stately, sacred dance, more than a performance for the worshipers, was intended to ward off evil. A prayer, Tara thought, the fugitives could surely use.

The alien harmonics of the monks' sonorous chant sent chills down Tara's spine. Although she couldn't understand much of the ritual, she deeply respected the ancient religious practices these people struggled to retain in the face of the authorities' outright hostility toward them.

She felt curiously drawn to the ritual. Perhaps because she, too, was wearing one of the monastery's treasured antiques. Her magnificent long-sleeved gown of dark green silk had once belonged to a princess whose ruling class had been swept away by the Chinese takeover. Tara wondered if the princess had ever sat, as she did now, in back of the carved wooden screen designed to allow members of the nobility to watch the proceedings below without being subjected to the curious stares of the commoners.

Kent's long legs were folded onto a cushion beside her straight-backed, red-lacquered chair. In honor of the occasion, the abbot had personally delivered to the protector of the Gendun Lama a princely *chuba* of heavy gold brocade that enhanced Kent's dark good looks. He'd left the diagonal fastening undone; only the silver belt hooked low on his hips held the garment closed, and when he bent forward the stiff fabric stood away from his body. Tara couldn't help but catch glimpses of the black curly hair outlining the squared planes of his chest.

For several minutes he'd seemed less interested in the ceremony than in perusing her face. "I wish I could see your hair the way it is naturally."

"I think these black braids are very becoming. They're uncomfortable to sleep on, but I'm getting used to that."

"They're attractive enough, but your bright hair is softer and it suits you so well."

The music stopped. A hush came over the crowd. Tara intentionally transferred her attention from Kent to the floor below. As the dancers slowly moved off, a group of monks and chanting, praying worshipers bore another huge butter sculpture into the room.

"They're bringing Kali's lover to her," Kent explained. The bearers of Kali's consort circled the goddess before setting his elaborately bedecked platform down before her. "The goddess and her lover will spend the night together sharing the Great Bliss." Kent had leaned close to her in order to be heard over the loud music. His quiet, deep voice caressed her ears. "In the morning the sculptures the monks have worked on for weeks will be taken out to melt into each other in a consuming fire."

Melt into each other. The phrase and Kent's intonation of it wove themselves around and around her thickening brain. She was all too tantalizingly aware of his hand on her knee, of the imprints of his palm and each one of his fingers. His nearness, more than the erotic symbolism of the scene being played out by the worshipers, made her heart thump erratically. And looking into the black depths of his eyes dizzied her more than did the heavy, musky incense wafting up to her nose.

The light drumming of his fingers on her knee in time to the slow beat of the music resonated through her pelvis like the pounding of a big bass drum.

It was sheer idiocy to want him. Only a masochist would become any more entangled with a man bound to leave her soon. Now, more than ever, she wished she could stop wanting him. But no matter how hard she tried to dismiss her dream as the product of a sick woman's wandering mind, she knew it held a truth. The truth that she—like people whose hearts stopped temporarily on an operating table—had moved partway into death. Like many others revived after a near-death experience, she'd fought for life and won. And she'd done so because of Kent.

She was in love with him.

She'd resisted facing that truth. Finally having the courage to admit it to herself brought a kind of relief. She'd known from the first that it would be stupid to allow her attraction for him to go any further. But all the logic in the world hadn't prevented it. She loved him.

That love should be driving her quickly into his arms. It wasn't. The way she felt about him made it painful to be forced to settle for no more than the simple sexual encounter he offered. She needed so much more from him. She wanted what he'd plainly told her he wouldn't give. She longed to hear him return the vow of forever she was so ready to offer him.

He squeezed her knee. "Tara."

She jerked her gaze away from him. "Jigme's down there, Kent." She heard herself speaking too loudly and lowered her voice. "See? He's sitting on the floor next to the abbot and Songtsen. Do you think it's safe?"

"Safe enough." She could sense his gaze remaining fixed on her face while she looked away. "The monks aren't calling attention to the boy in any way," he noted. "There are many children around. I'm sure that to the villagers Jigme's just another kid."

Kent's hand was moving slowly over the silk covering her thigh, provoking a tingling excitement in the rest of her that she didn't want to feel. "B-but one of them m-might have ties to the Chinese. We don't know."

The strange, exotic music rose in intensity. When Kali's consort had made his appearance, a group of women near the statue of the goddess had begun to sway. Now their whirling dance was becoming wilder and their cries more abandoned.

"Tara." The way Kent spoke her name told her he recognized her continuing evasion and demanded that she look at him. Slowly she turned to him. His heavy-lidded

eyes darkened with passion he made no effort to hide as his
hand spasmodically kneaded her thigh. "Tara," he murmured. "Come."

He stood and took her hand.

"Come." No more than a whisper, his gravelly command vanquished the tumult from the chamber below. She
was powerless to resist. Whatever warnings her mind threw
in her way, her body was already tuned to follow his lead.

"Come." With the lightest of touches he drew her to
him. Behind the shadowing screen, he took her into his
arms. She lifted her arms up and around his neck. On a
sigh of mingled defeat and anticipation, she surrendered
her mouth to his plunging tongue.

The pleasure rushing over her crowded out all thought.
Her heart filled with a yearning for his love as fierce as the
desire tightening her lungs and the raw need swelling within
her feminine core. His mouth remained welded to hers as
he carried her down the hall.

He set her down in the center of the room where the tiny
flames of dozens of butter lamps shimmered over the
lovemaking figures on the wall and set them into lifelike
movement.

As if the satisfaction of plundering her mouth had taken
little of the edge off his desire, Kent bracketed her face
with gentle hands and dropped soft, delicate kisses on her
eyes, her nose, her cheeks. One by one he pulled from their
loops the jeweled buttons angling across her dress from
neckline to underarm and brushed the soft fabric from her
shoulders. Her bent elbows held the light fabric draped
around her waist.

His hands moved at first reverently and then with increasing familiarity over her breasts, sending waves of delight quivering through her. "Lord, but you're beautiful,"
he murmured in a husky voice.

She was thinking the very same thing about him. The
golden threads woven through his robe glinted in the light,
entering him in a glittering web. And the black-agate
pupils of his eyes reflected the small, wavering flames of
the nearest candles. This night would be all she'd ever have

of him, but she determined to make the most of it. Slowly
she straightened her arms. With a whisper of silk, the gown
rippled down her body to the floor.

Her lips hovered teasingly at the center of his collar
bone as she unfastened the silver buckle at his hips and let
the belt drop. His robe fell open, revealing the burnished
glow of tanned skin. Like her, he wore nothing beneath his
robe. When they'd made love at the mountain, his body
had been hidden in shadow. She wanted to see him in the
light.

Her hands traveled slowly upward over his chest, pushing aside the golden fabric. A flick of her fingers tumbled
the brocade from his shoulders and the stiff material piled
around his feet. Her eyes feasted on the beauty of a male
body the trek had left steel hard and whipcord lean. The
fullness of his need for her thrust forward as proudly as did
the maleness of Kali's sculpted lover. She slid her hands
from Kent's shoulders to his taut midriff, and lower. When
her fingers closed gently around him, he gasped and
clutched at her arms.

His arms went around her, and she could feel the tension in him as if he were striving to keep his embrace from
hurting her. On fire for him, she wanted no cautious, controlled lovemaking.

"You don't have to be so careful of me, Kent. Don't
worry, I won't break." To let him know that she wanted
him the way he'd been at the mountain—passionate and
almost mindless in his need for her—she wound her arms
tightly around his neck and brazenly burrowed against
him, crushing her breasts against his chest and burying her
nipples in its soft, curly mat.

As she'd hoped, her wanton provocation unleashed his
hunger. With a groan he spread his hands wide and moved
them over her bottom, finally cupping it to lift her off the
floor. She drew up one leg and then the other to cage his
hips.

A few steps brought him to the bed where he laid her on
the fur spread and knelt between her thighs. His hot, wet
mouth burned over her whole body, catapulting her into

azzle of sensation and turning her sensitive center to a
aolten core. Awash in a sea of exquisite sensation, she
rove to return to him everything he was giving her—and
aore. Locked in a mating as sacred as the gloriously sex-
al dance played out on the walls around them, she let slip
ae last reins of reason and abandoned herself utterly to
im.

Kent worked to hold back the fire threatening to con-
ame him. Making love to this woman was like learning a
ew language. A language of cherishing, of tenderness, of
agaging in a deeper, more intimate communication. He'd
aspected that because of what had happened to him with
er that first night in Yonten-La, their lovemaking this
me would be different. And it was. This time losing him-
lf in her was propelling him into uncharted territory a
art of him was loathe to enter. But all choice had been
arn from him. Rocked by need, he buried himself deep
ithin her warm, welcoming womanhood.

Tara heard Kent moaning her name over and over like a
aantra. The driving rhythm of the haunting ritual music
choed through the room, counting cadence to his thrusts
s he pulsed within her.

I love you. I love you. The words throbbed through her
ind. Before they could reach her lips, she shattered into
thousand pieces, each tiny bit a mirror reflecting the man
ho gripped her so tightly in his arms.

An eternity later, she became conscious of those arms
ill circling her, though loosely, as she gathered up all the
agments of her self. Again and again they turned to each
her, in gentleness, in wonder, in frenzy, never noticing
hen the music and the chanting slackened off and died
vay. Downstairs, the image of Kali, resting silent and
otionless in mystic union with her consort, benignly ac-
pted the homage paid her by the two foreign lovers un-
er her roof.

Hundreds of miles away from the monastery of Yon-
n-La, Colonel Wu Chen's stubby fingers trailed across
e lower half of the large military map of Xizang tacked

to the wall in back of his desk. Yonten. Yes. There it was
Apparently no more than a tiny village at a place he'
never heard of. The map did not show a pass there
"Yonten-La" did mean "the pass at Yonten," but Xizan
was full of "la's." He needed to know if this "la" indi
cated an unknown pass out of China. The place was far t
the west. It didn't seem likely that soft Americans woul
choose to make their escape that way. Still, it was possibl
that the boy had been sent there. The nearest garrison wa
at Sa-Ga Dzong, he noted. At the colonel's command,
squad of troops at the large camp piled into two armore
personnel carriers and hurried to find and investigate th
hidden valley of Yonten-La.

Chapter 14

An uncomfortable chill skittered down Tara's body. Sleepily she sought the fur throw to pull it over her. But it wasn't close at hand and she didn't have the energy to wake up fully and sit up to recover the blanket from the foot of the bed where she could feel it at her toes. A snatch of memory of the night's magic snaked into her sluggish mind and a much more pleasant solution to the problem of the morning's chill presented itself.

She wriggled over a little, meaning to snuggle into Kent's warmth. Instead of encountering a comfortable masculine body, she felt the edge of the bed. Mumbling a soft objection she sluggishly heaved herself onto her side and pulled open reluctant eyelids. Her unfocused gaze contained only a few guttering candles.

Pushing her herself up on an elbow, she brushed a couple of black braids from her eyes and looked around the bed. She was alone. A huge sense of disappointment blasted with growing outrage swept over her. After last night's glorious lovemaking, the least she'd expected from Kent was a little morning sensitivity. But evidently he didn't share her lingering afterglow. The man couldn't

even slow down long enough to stay in her bed until s
woke up.

The room smelled of stale candle smoke, and a gr
morning light filtered through the draperies to flatten
self on the washed-out colors of the back wall. The co
breeze that stirred the white panels at the doorway pr
voked another chill and she reached down for the thro
A vivid memory of the lovely warmth Kent had provid
when he'd covered her with the heated blanket of his bo
pushed into her mind. That pulled up another picture
him resting his head on her breast. Under the barrage
unwanted but still arousing scenes parading through h
mind, she discarded her plan to lie in bed for a while.

Her gown still lay in a crumpled heap on the floor whe
she'd kicked it aside before surrendering herself to Kent
arms last night. She slid out from under the cover ar
scurried over, naked and shivering, to pick up the ga
ment. She clutched the wrinkled silk in front of her whe
Kent, fully dressed, swatted away the draperies and stro
into the room.

His eyes darkened when they lit on her. "Good mor
ing," he murmured. His fingers trailed slowly over h
naked shoulder, evoking a tremble that had nothing to
with the cold. "I let you sleep as long as I could. After la
night I thought you could use the rest." The softness of h
smile, she assumed, had less to do with his seeing her tha
it did with his memory of the long hours of pleasure she
given him.

Her unwarranted expectations about Kent were h
problem, Tara reminded herself, not his. She had no i
tention of staging a replay of the incident in Kenya whe
an unsophisticated young college student had mistaken
male tour guide's acceptance of what she'd offered as
sign of his love. When the affair ended with the trek, tl
girl had been devastated, and Tara had been left to de
with the young woman's tears and recriminations. She
refused to fire the guide, one of her best, but ordered hi
to keep his amorous excursions confined to women wl
knew the score.

As she did.

She'd always known that ultimately Kent would go his way and she hers. A little late now to demonstrate any regrets that she'd never have more of him than a few nights of admittedly wonderful lovemaking. More than a little foolish to wish the man who'd come to mean so much to her might actually return her love. She was a grown-up and knew that wishes didn't always come true.

"About last night," she said, forcing herself to step out from under his hand, "which by the way, you were very good at." No more than the truth, she admitted, hoping he hadn't heard the little catch in her voice. "I'm sure you know it happened because of the music... and the incense..." She waved vaguely at their surroundings. "And the general erotic atmosphere around here."

One dark male brow shot upward. "Did it?"

"What else? I'm not naive enough to believe it signaled any great change in your thinking—or mine, either, for that matter." She struggled to keep her voice as dispassionate as possible. He hadn't deliberately set out to hurt her. "It's not as if either of us is about to make any silly noises about...about forever...or love...or anything like that."

Kent's eyes flashed dark fire and his hand shot out to grab the silk she was using to shield herself. For a moment she thought he might rip it from her. Then he stepped away.

"Get dressed," he ordered. "Put on your nomad clothes. The monks are loading the pack animals, and we're just about ready to leave."

"Leave?" Tara echoed, surprised.

"Yes. The high lama sent for me early this morning. At the ceremonies last night the abbot received reports that the Chinese have been rounding up nomads."

"Rounding up nomads." Her ambiguous relationship with the wandering photographer had to be relegated to second place as their basic problem of getting out of China again thrust itself front and center. "That's not good. It

sounds as if our Colonel Wu has discovered that we'r
traveling in disguise.''

"Perhaps. But the villagers said that the soldiers wer
most interested in questioning nomads about the exis
tence of secret passes like the one here.'' Kent's mouth
hardened into a grim line. "There are even reports of tor
ture.''

Tara gasped. "Oh, my God, Kent. People are bein,
tortured because of us? We can't let that go on.''

"I agree. If I were alone I'd...'' His hands clenche
around the handle of the knife at his waist. "But we hav
more than ourselves to think of—there's the boy and th
old man. The best thing we can do for everyone is to ge
the hell out of Tibet as quickly as possible. We've got to ge
through that pass before the authorities find out about i
and show up here. I'm sorry, Tara. I'd hoped you'd hav
a few more days to recuperate before we had to get back or
the road, but it's not working out that way. Do you thin
you're well enough to ride?''

"I'll manage.'' Right now the weakness she felt in he
limbs had less to do with her injuries than it did the nigh
of strenuous lovemaking with Kent. "As you say, we hav
no choice.''

"You'd better put a little more dye on your face an
hands,'' he advised. "The color is wearing off in places
And there's a ring of red hair showing around your face.'

Tara nodded. "I'll do what I can, but I don't have muc
makeup lotion left.''

"With any luck, you won't need much more. From wha
Songtsen has told me, once we trek through this pass we'
be free of Chinese patrols—or of anyone else, for tha
matter—all the rest of the way through to Nepal.''

Kent turned and made for the door. At the chapel en
trance he swiped back the curtain and looked enigmati
cally at her over his shoulder. "By the way, your commen
about me being good last night? I'm flattered, but I'd hav
said we were pretty good together.'' The cotton panel fe
behind him and swung back and forth as she listened to th
sound of his footsteps fade away down the corridor.

She threw the silk gown on the bed and retrieved her black skirt and top from the chest where a monk had packed her things away after cleaning. A half hour later she hurried down the steps at a side entrance to find preparations for putting the little party of fugitives back on the trail almost complete. The monks had replaced Songtsen's lost belongings. They'd even made him a gift of another book of scripture, which he was fastening securely to the saddle's high seat back.

In the main courtyard a group of the pious chanted before the dying flames of the holy fires consuming the last remnants of the butter sculptures. She hadn't been up when the final festival rituals had begun.

The monks turned toward Tara and bowed as she approached, and Jigme stopped whacking at his *chibi* to run to her. The beauty and serenity of Yonten-La had almost made her forget that the child—and all of them—remained in grave danger. But the worry that clearly gripped everyone in the courtyard now descended on her in force once more.

"Good morning, Rimpoche," she said.

"Good morning, Tara. I'm sorry that you must so soon resume the ordeals of travel. Kent has told you the disheartening news?"

She nodded.

The smile that had creased the old man's leathery face on greeting her departed as he looked worriedly down the valley. "Even without the increased efforts of the Chinese to find us, we dared not linger here much longer. The gods were kind in granting us fine weather for the ceremonies but it cannot last. And another storm like the last one could close the pass."

"I know. And I'm quite ready to leave." That was truer than the lama knew. Maybe when she'd put the magical atmosphere of Yonten-La behind, she'd be better able to maintain a more realistic outlook on her feelings for Kent.

After Kent had helped Tara mount her horse, Songtsen and the abbot were assisted to their saddles. Their guide, a man from the village who would help the fugitives thread

the difficult passage across the trackless frontier, took the
lead, followed by two of the abbot's assistants.

The pungent smoke from burning butter wafted through
the valley as they wound their way down from the monastery. Jigme showed no disinclination to be back on the
road, skipping down the trail and playing catch with himself. Tara thought the child a particularly adventurous
youngster. And fortunately one who adapted easily to
changing circumstances. Maybe the special life fate had
carved out for the boy was the right one for him after all.

The pass to the south was doubly hidden. Not many
strangers would ever locate the cleft in the rock that led to
the monastery itself. And certainly no motorized vehicle
would ever make it up the trail, let alone through the narrow opening. When Chinese troops finally located Yonten-La, they'd have to march in on foot and then search
the valley for the well-hidden entrance to the pass.

No wonder the pass at Yonten-La had for so long remained a secret, Tara marveled. She'd been carefully
looking for its entrance and still hadn't been able to locate
it. Until the abbot pointed it out to them, neither she nor
Kent had noticed that in one spot the base of the massif
that formed one wall of the valley had folded back on itself like a pleat. The small gap at the bottom of the fold
was barely high enough to let her through. Kent had to
bend low over his saddle to make it.

After a few minutes the long, womblike cavern they'd
entered gave onto the meager daylight of an oppressively
narrow, steep-sided canyon. For several hours the entire
party trailed through the crevasse that zigzagged ever
higher through the dark, ice-streaked granite cliffs loom-
ing above them. Tara peered up from the deeply shad-
owed fissure in which they rode to the slash of blue sky in
the opening so high above them and wondered if she was
the only one feeling claustrophobic.

Apparently not, because her companions spoke little
and only in low tones. For long stretches the only sounds
to be heard were the complaining moans of the yaks and
the clip-clops of the horses echoing from the confining

walls. Whenever a few stones clattered down from above, all eyes anxiously flicked upward to learn whether the small rockfall was a portent of anything more ominous.

When the guide had led them into yet another dogleg around the rock, he came to an abrupt halt, and Kent's hand shot warningly into the air. Tara kneed her horse forward next to his to find out what was holding up their progress. A cry of dismay escaped her lips when she saw that just ahead of them a massive avalanche had crashed down to the canyon floor. Tons of snow and rock totally blocked the pass. She needed no more than one glance to know that their single unguarded escape route from China had been slammed shut and locked tight.

The Tibetan guide hurried back to the abbot and delivered the verdict already clear to all of them. "The villager says we cannot pass," Songtsen translated. "He says that this has happened before and that in the spring the snow will melt and he will try to find a way over the rock pile." The high lama also reported that the abbot had quickly voiced his willingness to continue hiding the fugitives until spring.

"Until spring," Kent repeated. "Thank the abbot for us, Rimpoche, but we can't wait that long. Every hour we stay in this area we risk discovery by searching Chinese troops. Eventually they're bound to find Yonten-La. And it will go very badly for the monks and the villagers if we're still here when they do."

Slowly the party turned and made their dispirited way back. "There's no safety for any of us anywhere in Tibet," Kent said when they'd once again broken into the fading green of the valley. "We've got to get out."

Songtsen shook his head dubiously. "The only way left to us poses great danger. The main pass lies over a hundred miles farther west and its checkpost is manned by troops."

Tara seconded Kent's assessment of their situation. "What other choice do we have, Rimpoche? It's kind of the abbot to offer to hide us, but we can't possibly stay at Yonten-La through the winter. Except for my injuries, we would already have been long gone from here."

"But the guards, Kent," Songtsen protested. "There is no way around the guards. Perhaps it would be wisest for us to wait. The boy may get by at the checkpost. He is Tibetan, and border-crossing permits can be obtained for Tibetans. We must be realistic. It is one thing for the Chinese to see you and the Tara from a distance. I doubt if either of you can fool a soldier who gets a good look at your Western features. And you can be sure the guards are now carefully checking the papers of everyone who passes."

"I haven't figured out any way around that yet," Kent admitted. "But as Tara says, we've got no other choice. We face danger whether we go or we stay. Personally, if I'm to end up a Chinese captive, I'd rather go down fighting to make it to freedom than sit around waiting for the army to come and haul me away."

"I feel the same way, Rimpoche," Tara agreed in a tone as decisive as Kent's.

"It's a different matter for you and the boy, Songtsen," Kent added. "The monks can hide you two more effectively than they can Tara and me. Perhaps it would be safer for you to stay here and get Jigme out later when the track becomes passable. If we make it out, I promise that come spring I'll be waiting for you in Nepal with American visas for both of you."

From his saddle, Songtsen gave Kent a deep, respectful bow. "Your courage shames me, Kent Masterson. And your words about not waiting for our enemies to find us remind me that we must continue to place our trust in Buddha. Your strong spirit—the same spirit that brought your grandfather to Tibet—is why you were chosen to be the child's protector. I am content to leave the matter in your hands. The abbot has suggested we return to the monastery for the night. What is your wish?"

"There's no point in returning to the monastery. I vote we keep right on going."

No vote was required. All acknowledged that Kent was the commander of their little troop.

The long bilingual discussion concerning their fate hadn't interested the boy all that much. Jigme had just continued batting around his feathered ball. Now, noticing that the group was again ready to move, he glanced at Tara quizzically. "We go, *Ama?*"

"We go, Jigme."

The prayers of the monks of Yonten-La faded on the wind as the four, Jigme seated in front of Kent on the horse, made their way through the oval-shaped entrance to the valley and continued down the coiling track to find the main trail west. Once on that trail, the mountains herded them like wild animals into a pen toward the only opening left them.

The mood of the little group was noticeably different from their generally upbeat spirits on the trek to Yonten-La and safety. This time they were heading directly for a confrontation with Chinese troops. And although, to keep the boy from worrying, none of the adults spoke of their apprehension, Tara was sure the others shared hers.

As they came down the upper reaches of the Tsang Po, a long caravan of yaks trailed across their path. The beasts carried bales of wool to market, to be traded for rice and barley and supplies to last through the winter. If the shearing was particularly good, there might be enough to purchase a luxury item like one of the music tapes that had laid the groundwork for the help they'd received from the Qinghai miners.

The fugitives gave the caravan a wide berth, as they did the sheep-driving nomad group they came upon the following day. The four kept apart to avoid revealing themselves, but one of the vicious mongrels accompanying the herd spotted the intruders and raced across the stony ground toward them.

Before Kent could move to stop him, Jigme leaped down from the horse and ran at the dog, shouting and waving his stick. Whether as a result of the dog's training not to attack a child, or the fact that the boy's stick landed sharply on his snout, the animal turned at its owner's commanding whistle and headed back to its place in the herd.

Tara quickly slid from her horse and hurried after Kent to the boy. "Jee-mee not afraid of *kyee*," the child announced, grinning broadly. Maybe he wasn't afraid of these Tibetan mongrels, but she was. Frightened for the boy, she'd watched the worrisome scene with her heart in her mouth.

Neither she nor Kent returned the boy's grin. "Maybe not, sport," Kent said sharply. "But you're not to do such a thing again. Do you understand? *Hoko song nay?*"

His Holiness the Gendun Lama wasn't accustomed to hearing rebukes of his actions, but he took this one with good grace and hung his head sheepishly. *"Hoko song."*

Kent went down on one knee beside the child. "The Gendun Lama is important to his people," he said in a milder tone. "And must take care of himself. But also we don't want our Jimmy to get hurt."

"Jee-mee no more tell *kyee* go away, Missa Massaton," the boy promised.

"Good." Kent curled his big hand around the boy's tousled black head and gave it an affectionate shake. "Look. One of the yaks is wandering off. Can you fetch it back?"

The child instantly took to his heels after the errant beast.

Kent might consider himself a lone wolf with no interest in developing ties to keep him from the constant travel he loved, Tara pondered. But she'd observed before now that he was forging strong bonds between himself and Jigme. And the little Tibetan boy was weaving delicate strands of his own to hold the man in one spot for at least part of the time. That developing relationship, she was convinced, would prove to be as good for the American rover as it was for the child torn from his family and country.

The trail took them down to levels where the climate was milder so they only needed to break out the tent when rain threatened. Fast travel was now their main priority, and that meant unpacking as little as possible. At night Tara lay a few feet away from Kent and tried to keep from thinking about a tomorrow with him that would never come.

He never broached the subject of their relationship or of what it might mean other than the obvious strong sexual attraction between them. And she was no longer even sure how strong that attraction remained. Since leaving Yonten-La Kent seemed to be going out of his way not to touch her. She'd known men for whom the pursuit of a woman provided the major thrill. After the conquest they lost interest. She hadn't judged Kent to be that kind of man, but maybe she was wrong.

Whatever his unspoken feelings toward her, her own toward him were clear. If they did overcome the odds and make it through, she wanted to stay with him forever, though she knew her forever with Kent would last only a few more days. Then either they'd find themselves in the hands of the Chinese or they'd be free. Either way their time together would be over.

The little group was sitting around their dung fire when Jigme cuddled into Tara's lap. "Jee-mee come visit *Ama* and Missa Massaton in tent in Amayriga?" he piped up.

"We don't live in tents in America, Jigme," Tara explained. "We live in houses."

"Houses like Lhasa?"

"Well, something like those."

"Jee-mee come live in house of *Ama* and Missa Massaton?"

Tara lifted a brow in Kent's direction to let him know he was to field that one.

"Tara and I don't live in a house together, Jigme. I mean, Tara has a house and I have a house, but it's not the same house."

"You have two house?"

"Uh, yes." Kent decided that trying to explain to the boy about the New York condo and the London flat in addition to the Philadelphia mansion the child would visit would be too confusing.

"Two house." Jigme looked impressed. "You rich, *Ama*."

"Missa . . . uh, Mr. Masterson is rich. I'm not."

"You have house, you rich," Jigme returned flatly. "You have childs with Missa Massaton?"

"No, Jigme. Mr. Masterson and I don't have children."

"My brother has two boys you can play with," Kent interjected hurriedly as if anxious to get off the subject of his and Tara's nonexistent offspring. "When you're not studying with your own people, you'll be staying with them."

The little boy's downturned mouth indicated his unhappiness with this situation. He looked at Songtsen for explanation. But either the lama was as deeply into his meditations as he seemed, or he was letting Kent and Tara work their own way out of the sticky situation.

Jigme scrambled out of Tara's lap. With determination written clearly in the pushed-out lower lip and the fixed stare of the bright black eyes, he stood boldly in front of Kent.

"I want stay with you and *Ama.*"

Kent whipped out an arm and pulled the child down over his knees. "Hey, sport. I want to stay with you, too. Don't worry about it. We'll work something out."

"While you're working that out," Tara said, "can you work me into some of those visits? I want to stay in touch with Jigme. He's come to mean an awful lot to me." The little fellow had given her a taste of what it would be like to have a child of her own. She enjoyed being with her nieces and nephews of course, but there'd never been any question of her actually playing a mother role with them. Those kids had real mothers. This endearing little guy had only her.

Over the child's small, wriggling body, Kent sent her a long look she couldn't fathom.

"I've been thinking about that, too, Tara. The kid has fixed his need for a mother figure on you. He's already given up one mother—we can't have him losing two. Back in the States, we'll stay in touch."

Stay in touch, she thought. Not exactly a vow of forever. But she'd have to be content with Kent's small romise.

The boy's happy shriek cut off that depressing line of ought. Evidently Jigme, with his boundless energy, was ady for some roughhousing. His arms whirling like little indmills, he tumbled over Kent like a puppy over its sire, hile Kent tried, not very hard, to fend him off.

Songtsen, she noticed, had come out of his meditaons. His long look jolted Tara with its puzzling intenty. In a moment the lama transferred his attention to the rown man playing laughingly with the little boy. He gave e scene a slight nod of approval before withdrawing into imself again. Almost as if, Tara thought, some plan of e rimpoche's was working out just as he'd intended. Alost as if he'd already passed the child completely into ent's hands.

The old man had done so a little too early, she thought, onsidering he was going to Nepal with them. And there as no reason he couldn't continue on with them to the 'nited States. With her contact in the intelligence comunity and Kent's family ties to the diplomatic corps, they ould easily get the priest a visa. But there was no point in ringing up the subject before finding out if they were all end up in the hands of the Americans or the Chinese.

Not long after dark both Tibetans curled up near the ying fire while Kent poured himself and Tara another owl of the salty tea she'd learned to enjoy.

Tara's gaze wandered beyond the fire to where the child y sleeping. "Kent?" she ventured in a tone that couldn't e heard by the others. "Do you believe in reincarnation? o you think it's possible that cute little boy could really e another incarnation of a man who first lived four undred years ago?"

"Damned if I know, Tara." Kent's thoughtful look sted on the child. "A couple of months ago I'd have anwered with a resounding no. But after living awhile in this credible place, walking in the shadow of these majestic ountains, learning more about Songtsen and Jigme's re-

ligion, I'm not as sure as I used to be—'' his dark glan
flicked back to her "—about a lot of things.''

"That's how I feel, too. To me Jigme's just a darlir
child, but sometimes..." She gave a puzzled little laug
"Sometimes I've almost caught a glimpse of something
his eyes. I don't know...an acceptance...a wisdom b
yond his years..." She trailed off, unsure of her ov
thoughts.

"Who can say for sure, Tara? For certain, Jigme's
very special child. Songtsen wants the boy to grow up
home in both Tibetan and Western cultures. These peop
have a centeredness, a wholeness about their lives th
many back home might envy. It wouldn't surprise me
find that when the little guy does become a man, he ar
the culture he represents may have something of gre
value to offer the rest of us.''

If the Chinese waiting for them at the border gave t
boy the chance, Tara added silently. Strangely, even wit
everything that had happened to her since arriving
Lhasa—even facing whatever might happen to her at t
checkpost—she didn't regret taking on Elliott's mission.

By noon the next day they were nearing the end of the
long, hard journey. They'd climbed up and over the fin
high pass leading down to the southern edge of the T
betan plateau and straggled to a halt within sight of t
border town that was their final destination. To the north
out of sight on a great empty plain, lay the great twin lake
forming the gateway to the sacred mountain.

When Kent dismounted, Tara did too. As she stoo
looking into the distance at the small, dusty town tha
would decide their fate, her mouth went dry. Maybe Ker
had sensed the tightening of her stomach muscles becaus
he threw back his shoulders and announced in a stron
voice, "Look, everyone. I want you all to realize that w
do stand a chance—I can't honestly claim it's a very stron
chance—but some chance of making this.

"We have a couple of things going for us. First is tha
very few individual Western tourists are given permits t
travel to this area. I only got mine originally because the

were anxious for me to bring out my book on Tibet and so were willing to bend the rules a little."

Songtsen and Tara were listening to Kent attentively. Jigme was more interested in watching the herd of antelope grazing in the distance.

"Even CITS groups are discouraged from entering or leaving Tibet from this part of the country," Kent continued. "That means that neither the guards nor the people down there expect to see any Westerners, so we won't show them any. At this time of year the place is crowded with nomads and traders and pilgrims anxious to make their meals or their walks around Kailas before winter clamps down on the passes."

Kent pointed to the part of the village nestled against the base of the mountain across a narrow river whose edges showed a bit of green. Several cave dwellings were carved into the gray cliffs above the few squat, whitewashed houses jumbled haphazardly along the riverbank.

"Look at all the tents pitched there. The town is jammed with strangers. We'll just be four more. So let's all try to keep our wits about us. There's no reason to suppose the authorities in this particular town have set up a stringent watch for us. We'll just strut on down there looking for all the world as if we belong."

Apparently Jigme had caught the drift of Kent's last words. "*Ama* not look like my people," he pointed out with a child's directness. "You face different. You eyes different. You not look like me and Rimpoche."

"The kid's got a point, Tara," Kent conceded. "This is where the color of your eyes will present a real problem. Try as much as possible to keep them lowered. If a soldier gets a look at green eyes, that'll be it. And can you put a little more of that dye on your face before we hit the town?"

"I'm afraid not. It's all gone."

"Well..." He shrugged. "Then we'll just have to go with what we've got." Kent looked at the tense faces around him and broke into a grin. Perhaps a little forced, Tara thought, but still a grin.

"Hey, tour group," he said jokingly. "One last though before we get this show on the road. These rolls of film I'm carrying will make some dynamite photographs. Maybe should send Colonel Wu Chen a thank-you note for invit ing me to take this trek. I've been able to get some fantas tic shots of places I otherwise would never have seen. Since the Chinese went to so much trouble to help me get thos photos, I want the world to see them. So, by golly, we'r going to get ourselves and that film out of here."

Kent's attempt to send them off on a positive note with a bit of humor made Tara return his grin with a lightnes she didn't really feel. "And don't forget," she said as Ken helped her remount. "I've got the film of their secret con struction site. Colonel Wu will never forgive me if I don' let the world know what wonders they're performing ou there in the Qinghai wilderness."

"Right." Kent swung himself back into the saddle. "I'n sure the colonel will be thrilled to see those picture splashed across the front pages. All right, folks. Are w ready?"

Jigme looked confused. But ever ready to agree with Kent, the boy shouted "Yah!" and skipped on ahead.

"Ready." Tara nodded. Songtsen's muttered praye answered for him.

Colonel Wu Chen cursed the underling who had de cided the marketplace gossip overheard in a remote tow wasn't important enough to rush to his superiors in Lhasa If the reports of Tibetan whispers that the goddess Tara had miraculously changed a Western woman into Tibetar had come in earlier, he could have figured out before nov that the nomad family who'd left Yonten-La before hi men had arrived there were in reality the disguised Amer ican spies, the boy and the damned high lama. Who coulc have guessed Songtsen would send the boy with the for eigners?

The colonel gnashed his teeth. At the time of his las verbal battle with the irritating priest, the boy very likely had been in hiding at the monastery. Perhaps he shoulc have foreseen that all the fugitives would be traveling together. All shared a common link with Songtsen. He'd made another mistake, Wu conceded to himself, if to no one else, in thinking he was dealing with two separate security cases. All along there'd been only one.

But now, for once, luck was working in his favor. The fugitives hadn't made it through the sealed pass—no longer a secret. That meant they'd be forced to deal with the main pass in the western part of the country. He'd already sent a message to the guards there to be on the lookout for an old man traveling with a six-year-old boy and two Westerners trying to pass for Tibetans.

The colonel mentally counted up the days since the fake Tibetan family had been seen leaving the monastery. He could make it, he thought as he strode toward his automobile for the short drive to the helicopter pad. Even with stopping at Sa-Ga Dzong for refuelling, the Z-9A would leave him in the western border area within a few hours. He would cut the traitors off in their bid to escape the punishment they so richly deserved.

Chapter 15

Besides the newer, uninteresting Chinese compound an
the poorer, half-destroyed Tibetan section, the tow
boasted several restaurants, a Chinese hospital and a newl
built guest house. Within a few weeks the dozens of tent
pitched on the riverbank would disappear, the hotel tout
ing hot showers would be virtually empty of customers and
the pilgrimage guides would retire to their village for th
winter. But for now, the streets of the border tow
thronged with people.

"Songtsen," Tara observed worriedly as they passed th
outskirts. "There are many Chinese here."

"Yes. But they mostly stay in their own compound or
the other side of the river. We will remain in the Tibetan
and Nepali sections where I will sell the animals and use the
money to purchase the necessary exit permits."

"I thought exit permits were only obtainable in Lhasa,'
Kent offered.

"For foreigners, yes. But there are men here who I hop
can help me. We will see what the gods provide." Appar
ently, Tara thought, the old man who seldom left hi
monastery had a network of contacts all over the country

that Roger Elliott himself would envy. "It is best if I go alone to the truck stops around the Tibetan market to arrange transportation. I will try to find places for our group in a bus, or more likely a truck."

The bazaar set up on the south side of the stream where they left Songtsen with the yaks and horses resounded with cries of men loading and unloading caravans of yaks, sheep and goats. Their earthy barnyard smells mingled with the delicious odor of grilling chicken wafting from a nearby open-air vendor's stall. Half a dozen women trailed in, lugging on their backs planks of lumber into the treeless area. Their heavy loads clapped to the ground not far from Kent, Tara and Jigme.

"Instead of standing out here in plain sight," Kent said, shepherding Tara and the child toward the nearest buildings, "we'd better find a less noticeable place to wait."

A Nepali trader called to the passing nomad family to inspect his bolts of colorful Indian cloth. Kent shooed the man away, and Tara remembered to look aside while shaking her head.

They stopped behind a low, whitewashed building across from a line of busy, canvas-roofed market stalls. While they were partially hidden from view, they were close enough to the meandering shoppers to seem part of the crowd.

The sun was disappearing behind a line of dark clouds that had managed to scrape over Himal's jagged peaks. Tara wasn't sure whether the approaching storm would help or hinder their escape. But the grayness descending on them certainly didn't inspire cheerful thoughts.

"I want to take a look around," Kent said. "You two stay here out of sight with our bags." Their packs had dwindled to Jigme's and Songtsen's smaller bags, Kent's camera bag, hidden inside a large woven Tibetan carryall, and her own tote, with its precious cargo of intelligence film. By now the bag was so scuffed and dirty no one could guess it had originated in an upscale American department store.

It was frustrating to know themselves so close to freedom, at least on the map.

Tara gasped as a man wearing the gutted carcass of a large goat over his head like a hat passed them. Following the goatman's progress down the narrow street, she noticed an elderly woman seated cross-legged behind a row of small bowls. Peering into a small round mirror, the woman was painting a bright yellow geometric design on her forehead to go with the red triangles on her cheeks. The woman's beauty regimen gave Tara an idea.

"Jigme," she said when it looked as if the woman had finished applying the local version of cosmetics. "Do you see that old lady down the alley?"

The boy stuck his head around the corner. "Grandmother make face pretty."

"Yes. Here, take this." Kent's gold watch had gone to buy their safety from the miners. She hoped her own much more moderately priced, leather-strapped timepiece would be enough to purchase the materials to fashion herself a mask. "Ask the woman if she'll trade the watch for those pots of colored sugar paste makeup." Tara rummaged in her bag for the lipstick she hadn't used in weeks and folded the silver tube into the boy's grubby little hand. "And she might be interested in this, too."

"Jigme do," he declared with enthusiastic nods. Evidently to the little boy, engaging in a bargaining session with a grandmother was more fun than just waiting around doing nothing.

Tara kept out of sight until the child returned from his successful foray, his short arms laden with bowls. He'd even managed to include the mirror in the trade. As Tara used her little finger to apply the sugar melted down with food dye and butter to form a paste, Jigme offered his critical suggestions for another blue circle here, an extra yellow squiggle there. Coating the half inch of red hair showing at her hairline with sticky black paste might not be authentic, but it did the job of hiding the telltale color.

Her mask was so effective that when Kent returned he did a double take before recognizing her.

"Clever idea, Tara. I've never seen a nomad woman with quite so much color on her face, but it works."

Songtsen was away so long all three were beginning to get worried that he'd been picked up by the police. With great relief, Tara finally spotted the old man wading toward them through a flock of sheep.

The lama, too, smiled when he saw Tara's transformation. "Ah! Good, Tara. But you must not forget that it is still of great importance to keep your eyes lowered."

"I'll try, Rimpoche." She'd already discovered that it was so ingrained for a person to continually glance around that it took great concentration on her part to keep her gaze modestly on the ground.

"I have purchased places in the back of a truck carrying Nepali pilgrims and a few Tibetans returning to their refugee village not far past the border."

"Good, Rimpoche," Kent said. "I'm afraid that what I have to report isn't quite as positive. Our chances of slipping by unobtrusively don't look as good as we'd hoped. I went down to watch the activity at the checkpoint for a while and the guards are scrutinizing everyone's papers. They're taking so much time with people, there's already a backup around the crossing." Kent made no mention of his suspicion that the guards had been specifically alerted about the four fugitives because they were paying particular attention to Tibetans.

Tara slipped her hand around the boy's head and drew him to her. Songtsen apparently refused to let Kent's news depress him. "There's still a chance, my son. Besides travel accommodations, I've obtained exit permits which are legitimate, not forgeries. They were issued to a real Tibetan family, and the guards will find no fault with them. But come now. We must hurry. The truck is ready to leave."

Kent hoisted the bags over his shoulder and Tara took the boy's hand. Songtsen carried his precious book. After he gave them each their papers, the fugitives proceeded toward the staging area not far from the barriered checkpoint manned by several uniformed Chinese. Halfway there the lowering clouds tore open, splattering people and animals with large, heavy drops of icy rain.

To protect her washable mask from the shower Tara pulled her checkered scarf low over her face. Caravan workers indifferent to the downpour kept on loading animals with piles of sheepskins or baled ropes of undyed wool. Everyone else dashed for the nearest tent or shop. Tara quickly relieved the lama of his book, and Kent took his arm to help him run toward their transport.

A group of Indian pilgrims were converging on an ancient, already crowded bus parked beside a couple of elderly trucks. Most of those seeking to cross the checkpost were on foot, many pushing two-wheeled carts or leading strings of pack animals. Some had broken out umbrellas. Others protected their heads from the drenching rain with plastic bags.

Songtsen pointed toward a truck whose passengers were already starting to clamber in. "This one."

"I've made a decision," Kent announced with quiet determination. "And I don't want to hear any arguments about it from anyone." Since his gaze was holding Tara's strongly in check, she understood that Kent was aiming his warning primarily at her. "You three get into the truck. I'm going to stay behind to stage a diversion when the guards begin to investigate this truck's passengers."

Tara's hand shot out to grab his arm. "No, Kent—"

"You not come, Missa Massaton?" Jigme sounded on the verge of tears.

Only the lama retained his usual air of calm. "No, my son. You will go now."

"Rimpoche, I promised my grandfather I'd get your religious treasure out of the country. I didn't make that promise lightly and I'll do whatever it takes to keep it. Surely you understand why some kind of diversion is necessary."

The lama nodded. The truck's motor chugged to life. The Nepali driver leaned out of the cab and hollered for his passengers to get in.

"Look, people." Kent's face took on an encouraging smile as he bent closer to them to be heard above the rain. "While I do plan to give the guards somebody other than you three to pay attention to, I don't intend to get caught doing it. Don't worry, I'll get out later."

"No way, Kent." Tara launched her protest immediately and with vehemence. "If you raise any kind of ruckus around here, you'll never get out. They'll catch you. You've got to come with us now." Oblivious to the cold rain, she thrust up her chin. "If you don't go, I don't go."

"Of course you'll go, Tara. You've got to. Think of the boy and the old man. They'll need an American to intercede for them at our embassy."

She was thinking only of Kent, and that she'd never see him again. Their chances of making it out together as a Tibetan family were slim. His chances of escaping alone once the guards had been alerted were virtually nonexistent.

"Kent, please. Don't do this." She could taste a hint of sweetness on her lips from the melting sugar paste trickling down her face.

Kent ignored her plea. "Elliott's waiting for that intelligence film you're carrying. And here—" He pulled out the camera bag containing the rolls of exposed film he'd taken on the road and shoved it into her tote. "Carry this for me."

"No. You—" Her continuing objections broke off under the noise of an engine echoing through the hills. The loud, rapid *whuck-whuck-whuck* drew the crowd's curious gazes to the rain-filled sky. Tara had recognized the sound of an approaching helicopter even before the small flying machine with the red star painted on its side rose ominously over a hill.

"Military," Kent said, grim-faced.

"Wu Chen," Songtsen pronounced with certainty.

"Okay. That tears it. We've run out of time. Into the truck with all of you." His hand closed around Tara's arm.

The high lama didn't move. "No, Kent. You are a brave man, but it is not you who will create a diversion. The soldiers would only take you quickly away.'' A frail but steady hand stemmed the flow of objections erupting from his distressed companions. ''I am an old man. I never in-tended to accompany you out of Pö. It is my karma to die in the land of my birth. Perhaps soon, perhaps not. That will be as fate decrees. It is your destiny, my son,'' he said with complete finality, ''to stay with the Gendun Lama and the Tara.''

The ear-pounding roar of the helicopter crescendoed as it approached. Everyone instinctively ducked when the chopper swooped low overhead, its rotors whipping the air. Animals skittered nervously. A train of donkeys bolted, dragging their cursing handlers behind them. Tunics and saris flapped around their wearers and Tara clutched at her kerchief.

When she looked back the old man was gone. ''Kent!'' she cried over the racket made by the aircraft. Her eyes darted over the crowd. ''Songtsen. I can't see him any-where.''

The truck driver again bellowed for people to take their seats—meaning whatever piece of truck bed one could commandeer. The escapees weren't the only ones linger-ing. Two or three men had leaped down from the truck to investigate the helicopter landing, a not-unknown, but still unusual occurrence in this area.

''The high lama made his choice,'' Kent declared. ''We've got to respect it.'' He scooped Tara up and de-posited her on the floor of the open truck, then swung the boy up before vaulting in himself. The vehicle was already moving when the three found places next to a large oil drum. A black-clad Tibetan woman with skin sunburned to rawhide squinted at the three of them suspiciously, but said nothing.

With a series of loud squawks on its horn, their an-cient, rickety truck lurched with painful slowness through a flock of bawling sheep. Coughing and sputtering, it lumbered toward a place in the line waiting to get through the checkpost. Kent kept his eyes glued to the military helicopter touching down on the flat riverbank in the distance.

Tara's heart plummeted at the sight that greeted her careful glance around the rusted oil drum. Even in the rain, the border guards were taking time to carefully screen everyone's papers. And they were thoroughly searching even small carts that couldn't possibly hide an escapee. She had little hope left that the three of them could slip by unnoticed.

The din grew louder as travelers waiting impatiently in the pelting sleet shouted their irritation at the delay. Several incensed Nepali traders, accustomed to quick border crossings, hurled epithets that needed no translation at Chinese officials, who angrily hollered back.

Tara sidled a glance around the scarf shielding her face to see a dozen armed men quick-marching toward the two uniformed men who'd bounded from the helicopter. At a gesture from one of the officers, the troops fanned out behind him. Their boots splattering mud as they ran, the military contingent headed straight toward the checkpost. Tara had no doubt that Colonel Wu Chen had finally caught up with them.

The bus immediately ahead, jammed with Indian pilgrims, some even clinging to the roof, would take forever to get past the guards. The colonel and his men would reach their quarry in minutes. Kent's face remained impassive, but his grip on Tara's hand tightened.

The little boy sitting between them, quite aware of their peril, slid his arms around Tara's waist and buried his face against her breast.

The sounds around them were changing, Tara noticed. Irritated shouts were dying away under an increasing flood of awed murmurs sweeping through the crowd. At Kent's gasp of surprise, she risked another quick glance in the direction of his gaze.

On a low, grassless hill not far away an old man was moving in a slow, prayerful dance. Songtsen! She'd barely recognized the lama, who had doffed his heavy robes for a thin yellow cotton wrapping, already soaked through.

Oddly, the freezing temperature and sheeting rain seemed to have no effect on him. Apparently oblivious to his surroundings, the elderly priest was ringing the small bell he held in one hand. In the other he held a curiously fashioned drum that looked like two shallow bowls stuck together end to end. With each twist of the drum, a small weight swinging on the end of a string fastened to the top thocked out a rapid rhythm on the twin drumheads.

As he circled the hilltop, Songtsen chanted a mantra in a voice surprisingly strong for a man his age. The strangeness of the sight, heightened by the storm, had pulled everyone's attention away from the checkpoint and to the chanting priest.

The rest of the crowd quickly took up the cry of *nagpa, nagpa* from the Tibetans in their midst. Hearing the words of his countrymen, Jigme gave up his fearful position pressed close to Tara and craned his neck to see what was going on. No one was paying the least attention to a Tibetan family huddled together in a truck.

"What's happening, Kent?" Tara asked anxiously. "That's Songtsen up there."

"Damned if I know, Tara. But the high lama's diversion seems to be working a lot better than mine would have."

"What are they shouting? Sounds like *nagpa*."

"A *nagpa* is a holy man who possesses seemingly magical powers. Some have gained such mastery over their bodies that the coldest of weather has no effect on them. I'm not too surprised to find that our friend over there is one of them. They believe such a yogi can pass through solid objects and even walk in space. But the Chinese frown on this kind of thing. I imagine it's been a long time since anyone in Tibet has witnessed such a saint."

The cries and rising prayers of the crowd grew louder and more frenzied. People who'd already passed through the checkpoint were hurrying back, curious to learn the cause of the commotion. Everyone within sight or sound of the growing hubbub was surging toward the hill where Songtsen, unruffled, kept up his singsong performance.

Shopkeepers and pack loaders abandoned their work and splashed across the river. A small group of troops spilled out of the nearby guardhouse and ran toward the high lama, rifles at the ready. Wu Chen and his men had reached the outskirts of the throng, and veered off toward Songtsen.

Religion played an integral part in the lives of most of the people in this section of the world. Hindu, Buddhist or Lamaist, all respected each other's holy men. Seeing that the soldiers meant to arrest the yogi—or do something even worse to him—the crowd's mood turned from awe-struck to angry.

Shouts in several languages warned the soldiers to let the old man be. The troops looked utterly confused by how quickly things were getting out of hand. Furious unarmed Tibetans threw themselves in front of the soldiers and tried to wrest away their guns.

"Oh, God, Kent. Somebody's going to get killed."

Troops bellowing orders continued to struggle into the mob in a vain attempt to hold it back. Tara could still hear, stitched within the growing tumult, the faint tinkling of Songtsen's bell and the patter of his drum.

The truck's sudden lurch toward the checkpost surprised her. She'd expected the inspection of the pilgrim bus to take much longer. The lone guard left to deal with border crossers must have waved the bus through without a thorough check in an effort to lessen the crowd that looked on the verge of full-fledged riot.

Tara cringed when the Tibetans in the truck screamed their opinions of the Chinese at the guard ordering their driver to show his papers. She could understand their rage, but wished they hadn't picked this moment to demonstrate it.

Keep your eyes down! Tara warned herself. *Keep your eyes down.* With her eyes half-closed she could see only the bottom half of the guard walking slowly beside the truck as he inspected its passengers. She pulled the boy closer and Kent wrapped an arm around them both.

Another impassioned cry burst from the crowd. People were searching for anything to serve as weapons against the soldiers. Some were picking up stones and hurling them at the uniformed men. Others were flailing about with poles used to carry goods on their shoulders. Some were even pulling food out of their luggage and tossing potatoes and cabbages at officials. Tara saw the border guard turn and furiously wave the truck through the gate.

What did that last great shout mean? Why the crowd's sudden violent rage? Had something happened to Songtsen? Tara's eyes automatically flew wide to find out, and she found herself staring directly into the guard's frozen, black-eyed gaze.

She instantly clamped her telltale green eyes shut, but not before she'd seen the soldier grab for the police whistle hung around his neck. The truck chugged under the lifted barrier, but its old motor could never manage any great speed. Technically they were still in China. The actual border ran across the perilous narrow ledge of road carved into the mountain. Plenty of time for soldiers to surround their truck and haul the fugitives out. Her stomach knotted. The tensing of Kent's body told her he knew what had happened. Her eyes squeezed shut, she dropped her forehead against his shoulder. Holding her breath she waited for the piercing signal that would deliver them to Wu Chen.

She waited until she had to let out her breath in a whoosh and drag in another lungful of air. She didn't understand. For excruciatingly long minutes she'd been braced to hear the guard's shrill whistle and the sound of soldiers' boots slamming against the pavement as they came for their prisoners.

But all she could hear above the rain was the grinding of the truck's gears as it strained up the pass. And the vehicle hadn't stopped. It still jostled her from side to side against Kent and the oil drum.

Tara slowly opened her eyes. No uniforms in sight. The only entourage following in the wake of the truck were a couple of goatherds and their meandering crew interpersed with a handful of Nepali wandering home to their villages. "Kent," she murmured dazedly. "The guard saw me. I'm sure he did."

"I know."

"Then why—?"

Kent shook his head. "I don't know, Tara. Maybe he's just a conscript with a grudge against his superiors. Maybe he had a friend in Tiananmen Square. Or maybe his heart yearns for the freedom he can never have, so he opted not to take away ours."

They owed their lives to an unknown Chinese soldier, Tara thought in amazement. And they'd never discover why. Even as they left Tibet, the land of magic and mysticism had presented them with one last mystery.

"Yes," Tara said softly. "We're free. But what of Songtsen?"

"I'm thinking of him, too. The high lama is a very brave man, who I suspect possesses resources his enemies can never counter."

"Buddha take care of Rimpoche," Jigme affirmed.

Kent smiled and tousled the boy's hair. "I believe you're right, Jimmy. Buddha will take care of Rimpoche."

The truck rumbled down the long serpentine road from the harsh, barren uplands of Tibet into pine forest and then into valleys lush with color and greenery on the sun-drenched, southern slopes of the Himalaya range.

"We okay now?" the boy questioned.

"We okay now," Tara and Kent answered in unison. Over the child's head, Kent clasped her in a happy bear hug. Jigme laughed to find himself sandwiched so tightly between his two embracing *parents*.

The old woman next to Tara gave her a congratulatory wink and nudged her in the side with an elbow. When the road degenerated to no more than a rutted track they, like most of the truck's passengers, decided to walk the rest of the way. Nepali officials in the first village of any size they came to didn't know what to make of the two curious-looking Tibetans with their clearly Tibetan child. But

Kent's curt order to contact the American embassy i
Kathmandu brought immediate results.

The STOL aircraft on the short-takeoff-and-landin
field nearby was held for three extra passengers bound fo
the capital, Kathmandu.

Tara's elation at their breakout from the trap th
Chinese military had set for them lasted only until the
were airborne. Her exhilaration fled the moment she re
membered that their escape marked the end of her Shan
gri-La adventure with Kent Masterson. And of thei
Shangri-La love affair.

Chapter 16

igme, ecstatic over his first plane ride, pressed his nose against the window of the seat in front of them. Tara sat beside Kent on the STOL. They'd doffed their heavy *chuƨs* in Nepal's warm climate and she was acutely conƨious of her arm brushing his. The drone of the aircraft ᴇgines, as they skimmed in a few short hours mountainᴜs terrain it would take weeks to traverse on foot, underᴏored her realization that the high-tech world in which ᴇy belonged had already claimed them. Far behind lay ᴇ beautiful, secluded valley of Yonten-La where the ᴇntle rhythm of life still held to its ancient, seasonal pace.

What could her love affair with Kent have been but a ᴠely, romantic fantasy raised by that magical world? ᴀra asked herself. Like all fantasies, in the end it had to ᴏve illusory. For Kent their romance had been merely a ᴜnction of an uncommon time, a unique place. A time ᴅd place where the normal rules of their busy lives had ᴇen temporarily suspended. The special connection ᴇrged between them on their long, arduous journey must ᴇntually melt away like the butter statues of Kali and her ᴏnsort.

"Your boss is waiting for us in Kathmandu." Ken raised his voice over the roar of the engines.

"Roger Elliott is here in Nepal?"

"Has been for weeks, moving heaven and earth, appar ently, in an effort to get information on our whereabout According to the ambassador they'd just about given us u as captured or shot."

Tara shuddered. They'd come close to that end.

"I want to be there," Kent continued, "when you de liver the intelligence film to him. I intend to tell him th courier he sent me did a damn fine job."

Kent circled his fingers around her wrist. Though he' most likely meant the gesture more in the line of a hand shake, she always felt any touch of his like a caress. Tha hadn't yet changed.

"I'm going to tell Mr. Elliott," she said, "to find him self another courier. From now on I'll stick to managin tours. It's a little easier on the nerves." Not at all easy c the nerves was sitting here next to Kent without grabbin him and demanding, *Didn't what we shared mean an thing at all to you?*

"Frankly, Tara, I'm glad about that. You've said th jobs aren't usually dangerous. But any kind of intell gence work can involve some risk. As we've both foun out."

It wasn't so much the risk that bothered her, but th unintended byways down which a simple thing like carr ing a package from one place to another had already le her. She'd lost her heart, along with her good sense, dow the road that led to Kent Masterson.

No longer a pretend Tibetan nomad, Tara donned th pale green silk blouse and matching linen skirt purchase for her by one of the embassy staff. A hot, soapy show and heavy latherings of shampoo had removed most of th color from her skin and hair. It had taken over an hour unravel the dozens of skinny braids.

"Come in," she answered to the knock on her door.

Kent, divested of his romantic costume and wearing a
own batik-printed sports shirt and tan slacks, strolled
ward her. He smiled when he saw her loosened hair and
ted a soft, curly strand. "Yes. This is how I like your
ir—loose and fiery."

Though he touched only her hair, she could feel the
armth of his hand by her cheek. Maintaining her precar-
us equilibrium about their parting would be so much
sier if he wouldn't touch her, wouldn't stand so close.

"Sure you won't come to the press conference?"

The Masterson name alone was enough to spark inter-
t among journalists, but Kent's disappearance, along
th that of an American travel agent, had resulted in
adlines all over the world. Every reporter in Kath-
andu, and several hurriedly flown in from India, guar-
teed full attendance at the news conference slated for
is morning.

"No," she said tersely. "I've got to call my agency." Her
al reason for skipping the press conference was to avoid
e questions sure to be raised about her relationship with
nt. She'd probably lose her temper and provide report-
s with a sound bite all the networks back home would
unce on for the evening news.

Kent's mouth tightened. He dropped his hand from her
ir and shoved it in his pants pocket. "I see. It's back to
siness."

Tara looked away, fussing with the charm box now
oped around her neck only as a beautiful piece of jew-
y. "I've been out of touch with my partner a long time."

hat was the matter with her? She'd been addressing Kent
that short, impatient tone ever since landing in the city.
e hated the way she sounded, but hadn't been able to
p. Maybe because he also had been growing increas-
ly curt and tight-lipped.

"I wish you wouldn't subject Jigme to the press confer-
ce," she said. "A battery of screaming reporters and
otographers can be a tough thing for anyone to face, let
ne a child."

Kent waited a beat. When he spoke his voice w
strangely quiet. "I know."

Tara turned in quick regret. Of course he knew. "I'
sorry, Kent. I'd forgotten that you've been subjected
media attention right from the cradle." Might a sensitiv
essentially private man, she wondered with sudden i
sight, choose to wander the world in order to escape life
that kind of fishbowl? "I know you'll watch out for hi
You've done an excellent job of that so far."

Her apology and her light touch on his arm seemed
ease some of the strange tension that had arisen betwe
them since setting down in the ancient city.

"Don't worry, Tara. I won't be shy about running i
terference for the kid. And I'll only keep him long enou₂
for the press and television people to get some picture
Jigme needs the coverage to prevent any attempts on t
part of Chinese agents to recover him."

"It's funny," she said. "Jigme's only been gone ov
night and already I miss him." On arriving they'd deli
ered the boy to the Buddhist monastery in Kathmandu
Tibetan refugee community.

Jigme's absence wasn't the only thing jangling h
nerves. Kent's room in the embassy adjoined hers. S
really wasn't surprised—or disappointed, she told he
self—that he hadn't come to her last night. He'd be
closeted for long hours with Roger Elliott and embas
personnel. No doubt diplomatic cables were still flying fa
and furiously between Kathmandu and Washington.

"I miss the kid, too," Kent said. "But he'll be comi
with us on our flight home tomorrow. We'll spend a co
ple of days in Philadelphia to introduce him to Andre
boys and the rest of the family." Kent started to lift I
hand, and Tara thought he was going to touch her h
again. But he didn't. "I want you to come too, Tara." I
eyes slid away as if he wasn't ready to hear her answer, a
he glanced at the small gold clock on the table. "They
waiting for me. Catch you later."

Tara stared unseeing at the door Kent had closed I
hind him. She had to learn to do a better job of reme

ering that Yonten-La's shimmering promise of forever hadn't been real. It was foolish to try to take their relationship any further. Useless to hope that she could find happiness with a rootless man who wouldn't—perhaps couldn't—offer the permanent commitment without which she could never return him her complete trust. And what was love without that bedrock trust?

She'd found her own private Shangri-La within Kent's arms. The memory of that fantasy paradise, the lovemaking during which she, at least, had felt inseparably linked to him, was implanted in her mind. But a memory could never fill the aching emptiness in her heart.

After watching the press conference on TV, she decided she couldn't stand to spend another whole day mourning his growing chasm between them. She'd grab whatever flight would get her out of here the soonest and make connections for the States somewhere along the way. If only she could make a quiet escape from Kent, but it would be cowardly to leave without telling him a personal goodbye. And she certainly couldn't leave without giving Jigme a goodbye hug.

Kent looked up at the serene bronze face of the Temple's massive statue of Buddha and planned his camera shot. He'd been battling gloomy thoughts ever since he and Tara had arrived in Kathmandu. When he'd wanted only to be with her, he'd been forced into endless repetition of the details of the Chinese construction site.

He and Tara had talked a little on the plane about getting together later on. *After they'd caught up with their real lives,* was the way she'd put it. But dammit, he wanted more than to be squeezed into her busy schedule. A native honesty quickly forced him to the question, *Wasn't that more or less what he wanted to ask her to do for him?*

Or was it? Certainly the man he'd been a couple of months ago would ask no more. But he wasn't the same man who'd started on this incredible journey. He'd changed. Grown. Meeting a goddess will do that, he thought with a wry smile.

He wasn't sure exactly when he'd made the transitio
from wanting Tara temporarily in his bed to wanting h
permanently in his life. It had crept up on him during thei
trek. And had overtaken him completely in that shadow
centuries-old room where he'd fought death with her.

The thought of the moment when she'd leave hi
clamped down on his mind like a dark cloud. She'd give
him so much. Making love with her had tapped int
memories he'd never known. Had presented him with sou
stirring images of beauty he could never capture on film
He didn't want to leave her. Ever. He was in love with Tar
Morgan.

"They told me I'd find you here."

The thought of her so strong in his mind, Kent wasn
sure the sound of her voice was real. He whirled around t
find her walking slowly toward him through a smoky shaf
of pale gold sunlight.

"I've come to say goodbye," she blurted out, keepin
her eyes lowered. "I'm already booked on a flight tha
leaves for New Delhi in a couple of hours."

Tara hadn't been able to predict what Kent's reaction t
her leaving might be. She thought she might see his relie
She certainly hadn't expected his fury.

"You're what?"

A couple of Nepali nearby scowled their disapproval d
Kent's voice raised impiously in a holy place.

"I've already missed one of my agency's schedule
tours," Tara rushed on, trying not to react to the intim
dation of Kent's anger. "And in a couple of weeks I'll b
leading a group on safari in Africa." She didn't really hav
to go. Her Tanzanian contact could take over for her. Sh
might skip it. Watching the sun rise over Kilimanjar
would mean nothing without Kent Masterson by her sid
to enjoy it with her.

"Dammit, woman—" Kent agitatedly raked his finge
through his hair. "You can't go."

They were ending their affair as it had begun, Tar
thought ruefully—with an emotional collision.

"I'd like to know why not." Her throat tightened up.

"Because I'm in love with you. That's why not."

Because he . . . Had she heard him right? Was she losing it and imagining she was hearing words only because she wanted so badly to hear them?

As she stared up at Kent with mouth agape, all the fight went out of him. His eyes softened and he gathered her tenderly in his arms. Immediately her body fitted against him in the space that seemed made for it. "I love you, Tara. I want to marry you."

The flowerburst of happiness that swelled in her throat threatened to overflow into tears. "Oh, Kent," she breathed on a sigh. "Oh, my darling." She couldn't stop her lips from trembling. "I love you, too."

His arm tightened around her. "Then say you'll marry me."

Her heart railed at her to shout out her *Yes!* At the same time her brain whispered that someone in this crazy situation had to keep their wits about them. Someone had to hold firmly to reality.

"I do love you, Kent." She pressed the side of her face against his cotton-covered chest and reveled in the warm, hard strength of him. "Oh, I do." She pulled her face away. This wasn't the time to listen to the music of his heartbeat. She had to make him see that they couldn't allow their love to prevent them from acting like sensible adults.

"But surely you can see that a marriage between us would never work. What will we do? Make arrangements to meet occasionally in hotel rooms on our travels in opposite directions? What kind of marriage would that be? Eventually it would just destroy the love we feel for each other."

His fingers threaded into her hair. "It doesn't have to be that way, Tara."

"But I'm afraid it would. Look, Kent. For all their married lives, my mother followed my father around, just as yours did. When my dad couldn't take us to a posting, my mother was content to wait patiently for him to return. Both those solutions to my father's unanchored life style worked for her. Neither would work for me.''

"I know. And I'd never ask you to do that. I want us to be together on terms that suit us both.''

Tara noticed that two foreigners engaged in public embrace drew glances of disapproval from those near them in the temple.

"Maybe we'd better find a less public place to talk,'' she offered. Kent nodded, his arm hooked firmly around her shoulders as he led her outside. Though hundreds of people bustled through the square, Kent found them a private niche formed by the temple walls.

"On the trek,'' he continued, "I started getting some ideas for a new project. A project unlike anything I've ever done before.'' He reached into his camera bag and pulled out a photograph of Jigme caught in midskip as he tossed his *chibi* into the air. "Here. Take a look at this. I used the embassy's darkroom to develop a roll of my personal film.''

"Oh, Kent. It's a beautiful picture.'' The photograph of the laughing little boy drew her wistful smile. "I'd love to have a copy of this.''

"Keep it. That's the first photograph of a new book I'm planning—a book of photographs of Asian children at play. Westerners don't know a lot about the people of Asia. The book might help change that.'' Actually, the ideas for the book had just this moment jelled in his mind, but he'd tell her that later—after she'd given him the commitment he needed from her. "What d'you think?''

"I think it's a wonderful idea, but—''

"The whole thing will take a lot of planning. Decisions on what countries to visit. Itineraries to be set up. Travel arrangements made. Contacts with local authorities. Exactly the kind of thing you're so good at, Tara. We're talking about three years' work from start to finish.''

"You mean you want us to work on the book together?'' Tara's thoughts were spinning like a prayer wheel.

"I want much more than that. I realize I'm asking you to give up traveling for your agency, but I'd never ask you to give up your work. We'd be working and traveling and spending our time with Jigme together."

"Oh, Kent. It sounds like heaven, but—"

"Heaven, yes. Exactly the word." His deep, quiet voice caressed her ears. "If ever heaven meant any two people to be together, it's us. We have the prophecy of an oracle and the blessing of a goddess on our union. Who else marries with those kinds of guarantees?" He was crowding her with that soft, melting look in those deep brown eyes, and his clean masculine scent, and that lopsided smile that had snared her heart the first time it had flashed down on her. "Do you remember when Songtsen spoke of Jigme's karma?"

"Yes. I remember."

"Well, Jigme has his destiny. Ours is to spend the rest of our lives together. I'm more certain of that than I've ever been of anything. I admit two nomads like us won't have an ordinary marriage. And maybe the home we set up will be more like a base camp. But the way I look at it, our love will provide us with new exciting territory it will take the rest of our lives to explore."

Base camp, he'd said. She liked the sound of that—centers from which to plan excursions and to return to afterward. A place to rest and shelter from a storm. A place to meet your friends and talk over the day's adventures. Base camps. Elegant they weren't. Safe and comfortable they were.

Kent's lips gently brushed hers, capping his arguments with the action that always fogged up her thoughts. "Say you want to explore that new ground with me, Tara. Say you'll marry me."

This time his kiss hadn't turned her brain to mush. This time his nearness brought his words home with sparkling clarity. She'd been envisioning a relationship with Kent only in terms of her own failed conventional marriage and those of her parents and sisters. But why *couldn't* she and Kent fashion a marriage responsive to their own needs, their own similar personalities? It was their lifetime commitment to each other that really counted. And she saw that promise shining clear and steady in his eyes.

"There's a special bond between us, Tara. A connection, a tie that I've felt ever since that frightening night when Songtsen kept you from dying—"

"Songtsen didn't keep me from dying, Kent. You did. I knew nothing else, but somehow I felt you holding me. And I had to hold on to you."

"Hold on to me, Tara." His hands spread wide across her back, enclosing her in the gentle prison she never wanted to be free of. "Hold on to me the way I want to hold you every day of my life."

"Yes, Kent. Oh, yes! That's what I want too."

Holding on to each other was the only answer, Tara saw. What she and Kent had together was too precious to let slip away. Their journey to freedom through the timeless landscape of Tibet had also charted their own private road to forever. The road they would travel together.

Afterword

In 1989 Tibet's Dalai Lama was awarded the Nobel Peace Prize. From exile in India, His Holiness works tirelessly for the welfare of his people both inside and outside Tibet. An American woman recognized as the reincarnation of a three-hundred-year-old female Tibetan lama lives in a Maryland suburb of Washington, D.C. Both Chinese and Western scientists are investigating the mysteries of *Qi*.

* * * * *

IT'S A CELEBRATION OF MOTHERHOOD!

Following the success of BIRDS, BEES and BABIES, we
are proud to announce our second collection of
Mother's Day stories.

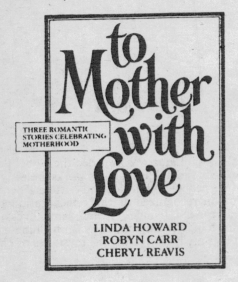

to Mother with Love

THREE ROMANTIC
STORIES CELEBRATING
MOTHERHOOD

LINDA HOWARD
ROBYN CARR
CHERYL REAVIS

Three stories in one volume, all by award-winning
authors—stories especially selected to reflect the love
all families share.

Available in May, TO MOTHER WITH LOVE is a perfect
gift for yourself or a loved one to celebrate the joy of
motherhood.

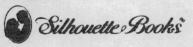

ML-1